Justice

Emily Conrad

Justice
COPYRIGHT 2017 by Emily Conrad

Contact Information: titleadmin@pelicanbookgroup.com

All scripture quotations, unless otherwise indicated, are from The ESV® Bible (The Holy Bible, English Standard Version®), copyright © 2001 by Crossway, a publishing ministry of Good News Publishers. Used by permission. All rights reserved.

Cover Art by *Nicola Martinez*

White Rose Publishing, a division of Pelican Ventures, LLC
www.pelicanbookgroup.com PO Box 1738 *Aztec, NM * 87410

White Rose Publishing Circle and Rosebud logo is a trademark of Pelican Ventures, LLC

Publishing History
First White Rose Edition, 2018
Paperback Edition ISBN 978-1-5223-0076-2
Electronic Edition ISBN 978-1-5223-0046-5
Published in the United States of America

Dedication

For Mom
Thank you for believing in me and, more importantly,
in God.

For the Lord is a God of justice; blessed are all those who wait for him. ~Isaiah 30:18

1

Snow floated onto Main Street, each flake large enough to catch the breeze like a parachute. A miniature army, launching a surprise invasion on March first. If it kept up, Jake would have to clear the sidewalk. As it was, customers had tracked in enough to leave a puddle trail across the hardwood floor.

He hefted the tray of dishes he'd gathered from Hillside Coffee's tables and headed for the back. The bells on the side entrance jingled, announcing at least one more North Adams resident needing a coffee to warm his or her hands.

Carrie, the manager Jake had scheduled for the morning, stepped toward the register.

As he slid the tray onto the workspace next to the sink, the silverware rattled against the stack of mugs. The scent of detergent rose, but the machine was silent now. The kid on dish duty, Ronny, was nowhere to be seen. As usual.

Carrie stuck her head around the corner. "Brooklyn's here to see you."

His stomach flopped. Amazing he'd known Brooklyn since fifth grade, yet she had that effect on him. He'd track down Ronny later.

Brooklyn Merrill stood at the end of the sales counter as if she had been about to come back to find him. She held a hat in one hand while she used the other to smooth her blonde hair. Since her business trip two months ago, she'd worn her long locks up without exception. Every time he saw her, he had to fight off the thought of kissing that spot between her spine and her ear, where her hair was soft and new. Someday, he'd coax her into giving love a chance. For sanity's sake, he had to.

He cleared his throat. "Took the day off?"

Brooklyn's mouth pulled into a tight grimace. For two months, sadness had infused her expression whenever she didn't seem to think he'd notice, but this was the first time she'd failed to tuck it away when he was obviously watching.

This could be the answer to his prayer that she would open up again. He led her a few steps away to a space by the display shelves. "You want to talk?"

A collection of tears glittered in her eyes. "I haven't been as good as I've been acting."

He would wrap her in the hug of her life, but their friendship rarely crossed the border of touch. He tried a gentle smile instead. "That's a problem. Because you haven't been acting very good."

A laugh caught in her throat.

He put his hand on her shoulder and guided her to the rear corner of the first floor, where she could sit with her back to everyone.

Even wrapped in privacy, she stared toward the wall and picked at her fingernails. "I planned what to say to you." Her voice quieted. "But I don't think I can do it."

His relief morphed into dread. What could be this

bad? *Father, don't let me mess this up.* "Just tell me the script. What'd you plan to say?"

"I need a ride to a doctor's appointment." She spoke in a flat tone.

He wanted to play along and say his lines, too, but all this over an illness? If she'd been sick since her mood froze over in January and couldn't drive herself, it was serious. His dad's problems had started this way—an appointment followed by a cancer diagnosis, months of treatment and supposed remission, and, finally, a funeral.

Brooklyn searched his eyes, tense sadness weighing down her features.

He kept his gaze trained on her beautiful, worried face. Maybe this appointment was something simple. He had to believe it, or he couldn't ask. "What kind of appointment?"

Brooklyn swallowed, neck ridged. "I'm three weeks late."

"To the appointment?"

"My body. My body is three weeks late."

"Your body..." Then it hit him. *She thinks she's pregnant.* How had he not understood sooner?

"I took a test, but maybe it was wrong."

She'd changed on that business trip. An image thundered to mind, and he willed it away. But the question remained. "You and Caleb?"

"It's not like you think, Jake."

"No kidding."

She taught Sunday school. She had worn a promise ring for years, but her finger was bare now. Caleb went on the New Wilshire trip knowing how Jake felt about Brooklyn, knowing he'd ended his last relationship to pursue her. Would Caleb have slept with her anyway?

"I can explain. There's not enough time right now, but I will explain."

He clenched his fist under the table. "I'm sure you could summarize." After all those years of pushing him away with the claim she'd never marry, never fall in love, she'd let someone else in. If it was just Jake she hadn't wanted all this time, she could've saved him years of trouble by being honest. "It's none of my business." He started away.

"Jake, please."

He turned back.

"I can't face this alone anymore." Her grip on the table turned her fingertips white.

The day Dad had died, when Jake reached home from the hospital, he'd found her waiting in the driveway. He and his mom had been together the whole time, but as soon as he held Brooklyn in his arms, he felt a million times less alone. Later, when losing Dad prompted him to question God, it had been Brooklyn who stood by him, her unshakable faith drawing him back to faith of his own. She may have brought this on herself, but he owed her company in her darkest hour. "Fine. When's the appointment?"

"I sat in the parking lot for half an hour before I worked up the nerve to come in."

He crossed his arms.

"Ten."

He checked his watch. "Fifteen minutes?"

She nodded, sighed, and stood. "I was going to talk to you sooner."

He trusted his managers, and he could leave with little to no warning. As he led the way to the door, he braced for snowflakes. Since he lived in the apartment above the shop and had no plans to go out, he'd worn short sleeves, and there wasn't time to run up for something warmer.

As they walked to the car, his peripheral vision caught the line of Brooklyn's dipped chin and the slant of her downcast eyes. He was failing her. He put an arm around her shoulders but felt no warmth when she leaned into him.

~*~

The seat Jake chose in the waiting area faced the door the nurse had led Brooklyn through.

She and Caleb were in the same place in life as Jake—hitting a stride in their careers, getting established. What would they do with a baby? *Do they really deserve this, God?*

One or the other would have to move if they were to be a family. If she relocated to Madison, where Caleb lived, Jake would lose touch with her. If Caleb came to North Adams, Jake would have a front row seat as the love of his life and his best friend played house.

He leaned forward in his seat. *Please, God, let there be some other explanation.* He was no expert. Maybe three weeks wasn't that significant. *Please, God, give her another chance. And show me what to do. I thought she was the one.* No one else's smile could light him up like hers, and no one else's problems made him wish he could change the world like hers. If only he could change it now. He stared at the speckled carpet, wishing for answers, but no Bible verses, no advice from his parents, and certainly no voice from God spoke to him.

Twenty minutes passed.

"Jake?"

He sat up.

Robyn Washburn took a seat. "What brings you here? Not sick, I hope." She was the wife of one of his church's elders. Everyone might have sin and secrets, but he didn't know any of Robyn's. How would her expression change if she knew why he was here?

"A friend needed a ride."

Caleb and Brooklyn had never shown signs of falling for each other. However, they'd stayed in the same hotel. No wonder the coward had feigned ignorance when Jake asked what could've changed Brooklyn on the New Wilshire trip.

Jake stretched his fingers. "How's the new car treating you?"

"Henry can't get over how I always get better mileage than he does. I keep telling him he needs to ease off the gas, but he just persists and then complains." She chuckled. "If he would slow down, it might save him a speeding ticket or three."

"You could get him a motorized scooter. They're slower and have great mileage."

"Oh, can you imagine?" She laughed again. Whatever her reason for visiting a doctor, it had to be routine.

The door opened, and Brooklyn ducked through. The only mascara left on her face was a faint smudge below one of her eyes. That could only mean one thing: she was pregnant.

She took an uncertain step toward him. He wrapped her in his arms, but even so, she'd never been further out of his reach.

"I can't do this," she said against his shoulder.

"You can." He leaned his head to look at her face. Her closed eyes seeped tears. "We'll do it together."

Liar. He couldn't help her with a baby. That job belonged to Caleb. Yet, he had the sense that the promise answered his prayer. It was God's direction for how he should proceed. *How do You figure I can help her?*

She scrunched her eyes tighter, and he placed a hand on the back of her head as she collected herself. When she stepped away, her gaze focused behind him, and her face reddened. "Can we go?"

Robyn stared at them, forehead furrowed.

Jake lifted a hand in a wave and turned toward the door.

Brooklyn followed him out to the car and buckled herself in. "I don't want people talking."

At this point, gossip was unavoidable. The time to worry about appearances was already weeks behind them. He started the engine and navigated to the road.

She gasped like they'd had a close call with another car, but the road was clear of everything but cottony snow. "I can't do this, Jake. I never planned to get married, let alone have kids all by myself."

"You're not alone." She had God if she wanted him. Or Caleb. He wouldn't turn his back on his own kid. Then again, Jake hadn't expected him to make a move on Brooklyn either. He and Caleb had been friends since high school football. That should've counted for something.

She remained silent.

Despite everything, he couldn't stand to see her cry, so he kept his eyes on the road.

She dug through the glove compartment for a napkin, which she pressed to her face. "The doctor said the baby is the size of a BB pellet. A bullet. Who compares a baby to a bullet?"

News that the baby already took up space was at the edge of his ability to grasp, but a bullet comparison was the most sense she had made all day.

"You're angry," she said.

A black SUV pulled out of a parking lot, and he slammed the brakes to avoid it. The car slid a couple of inches before the tires gripped. He ground his teeth. Anything he said would betray just how right she was, and she hurt enough without him piling on more wounds. As he parked in his spot behind Hillside, his phone went off. He took it from his pocket and answered.

"I think I messed up." Devin, one of the youth group boys Jake mentored, rarely bothered to introduce himself.

Join the club. Jake rubbed his hand over his eyes. "Why's that?"

"Do you have time? We could meet up?"

This had to be about Lauren, Devin's girlfriend. Or something could've happened with the kid's alcoholic parents. Or school. Jake took his keys from the ignition but didn't open his door.

Brooklyn sat still and quiet, probably waiting to say good-bye.

"Sure. Let me wrap up what I'm working on. We can grab lunch in about an hour."

"Who's buying?"

"Who always buys? I'll text you when I'm headed over." Jake pocketed the phone before turning his attention back to Brooklyn.

She collected her purse and tugged her coat zipper up to her throat. "I should get to work. I'll need the time off later in the year." The door clunked open.

"Let me know if you need anything."

She must've picked up on his hesitance because she nodded once and got out without another word.

You're a terrible friend, Jake.

He couldn't imagine doing better. Not when the woman he'd hoped to someday marry was carrying someone else's child. *God, what do I do now?*

2

Jake headed toward his apartment, his Bible, and some peace and quiet.

Two people waited at the counter with only Carrie there to serve them because, of course, Ronny was missing. Jake could go help, but why have staff if they couldn't handle making drinks?

"Good morning, Madame Durand. I haven't seen you in weeks."

The words halted Jake. Only Harold, owner of the bookstore across the street, would speak that way. Jake altered his course and stepped behind the counter, where Harold lingered next to Rachel Durand, one of Hillside's regulars.

With her back to the customers as she pumped syrup into Rachel's drink, Carrie raised her eyebrows and frowned in exasperation. She was one of the two employees Harold had reduced to tears on past visits.

The flush on Rachel Durand's cheeks signaled she wasn't immune to Harold's bullying either.

"When I was raising my boy, I made sure he read a book a week. That's how he got into—"

"Harold." Jake planted his palms on the counter. "Slow day over at the store?"

That his business might be lagging was a calculated blow to his pride. If it didn't send him packing, Jake would ask how he ended up estranged from the son he acted so proud of. No. That would be letting Harold get the best of him. *Love your neighbor. Even today.*

Harold slowly pivoted. "Mr. Davidson."

"That's Monsieur Davidson to you."

A laugh escaped Rachel Durand. She took her drink from Carrie and hurried off to a second-floor table.

At least he'd kept Harold from alienating one customer from Hillside.

"I came to check out the competition." Harold's voice boomed like his belly was an amplifier.

"Competition?" Their businesses couldn't have been more complementary. Though snow obscured the view of the glass and metal building now, Harold's Books stood on the corner across the street. When the bookstore had a signing, Harold's customers would visit Hillside for a latte before heading home. Jake's customers crossed the street and bought novels to enjoy with their coffee on Hillside's couches. "You're breaking into the coffee business?"

"Only seems fair if you're going to sell books." Harold's volume drew glances from customers.

Jake reviewed his shop for something that could've offended the man. Among the coffee and tea items, Jake stocked locally-made goods—caramel corn, soap, little clay dogs. A small gift book tucked in among the other products snagged his attention. There were three different books, mostly filled with pictures. "You're over here because of a frog book?"

"We had a gentlemen's agreement. A symbiotic relationship." Harold enunciated each syllable as if Jake needed to hear it slowly to understand.

He came out from behind the counter. "We have no agreements, Harold. Last I heard, making a deal to not compete is still illegal."

Harold's gray eyes narrowed.

"Besides. This? Over gift books? You've got three stories of books in a million-dollar building across the street."

Harold had demolished an historic bank building to erect the modern bookstore, something the city had allowed because of the pull of Harold's brother, the mayor. Bringing it up helped draw them closer to the windows and the main exit.

"Then you know I can't agree, either." The man finally hushed his voice. "Keep selling books, and I'll put in a coffee shop."

"I'll keep stocking them as long as customers keep buying them."

"Your father would call that downright stupid." Harold tugged on his belt, his puffed-up chest no match for the size of his belly.

"Next time I see him, I'll talk it over with him."

Harold lifted his hands, and his voice rose again as he pushed open the door. "Can't say I didn't warn you."

Jake stepped onto the mezzanine along the Main Street windows. Harold wasn't alone in the crosswalk. Vanessa, Hillside's best manager, approached from the opposite direction. From the looks of it, she chirped a greeting to Harold.

Just after they passed each other, Harold waved his hand as if to swat down pleasantries.

Vanessa swung open the shop door and stomped the snow off her boots. Laughing, she smoothed the snowflakes from her curly brown hair. "That's loathing if I ever saw it." She joined Jake. "Are we glaring at the snow or Harold?"

Jake owed the steady flow of customers during Hillside's first year to curiosity about Harold's construction project. If only the man hadn't proven to be such a difficult neighbor. "He says if I keep selling books, he's putting in a coffee shop."

"Selling books?" Vanessa surveyed the dining room then tossed him a helpless look.

"The gift books."

"Seriously? He wouldn't really open a coffee shop, would he?"

Harold, a business man, had to know there wasn't enough traffic on North Adam's Main Street to support two coffee shops. That would be the allure—the possibility he could starve out Hillside. But was Harold enough of a gambler to risk it?

"Let's say he does. He won't bring in live music like us. And he wouldn't source locally the way we do."

She raised her eyebrows. "You don't think a coffee shop would be a problem?"

He turned from the windows. "I don't know about you, but I was glaring at the snow. It's not supposed to happen in March."

She rolled her eyes. "It's only the first. Speaking of March, did you order the daffodils?"

"There's another thing Harold couldn't take from us."

"My marketing genius? Or my razor-sharp memory?" She headed for the back where employees stowed their winter gear. On the way, she said hello to every regular she passed.

Jake followed her.

She'd given away daisies on Valentine's Day with a little card tied to each one advertising that weekend's performer. The show packed the shop. He'd put off ordering the daffodils, which she planned to give out the first day of spring, but he hadn't forgotten.

"Either way." Tying her apron, Vanessa passed him. "I'm not working for Harold. I don't care if that means working here for the rest of my life."

"You say that like it'd be a bad thing."

She laughed but skipped offering a reply. Come May, when she finished her marketing degree, he was bound to lose his second-in-command, but he didn't have the heart to pursue it today.

He checked his watch. The idea that he could somehow help Devin might be farfetched, but the kid was counting on him. "I'll be back after lunch."

She waved good-bye and turned her attention to a customer.

~*~

Nearly an hour later, Jake and Devin lingered in a booth. They'd ordered a monster of a pizza and had managed to eat half. Jake's first guess about the teen's problem had been right. A bunch of the high schoolers had gathered for an offseason bonfire in the middle of a field of snow. Devin paid too much attention to his friends and too little to his girlfriend. Lauren, the girlfriend, was furious.

The teen took a third slice of pizza. "She says I don't love her."

Jake stopped halfway through moving his straw to his drink refill. "Do you?"

"Yeah."

He stabbed the straw in the new cup and swiped a napkin over the mess he'd made. Seventeen and in love after two and a half months. Jake wasn't qualified to help. He should've stayed at work to take his mind off Brooklyn. Not that distraction would change what she had done.

If only he could dredge up some good advice. He resorted to the question his mom had once used to help him straighten out his priorities. "Is this the kind of love you're willing to make some sacrifices for?"

Devin lifted one shoulder in a non-committed shrug, but his attention was fixed on Jake.

Now what do I tell him, God?

"Then Lauren needs to know that."

"How?"

Lord, give me wisdom. "Find a way to show her. Do something for her that you usually don't like to do. Go see a musical or a chick flick or a ballet."

Devin's lip curled in disgust, but he laughed. "A ballet?"

"Throwing it out there."

"So I go to the ballet." He lifted his pizza. "If I do that, you'll finally ask Brooklyn out?"

"Not that simple, buddy."

"We're going to die alone."

"Nah." Jake tossed his napkin on the table. "We'll always have each other."

Devin snorted, lifted his pizza as a toast, and went back to packing it away.

3

Brooklyn hesitated in the darkness outside Jake's coffee shop. She was going to be a single mother. No husband. Not even a boyfriend. Just one man, the man she'd come closest to letting in, who thought she had slept with his best friend. She was the last person Jake would want to see, but the conviction that Caleb's name must be cleared had dragged her here at six o'clock in the morning.

The bells didn't jingle as she eased open the door. She could sneak up to the second-floor balcony and wait for Jake to come down from his apartment.

"Gift baskets?" Vanessa was somewhere in back.

"Whether Harold gets into coffee or not, it's only a matter of time before we get more competition." Jake's voice jolted Brooklyn's stomach. Maybe he hadn't been able to sleep last night either. "Expanding Internet sales is one way to get ready for it. We missed Valentine's Day, but we could sell some locally-sourced Easter baskets."

Something scraped across the floor in back.

"We'll start simple," he said. "Just a picture on the website, only available to people we can deliver to locally. They can e-mail us to order. If it goes well, we'll expand. Then I might need someone managing that part of the business. Photography, marketing, shipping."

"You think it'll do that well?" Vanessa's voice grew clearer and louder as she approached the front.

"Counting on it." Jake's rich tenor was clearer now, too.

Brooklyn fought the pull to abandon her mission. She couldn't drag Caleb into this, and if she could undo some of the damage between her and Jake, she might earn another brief hug. From drama with her mom to everyday disappointments, she hadn't faced a trial without him by her side, believing the best of her, in years. What she wouldn't give to have his arms around her, comforting and supporting her right now.

Vanessa stepped into the area behind the counter with two trays of baked goods. "Internet Sales Manager?" Her voice bubbled. Smiling, she slid the trays on the counter.

"That's the thing with businesses like this." Jake appeared. "The only limit on what we can accomplish is us."

Brooklyn stepped toward the counter.

Vanessa spotted her. "You're accomplishing plenty already." She winked at Brooklyn and disappeared into the back.

Jake's dark hair flipped different directions as if he'd spent the night sailing instead of sleeping. She could run her fingers through it, straightening it, if she'd given in to the romance they'd both wanted.

When his gaze landed on her, he pulled straighter, hardening the set of his shoulders. "Would've figured you'd need rest."

Brooklyn cocooned her hands in her coat pockets. The black and orange of pre-dawn Main Street beckoned her to run. This was too far gone. Tears welled. How long would it be until she'd go a day without crying?

Jake stopped just feet from her, nothing between

them now but air and his crossed arms. Oh, and the baby of another man.

"You want to talk?"

All she could do was nod. Softness had marked his voice yesterday. Now, his tone hit with disapproval.

He started for the area where they'd talked yesterday. Instead of stopping at one of the tables, he took the stairs two at a time. On the second-floor balcony, he waited for her to pick a booth and then slid in across from her. "You said it's not like I think." He watched her like he expected to be disappointed.

How could she admit she took a gamble and lost so much?

Brooklyn ran her fingers over her scarf. During her sleepless hours last night, she'd read online that fifty percent of the women in her situation lost their primary relationship. Maybe she could keep them from the wrong side of the statistic. "You know it was on the trip, in New Wilshire."

He rubbed his hand over his mouth as his jaw flexed.

"It's not that I didn't want to tell you sooner." As if the delay were the problem. "I can't even tell you what the guilt has been like. You have to know this isn't what I had planned."

He sighed as if he was too tired to put up a fight. "Yeah? What did you have planned?"

She dropped her gaze. "Even I've had a hard time thinking of myself the same way since. Everything's different, but I liked the way things were. I liked the way they were headed."

"What are you saying, Brooklyn?"

Hadn't she been clear? This was torture. Maybe he meant it to be. "I'm saying I'm sorry. I know why you broke up with Sarah."

"That was months ago. Sarah and I are done because we want different things. She's moving out of state, and I'm not leaving."

As if she couldn't recognize that for a lie, but she couldn't blame him for the dishonesty after she'd lied about being fine for so long. "Would it be any better if I told you it wasn't Caleb?"

"I think I deserve the truth."

Watching him date Sarah had been a struggle. How much harder was it for him to think she and Caleb had been intimate? "You mentioned him yesterday, and I didn't set that straight, but I couldn't let you go on thinking it. Caleb's not the father." She scooted to the end of the booth to escape before he asked the obvious questions.

The skin under his eyes shivered with tension. Whatever happened in the coming months, he would want nothing to do with her. They'd landed on the wrong side of fifty percent.

"I don't know what I was hoping that would change, but I thought you should know."

"Then who?"

"Someone else." She braved one last look. He was too angry to risk the whole story, but this, he had to believe. "It's not Caleb. And I'm sorry."

A customer pounded up the stairs.

Jake looked that way.

She took the opportunity to get out before the whole thing came tumbling down.

4

Jake sat in his mom's kitchen, quizzing his nephew for a history test. Mom watched Taylor after school, but today she'd asked Jake to fill in. The thirteen-year-old didn't share Jake's interest in history, and Taylor's boredom was contagious. As soon as Mom arrived, Jake would move on his plan to figure out if Brooklyn had told the truth about Caleb. How much longer could shopping take her?

At four thirty, when the front door opened, Jake clapped the textbook shut.

Taylor hopped to his feet and hurried toward the living room.

Mom stood in the doorway at the end of the hall. One of her three grocery bags had hooked on the frame and kept her from entering.

Taylor took a left into the living room, leaving her to struggle.

Jake stretched to push the door open while keeping out of her way.

She took a step into the house with a grin. "Always biting off more than I can chew."

"That's not true." A few grocery bags may have tangled her up, but she and Dad started Contact Point Billiards years ago. Now that Dad was gone, the outreach continued to be effective under her direction alone. He took two of the bags and followed her to the kitchen.

"Thanks for stepping in with Taylor." She began to unpack groceries. "How're things?" Her gaze stopped on the keys he held in his hand. "Oh. We can talk another time. Where're you off to?"

They were due for a talk, but Brooklyn dominated his mind and only Caleb might have the answers he needed. "Madison."

"On a Tuesday?"

Because of Caleb's work schedule, he normally saved trips to Madison for weekends when they'd spend a few days hanging out and going to ballgames. But this couldn't wait.

"Is everything OK?"

He could tell his mom the basics, but then he'd never get on the road. "I'm fine."

She raised her eyebrows and took a bag of produce to the fridge. "That sounds carefully calculated."

"It is."

"Well…then let Caleb know I'm praying for him."

Mom had been pro-Brooklyn for years. Her promises to pray were never empty, so she ought to focus on the right person. "Brooklyn."

She shut the refrigerator, the produce only half unpacked. "What?"

Telling her this much was probably a mistake, but Brooklyn shouldn't have put him in a position where he had to lie to his own mother. "Pray for Brooklyn."

"You can't say something like that without telling me the problem."

He clenched the keys. "I'm sorry. I really have to go."

~*~

On the road to Madison, Jake shut off the stereo as the sun dropped closer and closer to the bare trees on the horizon. Brooklyn's last relationship—or, at least, the last he knew of—had ended five years ago. Jake's dad died, and he transferred to the college in North Adams following the funeral. Brooklyn's relationship ended less than two weeks later. Jake hadn't asked her about it until the night he found her sitting on the steps of Mom's deck after his college graduation party.

They talked for a few minutes about her plans. Caleb, who had crammed in enough credits to graduate the year before, was already working at Galley Paper in Madison. He fast-tracked Brooklyn for the recruiter position in Galley Paper's North Adams office and offered to keep an eye out for something for Jake, too.

Jake declined. If his life turned out to be as short as Dad's, he couldn't waste it in a career that didn't inspire him. The only thing he knew he wanted was Brooklyn. He'd sat next to her on the stairs. "Whatever happened to that guy? Eric?"

"Wow. That's been a while." She folded her hands between her knees. "It was bad timing."

He leaned back, hoping to appear nonchalant. "I had my issues, but you…"

"I had your issues, too."

"Not really."

"Well. He couldn't understand that I wasn't just going to let you…" She shrugged.

After losing Dad, Jake had been torn up by questions and doubts. How could God have allowed such a righteous man to die so soon? How could Jake follow a God like that? Brooklyn's quiet but strong faith had reined him back in, and he loved her for it. "So I had something to do with why it didn't work out."

She stretched her legs toward the bottom of the steps. "Most people aren't capable of the kind of love it takes in the long haul. Look at Eric. We used to be friends, and if we hadn't dated, I bet we'd still be. Friendships work, but love…once you cross that line, someone gets hurt, and it's never the same. I don't know why I bothered to try. I'm just glad you and I never lost each other that way." She smiled at him, as sweetly beautiful as ever, even as she relegated him to the friend zone. Again.

He'd swallowed three times before he could reply. "You'll never lose me."

As the sun set, Jake's headlights flipped on.

He wouldn't have made her that promise if he'd foreseen her having a baby with another man. *What do You want me to do for her now, God?* The father of her baby owned a part of her Jake would never have. She'd betrayed both him and the things they believed in. He should feel nothing but anger. Yet he longed for what he had always wanted. A future with Brooklyn. *Help me encourage her to go the direction You want her to go, not the way I want her to go. Make it very clear for me. I need Your wisdom. Kill my jealousy. Give me insight. Let me bring honor to You in this.*

He pulled up to Caleb's at six, but the windows were dark and the detached garage was still. He settled into his seat and cut the engine.

The snow that fell back home had missed Madison. Without the dusting, evening blackened the evergreen bushes along the white siding. Cold crept into the car as the night deepened. Much longer and he'd run the engine for heat. But then the distinctive headlights of Caleb's sports car shone in the rearview mirror. He grabbed the keys from the ignition and followed on foot as the car rolled into the driveway. On reaching the glow that spilled out through the garage door, Jake stopped.

Caleb got out and locked the car with a smirk. "Don't tell me you could smell the food all the way in North Adams."

Jake put his hands in his pockets and stayed in the driveway as Caleb crossed to the side door of the garage. After hitting the button to lower the garage door, he joined Jake in the dark. They started for the house.

Jake had considered calling instead of making this trip. Caleb wasn't the type to handle anyone with kid gloves. He would tell the truth, even if it hurt. But if Brooklyn was lying, perhaps Caleb would, too. Or what if he was the father, and she hadn't said anything to him? Jake couldn't risk breaking news like that over the phone. Not that he knew how to break it in person.

Caleb glanced back. "You OK?"

"I said Brook's been different since the trip to New Wilshire."

"Sure." His keys clinked. In one quick stride, he mounted the two steps to the back door.

"She's pregnant."

Caleb turned from the door, his hands still on the keys in the lock. In this light, his skin was about the same color as his sandy hair. His eyebrows drew together, cloaking his eyes in shadows. "What?"

Jake shrugged, and the fleece of his jacket brushed his neck. It was cold. Too cold and too dark for this. "They say the baby's the size of a bullet."

Caleb dropped his hands, and then put them on his waist, balled like rocks. "I don't get it."

"Yeah. Me neither."

"No. Like..." Caleb shifted his feet but kept his focus trained on Jake.

"Same thing I was going to ask you."

Caleb took a deep breath and raised his eyebrows. He completed half a shake of his head.

So Brooklyn had told the truth.

Caleb stood still and silent for a few seconds before he led the way through the door. In the kitchen, he flicked the light on and tossed his keys on the counter.

The scent of roast beef took Jake back to the meals Mom made when he was in high school. He glanced at Caleb, who stared at the spot where the keys had settled. Maybe a change of subject would help him through the shock. "Are you actually cooking?"

Caleb motioned to a corner of the countertop, where a silver slow cooker sat next to the toaster. "Got it for Christmas and broke it out three days ago." He shrugged off his coat and unknotted his tie.

Jake smiled. "You're quite the homemaker."

"One that could take you any day."

The reply was standard, but the bite in his voice was not. So much for humor dulling the news about Brooklyn. They ate at the counter in silence.

After dinner, Caleb pushed his plate away. "Still keep your gym bag in your car?"

In high school, when Caleb failed a test or they'd lost a big game, he'd convinced Jake to tag along on some pretty intense workouts. For the week following Dad's funeral, Caleb stayed in North Adams and took Jake to the gym daily. The exhausting sessions allowed him to sleep instead of tossing and turning. The perfect medicine for tonight.

Cold air grated Jake's throat for the first mile until the challenge of keeping up heated him through. Another mile later, traffic at a busier street forced them to stop. He stretched as he watched for a break in the passing headlights.

"You really thought you had to ask me?" The last two miles hadn't even winded Caleb.

Spotting an opening, Jake put his foot down. "It's either you or a stranger. It happened in New Wilshire."

The road cleared, and they started across.

"No way." Caleb extended his stride to miss a patch of ice. "She stopped talking to me for a month when she found out about Amanda back in college. A year later, she cried when I told her I'd come back to Christ. I talked to her the last night of the trip. She was into you. She wasn't off with anyone else. Especially not with anyone from Galley Paper."

"She was with someone."

"It couldn't have been on that trip. Not a chance."

"Be realistic."

Brooklyn had gone to participate in the job fair. Caleb and the other project managers had training all day.

"She wasn't being weird when we talked that night, and she's too sweet for deceit. Could be a virgin birth." Caleb pushed the pace faster, and Jake couldn't respond to ridiculous statements. "This is Brooklyn. She's the sweetest, most innocent woman I know. When I brought you up that night, she was relieved to let on that she has a thing for you. You should've asked her out years ago."

Jake kept his silence. Caleb would have to come to

terms with the truth.

"Why didn't you make your move?" Caleb asked.

"When she got back? I told you, she was different."

"It couldn't have been that fast. You're destined for each other. If you'd proposed to Sarah, I wouldn't have attended the wedding."

"Thanks."

Caleb might've saved Jake a wasted year if he'd spoken sooner.

"Come on." Caleb laughed. "I would've dragged you out of the ceremony. Brook's too well-mannered to object for her own sake."

"You're sure there's no chance—"

"What? Her and Steven? Or Alex? Have you seen them? Alex is old enough to be her father, and Steven's a lowlife. When she wasn't at the job fair, she stuck with me or Rosalie. That last night, we all had dinner at the hotel restaurant. The others left, and she and I stayed so long that she ordered a dessert to compensate the wait staff for holding up their table. That's how sweet she is. At eleven, she was tired. I offered to pay the bill, and she left. She yawned twice before she made it out of the room. That was not a woman on the prowl."

"Then I don't know how to explain it, but she wouldn't even look at me when I met her flight." Jake had to wait before he had the breath to continue. "Yesterday, she showed up at the shop and asked me to take her to a doctor's appointment."

"I'm telling you, virgin birth."

Impossible. That miracle was a unique event in history. Caleb wouldn't be any help until he figured that out.

5

The shake of elderly voices carried through the church hallway on Tuesday night. Brooklyn had come because the knitting club, Closely Knit, announced on Sunday that they wanted to share their skills with the younger generation. If these voices were any indication, she'd be the only woman under eighty, but her mind would keep spinning if she didn't find something to occupy it.

The conversation came into focus as she neared. "All respect to that pastor, but do you think he did right in his sermon on Sunday?"

Three women sat around the table in the middle of the room, a pile of yarn, hooks, and projects scattered over the workspace. What were these women's names again?

"Well, what do you know?" The one with tight, white curls beamed at the others. "All's not lost, gals."

Another woman stood. "Brooklyn Merrill. Welcome. You know everyone here, right?" She pointed out the others at the table. "Nora Schilling, Roberta Connors, and of course, Elizabeth Stein." She indicated herself.

Brooklyn silently recited the names again. "No one else wanted to learn to knit?"

Nora shrugged. "Knitting's not accurate, anyway. Betsy was the only knitter. She started the group, so she named it. The rest of us crochet. Never got around to renaming ourselves after she died. Roberta knows some knitting, though, if that's what you've come for."

Brooklyn didn't know enough about either to have a preference. "Crochet's fine."

Elizabeth selected a ball of yarn, a crochet hook, and a booklet of patterns. "What have you come to make, dear?"

She wanted to make clothes for the baby. What would these women think if they knew she was pregnant out of wedlock? "I have a friend with an afghan. I thought it would be neat to learn."

The blanket belonged to Jake. His grandmother gave it to him for his high school graduation. She'd never met her own grandparents, and the symbol of family and care drew her every time she entered his apartment. To think he'd let the blanket sit in a box until she found it. Now that he kept it out, the yarn smelled of the same rich coffee and vanilla that permeated the apartment from the shop below. No other scent made him feel so close. She'd tried dozens of candles in her own home, and all failed to give her the illusion of his embrace.

Elizabeth flipped open the booklet. "You've come to the right place, but let's start a smidge smaller than an afghan. How about a hat? Once you get the basics down, you'll be able to take on anything."

Something less likely to make her think of Jake would be best. She applied herself to following Elizabeth's instructions. Once she had gotten far enough in the spiraling pattern to satisfy the older woman, Elizabeth returned to her own project.

"Out with it, Nora," Roberta said. "What's the problem with the guest pastor's sermon?"

Brooklyn lost count of her stitches at the question.

Did she have to start over? Maybe she could guess her way through.

Nora raised her eyebrows without taking her focus off the little sweater she was making. "He said people who are in the midst of trials usually have brought the trial on themselves."

"And they have," Roberta said. "The sooner they admit their sin and ask for forgiveness, the sooner they'll get out of their trials."

Nora's voice lost some of its meekness. "Innocents suffer, too. That could've been stressed more. Look at Job. And Jesus. They followed God's will, and they suffered. And don't forget the man born blind. It wasn't because he or his parents sinned, remember?"

Elizabeth chuckled in agreement. "Not everybody's Jonah."

Brooklyn pulled out a few stitches. The pattern seemed hopeless, but she needed to hear this conversation more than she needed to ask for help.

"Trials are like jails," Roberta said. "Everybody in them says they're innocent, and very few are."

Brooklyn abandoned the pattern and did one simple stitch after another.

"The Holy Spirit doesn't let a true believer get away with sin." Nora grabbed for a different color of yarn. "But you go telling them they've done something wrong, and some of them carry a burden they were never meant to carry."

Brooklyn tugged out the simple stitches. Perhaps her trial wasn't a punishment. She'd done nothing wrong. She could tell Jake without fear. How welcome his help would be. Their relationship could still survive the fifty percent statistic. The stitches began to pour from her hook, but then her hands froze. What if God allowed the pregnancy in order to break up her friendship with Jake?

Even before New Wilshire, she'd been damaged goods. After watching her mother fail at marriage so many times, she'd learned to fail at love, too. Her few adventures in dating had confirmed as much. Jake, on the other hand, had grown up under the wings of his parents' solid marriage. If anyone could commit for a lifetime, he was that man.

If this trial broke them apart, he could focus on his work at Hillside and with the youth. He would grow to be a leader in the church and in the community. A wonderful Christian woman would come into his life, and they'd get married and have kids, all of them his.

"We can't often tell what purpose our trials serve," Nora said. "But we can be faithful to what we do know."

Elizabeth nodded. "Faithful to Jesus."

Brooklyn had tried to be faithful to Jesus. She'd drowned hours in prayer and study, but now she was pregnant. Did God really want to separate her from Jake? If the pregnancy was a redirection, not a punishment, and if she wasn't guilty, it'd be nice for Jake to know that. She hadn't been this desperate for anything since her last night in New Wilshire. *Lord, could You at least explain to him what happened? Somehow?*

Her sniffle drew glances from Roberta and Elizabeth. The yarn in her hands looked nothing like the picture. She removed her hook and reached to pull out her work.

Elizabeth touched her hand. "You have to give the pattern time to develop. Sometimes, you can't see it's working all right until you're a few rows into it. Let me see." The older woman prodded at the stitches, leaving the work intact. "You're doing all right here. Don't try to be perfect. Just try to be faithful to the directions and keep going. It'll fall into place."

Brooklyn blinked and a tear fell to her cheek. "It looks like a mess."

"Always does at first. Have a little faith." Elizabeth passed back the start of the hat.

Nora rose from her seat and set a box of tissues next to Brooklyn's yarn. "My Henry used to get a cold every time the seasons changed. The runny noses have started. Spring is coming."

Elizabeth smiled at her project, and Roberta diverted her eyes.

"Thank you." Brooklyn used a tissue and then did her best with the pattern.

Elizabeth lowered her work. "There is therefore now no condemnation for those who are in Christ Jesus. For the law of the Spirit of life has set you free in Christ Jesus from the law of sin and death."

"So if the Son sets you free, you will be free indeed," Nora said.

Elizabeth worked her hook in and out of the yarn with deft strokes.

Roberta nodded once. "Amen."

6

Caleb claimed their run had taken them seven miles, but Jake could've sworn they'd covered twenty.

"Basement shower's yours if you want it." Caleb pulled off his knit cap. "If you want to crash for a day or two, you know you can."

"Only a day or two?"

"Couple reasons." Caleb held up two fingers without a smile. "One, Brooklyn may as well be my sister. If she had you take her to the appointment, she's depending on you, and I won't let you get away with running from that forever."

Jake filled a glass with water.

"Two, I mentioned Rosalie went with us to New Wilshire." His tone brightened. "We sat together on the plane home, got to talking. Not only is she a Christian, she's actually committed to it. She's involved with her church, goes to a Bible study and all that."

"I have to leave because you're going to a Bible study?"

"On a Friday night? No. Dinner and a movie, and you, my friend, are not tagging along."

Jake took his glass to the basement. Whether he stayed or left, he needed to shower. Afterward, he found Caleb settled on the couch, watching previews for a movie. By the time the credits rolled, Jake was half asleep and in no mood to drive home.

The carpeted basement had a TV and a couch with

a pull-out bed. With nothing but two small, high windows, the room was dark and quiet. No noises from the shop. No light from the street. No work waiting.

Jake tossed a pillow on the couch without bothering to unbury the bed. Minutes after he shut off the light, each breath drew his heavy body closer to sweet, dark sleep.

Thank You, God.

~*~

Jake dreamed of a cement stairwell. Across from him, there was a landing and a metal door labeled ten. Below him, at another landing, the stairs turned, and he could see all the steps from floor ten down to nine. The air was tainted with the smell of metal and paint.

A rhythmic shuffle sped faster and louder—climbing footsteps. Brooklyn appeared, dressed for work in black pants, a gray sweater, and heels. Her face was flushed. She leaned to see over the railing, and then climbed faster, fumbling with her purse. By the time she reached the landing halfway between floors nine and ten, she'd dug out her phone. A man came into view, following her.

His clothes, athletic pants and a half-zipped hoody over a t-shirt, suggested he ran the stairs for a workout, but lowered eyebrows and a bunched chin marked his face. Brooklyn was right to be afraid of him. The man skipped a couple of steps, narrowing in on her lead.

Jake tried to warn her but found himself mute and invisible, an observer only.

She lifted her cell phone as she reached the tenth-floor landing. She lowered it and checked over her shoulder, eyes wide with terror as the man climbed the last set of steps. She reached for the railing as if to continue toward the next floor. Then, she changed her mind and stepped away, heading toward the door marked ten. Her moment of indecision cost her the last of her lead.

The man latched his fingers onto her pants. She yipped, stumbling. She tossed her purse at his feet as she broke for the stairs to floor eleven. Her hair spun away from her shoulders, and he grabbed it. This time, she shrieked. She started to fall toward the man, but she twisted to stay on her feet.

Jake railed to intervene, but his body didn't exist here. He was helpless.

"I don't want your money." The man kicked her purse away. He let go of her hair, grabbing for her arm.

She bolted for the stairs again. His arms engulfed her, one around her neck, the other around her abdomen. His legs were close to hers, impeding her struggle for the stairs.

Jake panicked. He wouldn't be able to see them on the stairs, and he was desperate to know she was alive and getting away. If only he could break through.

She fought her way to the stairs then stumbled forward. The man fell after her, presumably on top of her, but they were now out of Jake's sight.

Brooklyn screamed. Jake had never heard her voice so raw. One of her shoes clacked down to the tenth-floor landing. The man commanded her to shut up, lashing her with a string of insults Jake could only half make out.

This was a dream. If he couldn't save Brooklyn, he wouldn't watch. He had to open his eyes and wake himself. He stopped fighting to get in and waged war against the sleep that kept him in the stairwell.

Brooklyn's other shoe fell over the edge of the stairs, coming from a point about halfway up. She must have made it farther after she fell.

The dream went black for a second, the result of his effort to wake. Then, he was back in the stairwell where Brooklyn gripped the bottom of one of the railing supports. Her knuckles were sharp, and the tendons on the back of her hand strained.

If I can run seven miles, I can open my eyes.

The blackness returned. As if one night were giving way to another, Jake could see the sliver of a shadowed room. Forcing his eyes the rest of the way open was like pushing through chest-deep water, but he refused to drop back to that dream.

He broke through to full consciousness with a jagged breath. Cold but sweating, he clicked on the lamp. The corners of the room lay drenched in shadows. The quiet was stifling. His muscles demanded something to throw or to hit to drain the adrenaline and fade the memory of the dream.

Snippets bombarded him, and as the details added together, he shook. Weren't dreams supposed to have holes and inconsistencies?

The movie he'd watched with Caleb had some violent scenes. None of them had involved rape, but his subconscious could've blended that action with his wish that Brooklyn wouldn't have chosen to be intimate with someone. He should be ashamed. And he was, first for having the dream and second for not being able to endure it. Since he'd been hateful enough to dream it, he at least could've refused to abandon her to face it alone. He should've kept fighting to save her. In real life, he would've. He was certain. Even if he broke every bone in his body trying to reach her.

But he had known it was a dream while it was happening. He couldn't abandon her to a dream in his own mind. He'd saved them both by waking. It didn't happen.

If her pregnancy had come about as he had dreamed, the rape occurred after she left Caleb at the restaurant. But she wouldn't have taken ten flights of stairs when she was as tired as Caleb described. Besides, she would have no reason to hide a rape. There would've been an investigation and a trial, and medical professionals wouldn't have allowed her to fly out the next morning. Even if, somehow, she had kept the secret of a rape—and she'd never lock him out of something that significant after everything they'd been through together—the pregnancy should've brought out the truth. Why would she let the world think she'd done something wrong?

The dream hardened like a real memory instead of fading like a nightmare. Guilt stirred his gut. Even if it was just a dream, his subconscious had created the rape of his best friend, the love of his life, and he had abandoned her to it.

He stood, desperate to forget the images. Damp with sweat, he needed to shower again. He rolled his shoulders to loosen up.

Get yourself together, man.

~*~

Caleb went to work, and Jake hung out, reading his Bible and trying to get his feet back on the ground. The vividness of the dream wore away by the time Caleb returned home, and Jake kept it to himself. His dream said more about his own jealousy than a reliable answer about Brooklyn. Caleb dragged him through another workout, but he bowed out of the movie.

At Hillside, no one looked his way as he climbed the stairs to his apartment. He took out a biography his sister had given him for Christmas and read until his eyelids began to dip. Setting the book aside, he risked sleep.

6

As Jake moved chairs and tables off the mezzanine by the Main Street windows, he suffered flashes of the rape dream. The shrill of Brooklyn's scream when the man grabbed her hair. The slur of insults. He could even smell the lacquer of fresh paint.

"Jake, the band's not gonna make it."

Ten or twelve customers, many there to see the band, sat in earshot of Ronny's announcement. He mentally counted down the minutes until Vanessa and her better judgment would come in. "They canceled?"

"They're lost." Ronny pointed at the phone.

Jake picked up the receiver. "Having some trouble?"

"We're at this thrift shop, across the street from another thrift shop, and GPS says there's no Hillside Coffee on this street."

No GPS should've landed them that far away. "That's because we're on Main."

"But the guy said Billings Avenue."

"What guy?" Jake turned to look for Ronny, but he was alone behind the counter.

"Whoever called us this morning."

"I don't know who you talked to, but—"

"King or something."

"There's no one here with that name. Nothing even close."

"This is crazy." Whining, the man sounded

Devin's age.

Jake's customer service experience demanded he apologize, though the fault couldn't rest with Hillside. He drew a deep breath, but then a calmer voice came on the line.

"Hey. It's Sam, the drummer. Tell me how to get there. We're at least in the right city. It can't be that bad."

With the band on its way, Jake helped a customer Ronny had left hanging and called the kid back to watch the counter. As he returned to clearing the stage, his mind circled the dream. Nightmares had superhuman villains, nonsensical plot twists, and staircases out of surrealist artwork. And they dulled quickly. Horribly logical, this one refused to fade.

What if it was a vision of what really happened?

If it was true, it changed everything. Being grabbed by the hair like that would certainly explain why she didn't wear her hair down anymore. Once Vanessa clocked in, he could go to Brooklyn, assuming he could explain he had come to see her because he'd dreamed she'd been raped.

~*~

Jake leaned against the rear counter.

The dining room was packed with high school and college students. The adults sat farther from the speakers, in the balcony.

Vanessa neared. "Standing room only. Nice." She was exaggerating, probably to get on his good side since she was late for her shift.

Jake had been stuck here, but it wasn't like he could go to Brooklyn when he couldn't figure out what to say to her.

"How've sales been?"

"Not good enough to make me bring these guys back. The lead singer didn't want to set up his own gear, and he wanted the office as a dressing room no one else could enter for the night. Bands are a dime a dozen."

"Most aren't this good. I heard they're about to get signed."

"Not if he pulls this diva act with a record company. He got the directions wrong and then said we'd told him we're on Billings, but anyone here can see the sign for Main Street out our front door."

"Ronny?"

"He said someone named King."

"King?"

Ronny, the band, Vanessa's tardiness, none of it was the real problem, and taking it out on them wasn't the answer. "If you've got this, I've got work to do."

In the office, he slouched in front of the computer and updated the website. At least his brain hadn't lost all functionality.

Vanessa opened the door and slipped behind his chair to get to the cubby she'd stocked with her own personal collection of sticky notes, markers, and cosmetics. "Are you and Brooklyn fighting?"

"What makes you say that?"

"She's been insisting on paying for her drinks."

He fumbled the mouse, caught it, and tossed it back onto the pad. "She's here?"

Vanessa smirked as she pocketed lip balm from her cubby. "No, but she stopped by yesterday afternoon and the night before that. She sat up in the balcony for a while."

"Both days?"

"I almost offered to call you for her, but I figured she would've done that for herself. If you weren't taking her calls, you certainly wouldn't take mine."

"She didn't call." She'd just sat silently in his shop. To tell him she'd been attacked?

"So you're not fighting?"

"No." He closed the website and pushed back from the desk. "What'd she order?"

"Cider." Vanessa dodged the chair to keep up as he left the office.

"But what size?"

"Um. 10 ounce."

As he exited the back, the band's lights scanned the dining room from ceiling to floor. "Both times?"

"Both times. I think."

"OK. I'll see you later."

She closed the gap between them. "Did you ever think King might be Keen? Harold Keen?"

Beyond the band, out the Main Street windows, the bookstore loomed dark and deserted.

"You said he was mad about the books."

"If he did it, why would he give his name?" If she knew where he was headed and why, she wouldn't bother with this right now, so he didn't wait for an answer.

7

Jake entered Brooklyn's apartment building through the garage. After he rang the bell, the muffled pad of her footsteps descended the stairs inside. The peephole darkened, but the door remained closed for another thirty seconds.

Once it swung open, Brooklyn's hair was loosely back, as if she'd just rushed to tie it up. If what he'd dreamed about the man grabbing her by the hair was true, hiding her hair was a way of protecting herself. But even from him? A cord of regret tightened around his neck. He had been longing to kiss her. If she really was recovering from a rape, reading desire like that on his face could give her plenty to hold against him. He tried to hold eye contact, but his gaze fell. "I heard you were looking for me."

"I got the message."

"What message?"

Her mouth lifted, but it wasn't a smile. "You didn't want to be found."

His absence had worsened her suffering. "Can I come in?"

With a weak nod, she started up the stairs.

He kicked off his shoes and followed her into her apartment, which was decorated in beiges and vanilla.

She waited by a chair at the counter without looking his direction.

His stomach twisted, but he had to follow through

on what he'd come to do. He pulled eight dollars and change from his pocket and set the wrinkled pile of bills on the corner of the table. "I don't want your money."

She put her palms together in front of her lips and blinked, face flushed. "Where have you been these last few days?"

The money matched the cost of two medium ciders. If the line from the dream hadn't meant anything to her, he would've told her she didn't have to start paying for her drinks. But he'd struck a nerve. "Why did you take the stairs at the hotel in New Wilshire?"

"How do you know about...is that where you went?" Her eyebrows pushed up, and panic carried her voice. She grabbed for the chair three times before her hand made contact. Tears came as she pulled the stool away from the counter. "You asked the staff questions?"

His dream was true. She'd chosen no one over him. In fact, she'd turned toward him. He could've been so much more help if he had known. "Brook, why didn't you tell me?"

As the sobs started, he circled his arms around her shoulders. She'd never cry alone again if he could help it.

"Tell me they caught him."

She shook her head.

"Why didn't you tell me?" He didn't need an answer—not now, anyway—but hearing his voice might reassure her she was no longer alone.

"He told me to go home like it never happened." Her voice went from loud to quiet.

He stroked her hair, careful to not loosen it from

its precarious bun. "He doesn't get to make those decisions."

"I went to the police."

"An officer told you that?" A sea of anger demanded someone to blame. Someone he could punish.

She jerked her head back and forth, pressing against his chest. "No." She coughed before she could continue, and the heat of her breath seeped through his shirt.

"OK." He led her to the couch where she curled up with her back against him. He handed her a tissue out of the box on the end table then left his arm on the back of the couch. The man in the dream grabbed her from behind. He'd have to be careful.

"He told me to go home and forget it. The police..." She gestured with the tissue. "The police did their jobs and—one said I shouldn't have been in the stairs. And he was right. And then I wouldn't take the pills, so even the doctor thought I was crazy."

"What pills?"

"Any of them. Some were for pain and other stuff, but one was the morning after pill. When I told the doctor I wouldn't take it, she insisted. And I didn't know which one it was, and I thought she might lie to me. She kept saying I didn't want to have that man's baby. So I didn't take any of them." She coughed again. "I guess I was crazy. I'm sure they couldn't lie to me. But at the time..."

The mental anguish—he bet the doctor had a pill for that. But she hadn't taken anything because she wouldn't abort the baby of a rapist. He brought his arm around her. She could push him off if she felt threatened, but he couldn't endure this distance any longer. "You're not crazy."

"I thought God would come through. I didn't think he'd let me be pregnant. I had faith, and I don't know what all of this is supposed to mean."

He grabbed two more tissues and handed them to her. Caleb had suggested a virgin birth. The truth was the opposite in all ways but one: Brooklyn had stayed innocent through it all.

"Why didn't you go to Caleb?"

"I couldn't have let him be there for the exam, and the police...I wanted to leave it all there. The exam and the questions took hours. All I could think about was how could I have been so stupid, and why did God let this happen. And why didn't I get out of the staircase as soon as I saw him or scream louder?" She balled her fingers, and her nails sank into his palm.

He didn't move to stop her. He deserved this and worse for making her go through this alone for as long as she had. "You did what you had to do. You stayed alive. That's what counts."

"But they didn't find him. His DNA wasn't in the system, and his face wasn't on the security footage. I shouldn't have been in that stairwell in the first place, and I wanted my life back. But everything was different, and the longer I waited to tell you, the less I knew how to bring it up, and I should've said it when you asked what was wrong. You gave me chance after chance. Even when you weren't asking, I knew you wanted to know." Her voice turned more ragged.

"OK." He touched her shoulder. "You don't have to explain. You're not to blame. Not for any of it."

"But I'm sorry."

"Sorry? For what?"

"For not telling you. For the mess I am."

The cord around his neck returned. "I'm the one who should be sorry."

She circled her hands on his forearm and lowered her face to her fingers. Minutes ticked by. After a deep breath, she said, "Where have you been? How do you know what he said, where it happened?"

"This will sound unbelievable." If only he could see her face as he measured out his explanation. "I had a dream. I saw it happen."

"You saw everything?"

"I saw you come up the stairs and struggle with him." Wait. When she'd said "everything," her concern likely rested on the next part. She worried about modesty. Tears pressed at his eyes. He ought to find that purity ring and slip it back on her hand. "I couldn't see higher than the tenth-floor landing. I woke up right after you grabbed the railing."

"The tenth floor." She repeated the words as if memorizing a secret. "You quoted him when you came in. About the money."

"The point was to rule out the dream. Those images drove me crazy, but I didn't believe they could be true. Didn't stop to think what it'd be like for you to hear me say the same words he said. I'm sorry. That was crass. Unacceptable."

She shook her head and tightened her fingers on his arm, clinging to him. She deserved justice. The police needed to catch the monster that did this. If they failed, he'd take up the hunt himself. She'd spent weeks scared and alone and hurting because of this man. *I could kill him.*

Unable to sit still, he offered to make her tea and stalked to the kitchen. What he needed was a session at the gym with Caleb, but he couldn't leave her.

He went through the motions of making tea until he splashed boiling water on his hand. He burned himself often enough at work, but tonight he struggled to keep from swearing. Cranking the faucet to cold water, he opened his fist under the stream to work out the pain and anger. *Keep it together. God, help me.*

In his absence, Brooklyn had moved to the corner of the couch, and her expression had smoothed out.

He placed the mug in her hands and sat on the edge of the chair. "What are you thinking about?"

"Your dream means God loves me." She held the steaming mug close. "I was beginning to doubt. This felt like a punishment for something I couldn't figure out, and that seemed so cruel." Tears collected in her eyes again. "I know it's wrong to doubt. I just—well, with the way things were turning out…"

"The man needs to be caught."

"God took care of telling you the things I couldn't bear to say, as if I didn't already owe Him everything. Whatever this is, it's His will, and He'll see me through. I'm done trying to figure it all out, what it means, what it says about me. I don't need anything but God."

"You deserve justice."

"For now, I'm happy with you." Her little smile pointed toward her tea, but the words hit his heart like a shot of adrenaline.

"I've always loved you. You know that, right?"

Her eyebrows moved closer together, but she didn't look at him.

"A few days ago, you said you liked the way our relationship was headed. This doesn't have to change our direction."

"You want to date a pregnant woman?" Sadness

muffled her voice.

"You can't believe something like this could separate us."

She heaved a breath and set the mug on the coffee table. "It's late."

He shouldn't have assumed New Wilshire was far enough behind her. Just when he thought his anger toward her attacker couldn't get stronger, it surged. *Not just death. He deserves torture. Hunt him down, God.*

Brooklyn rose and crossed to the top of the stairs.

He followed.

"It's not you." She offered a weak smile then stepped out of reach. "It's just late. I'll see you Sunday, if not sooner."

He hesitated, his hand on the railing that led to the door.

"Good night, Jake."

"Sweet dreams." He started down the stairs. If he managed to sleep, at least no dream could be worse than the last. On second thought, a dream could offer some release for this anger. If he caught up with the rapist, he would teach him a few things about pain.

"Oh. Hold on. I have something for you." She disappeared. When she returned, she hurried down to him, holding a gray lump. "I went to the Closely Knit demo at church on Tuesday. I said I wanted to make a blanket like the one from your grandma, but they said to start small." The wadded yarn straightened into the shape of a knit cap as she loosened her grip. "It's for you."

He didn't wear hats unless it dropped below zero, something unlikely to happen again this year. But he pulled the cap over his hair. "What do you think?"

She grinned and nodded.

If wearing the hat had that effect, he'd sport it all the way through summer into next winter. She might be kicking him out, but he wasn't leaving empty handed. As he walked to his car, he ran his hand over the hat. It must count for something.

~*~

After Jake left, Brooklyn sat on the highest stair. With a shaking hand, she called Haley, her closest female friend.

Voices rose and fell in the background on Haley's end. "What's up?"

She needed to rehash tonight with another woman, someone who might understand the rollercoaster of emotion, from elated peace at realizing God loved her to the guilt that resurfaced at the hope Jake would kiss her good night. Could the depth of her attraction to Jake mean she deserved what had been done to her? She'd repulsed the lie, but guilt left black prints on her conscience.

"You there?" Haley asked.

"Yeah." She couldn't rehash this with Haley. Their casual friendship wasn't deep enough for talk about rape. "OK, this is weird, and it sounds like you have people over. I guess I just wanted to talk to someone about, um, Jake."

Haley laughed. "You say that as if you liking each other is the best kept secret. I say go for it. He seems like a great guy."

Someone called her from the background. The woman had enough friends. She didn't need Brooklyn with all her baggage.

"I'll let you hang out with your guests. Sorry to

interrupt."

"It's fine, no problem. I'll see you Sunday. Maybe we can take a trip to the mall again soon. I could use some new jeans, and you can tell me more then."

"That sounds good." In the meantime, Jake knew and cared. God had orchestrated his dream. He'd even sent her to the ladies of Closely Knit, and the verses they'd recited had spoken to her more than all her hours of Bible reading had. She'd been lavished with enough hope and love to see her through tonight.

God, I trust you.

8

The next day, Jake met his mom for lunch at their usual Mexican restaurant to distract himself from the desire to call Brooklyn every few minutes and make sure she was OK. At thirty-five degrees, the weather frowned on wearing the hat, so he'd stuffed it in his jacket pocket. Just because it wasn't on his head didn't mean it had to be far away.

The waitress dropped off chips and salsa as his mom settled into the seat across from him. "Taylor aced his history test, thanks to you."

He banished thoughts of Brooklyn. She had the right to choose when and where his mom learned of the rape. Talk about his nephew would have to suffice. "I should spend more time with him."

"You have a lot going on already." Mom took a chip from the basket and quirked an eyebrow. So she wasn't going to let the other day go.

The subject might be easier if he controlled the conversation. "Have you ever had a dream that turned out to be true?"

"Like a premonition?"

"Something like that."

"Early in our marriage, your dad once took me out for the nicest dinner. He pulled out all the stops. On the car ride home, I remember sitting there, looking out at an intersection and thinking, 'This is too good to last.' I half expected a car accident before we got home."

"Thirty years…"

"Not as long as it sounds." She forced a smile. "The day we got his diagnosis, I remembered that thought so clearly. It was too good to last. I can still tell you the intersection where we were stopped when the thought came to me."

"This is different. I had a dream that turned out to be true. Even details I had no way to guess were an exact match. Of all the people who pray for miracles… I mean, take Dad's cancer. I prayed my heart out for a miracle and got nothing. Why would God move like this now and not then?"

He avoided her stare by taking an interest in the blue and red swirls of the painting across the room. He shouldn't have questioned God. Hadn't he learned better as he processed Dad's death?

His mom snapped a chip in half and went for the salsa. "What do you think it is?"

Jake glanced around the room before realizing she meant the painting. He shot another glance toward the smears of color. "I have no idea." He shouldn't have expected answers from her when she didn't know the whole story. After they ordered, Mom took up staring at him again.

He drummed his thumb on the table. He should've called Brooklyn instead of coming here.

"God is like that painting," she said. "It's hard to tell what He's going for sometimes. Jesus told a parable about a man who hired workers for his field. Some started work early, others he didn't recruit until the end of the day."

He had to interrupt before she related the entire

half-hour message. "I listen to Pastor."

"Then you know that God's logic is not our logic. Whatever He's given you or not given you, He did it purposefully. It wasn't an oversight when you didn't get miracles before. And whatever kind of dream or vision you saw, it didn't result from some accounting error in the miracle department of heaven."

He laughed in spite of himself and sat back as the waitress dropped off their meals.

"So this is about Brooklyn."

"Why the dream? Why not help her directly? It doesn't seem right to do it this way." Why not stop the rape? Or at least arrest the man. *God, where were You that night?*

"I'd ask what happened, but you wouldn't tell me."

"All I can say is, it wasn't fair."

She leaned forward. "God loves justice. Even more than you do. Trust that. It sounds to me like you're Brooklyn's direct help. Leave being God to God."

Easier said than done. He needed another distraction. Picking up his silverware, Jake related how the band had gotten lost. "Vanessa says Harold's responsible."

"He's estranged from his wife and his son because they became Christians, so I believe it."

"Where'd you hear that?"

"His ex-wife, Sylvia, is on the committee for one of the annual women's conferences in town. She's shared her testimony a few times, so it's no secret. He was furious when she accepted Christ. Even more so when their son, Andy, did. He made some threats, got physical, divorced her. Neither of them keeps in touch with him."

"OK, but his problem was books, not my faith. I don't make a big deal about Christianity in the shop."

"I seem to remember a certain interview where you talked about it."

He had done an interview with the newspaper after being named one of the area's "thirty under thirty to watch." The interviewer had asked for the key to his success, and he'd named Jesus Christ. He'd also mentioned trying to follow Dad's example. The man had had it all—family, career, active faith.

"That ran almost a year ago."

She sipped her water. "How are you going to handle him?"

"Besides stocking more books?"

"Jacob."

"I'm not backing off. We have a right to sell as many books as we want. He's lucky we only stock two or three."

"An eye for an eye, Jake?"

"I'm not letting him intimidate me out of running a good business."

"You really believe you've been called to sell books?"

"You think it would be better to laminate maps for my bands?"

"Someday, you'll be running two businesses on Main. The last thing you need is an enemy like Harold. He has family in pretty high places, and the Keens watch out for each other. Not to mention he has the ability to be a hassle all by himself."

She'd been talking about passing down the pool hall, Contact Point Billiards, since he'd opened Hillside. By the time she retired, Harold ought to be riding off into the sunset. If not, maybe the inertia of two businesses to Harold's one would give Jake the upper hand. "Family in high places? I don't care who his brother is. This isn't the Wild West."

"It's not just the mayor. He comes from a family of judges and representatives. I think there's even a congressman or a senator somewhere in there. Before his son disowned him, Harold planned a brilliant career for him, hence the fancy education.

"Regardless, Harold was never taken into custody when things got ugly and Sylvia called for help, and it wasn't for lack of bruising. She ended up being the one who had to leave and hide out at friends' houses. That is not supposed to be the way that works. Also, the city allowed him to tear down a landmark in order to build his store, and on his terms. Tell me that's not rare."

Opening the coffee shop, despite that it hadn't involved major construction, had been a maze of regulations.

"Besides," Mom said, "if this is about Christianity for him, this is your chance to represent what you believe."

Jesus hadn't only told the parable of the man who paid everyone the same. He'd also told about the shrewd manager. In the Bible, Paul claimed the privileges that went along with his Roman citizenship. Surely, Jake could claim the right to run his business. She'd just shrug if he pursued the point, but maybe God was calling Jake to be the one to stand up to Harold, to stop him from getting away with everything.

But none of that mattered when compared with Brooklyn. His mom's opinion, when added to what Brooklyn had said, made two votes for trusting God and the dream. *Lord, give me faith. Show me what You'd have me do.* The idea to reach out could be God's prompting. After he returned to Hillside, he texted her.

Dinner later?

9

Caleb hadn't stopped shifting around and staring at Brooklyn from the moment she'd let him set up his laptop in her office. She swiveled away from her recruiting spreadsheets. "Work didn't prompt this surprise visit, did it?"

His focus shifted to his screen, hands on his keyboard, though he hadn't typed a word in ten minutes. "I met with Terrence about the new software. It went great. Thanks for asking."

"You haven't talked to Jake?"

"Not recently. Why? He's got news?"

He must want her to talk without having to spell out whatever he'd heard. She'd rather act clueless. "What happened with Terry?"

"He's championing the worst program because it's the most like the old program."

"Change is hard."

The honesty earned her a calculating stare. "That's why you and Jake are still acting like ten-year-olds with cooties?"

Lord, I can't handle this conversation right now. She turned back to her computer, but the words onscreen blurred. "I don't know what I was thinking that night in New Wilshire. Under the influence of travel and long hours, I guess."

"Look, don't lie to me, OK?" This was the first

he'd ever spoken to her with this edge in his voice. "We both know you weren't under the influence of anything that night." His tone turned sad as if maybe he'd noticed her hands shaking. "Whatever it is, I'd understand. I've made mistakes, too."

"I don't want to talk about it."

"What?" The word carried his smile, the edge absent. "Do I have to get you away from town before you'll open up? Wanna take a road trip back to New Wilshire with me?"

Her heart hammered at the thought of going back there, seeing that place again. Surviving this would require all the friends and help she could get. But words to explain were just as hard to find for Caleb as they'd been with Jake. "Where are you staying?" She peeked over her shoulder. "Your parents'?"

"Jake's."

"He didn't mention it."

"He doesn't know yet." Caleb's phone sounded. He checked the display and stood. "My boss. I'll take it in the hall."

When the door shut after him, Brooklyn unlocked her own phone and typed her response to Jake's invitation.

Dinner, yes, if it's my friend asking.

She needed to see him before Caleb, but she couldn't risk not being clear about her intentions. Everything about him attracted her, but dating would plunge her into a nightmare of guilt.

His response lit the screen.

When your friend asks someone on a date, he doesn't do it in a text.

Was he angry? She tucked her phone away before Caleb could come back to see her staring at it. Who could promise Jake wouldn't fall in love with someone else while she had him on hold? She'd have to accept the risk.

10

Jake found Brooklyn settled at a table in the front of the restaurant, next to a window. Her smile on noting the hat faded quickly. He waited until after the waitress collected their orders to ask how she was.

"I'm OK." She poked the bottom of her water glass with her straw.

Fear she'd shut down their friendship like this had kept him from asking her out years ago. What had made him think last night would be an appropriate time to take the risk? "Nothing has to change if you don't want it to, Brook."

She glanced toward the rest of the dining room.

"In my defense, it was just a couple of days ago when you said you liked the way things were headed."

Ice clicked as she stirred her drink. "What did he look like in your dream?"

At least her distraction of choice might answer some of his questions, too. "Our age. White, round face, brown hair, flat nose. Heavy eyelids."

"You should've been the one to describe him to the police."

"I will if you want me to."

She shook her head. "They can't make an arrest based on a dream."

"Why did you take your cell phone out and then not use it?"

"No reception."

Right. Concrete stairwell. "Why not use the elevator?"

"I got in the elevator with some guys who had been drinking. They were obnoxious, so I got off on the seventh floor. My room was on the twelfth, but they were going all the way to fourteen and…" She checked around as if she were afraid of eavesdroppers. Empty tables surrounded them. "I didn't want them knowing what floor I was on, and I wanted to be left alone. It made sense at the time. In retrospect, I was so stupid. I brought it on myself."

"I wasn't blaming you. You have to know that."

"He was on the elevator, too. He followed me off, but I had no reason to think anything of it until I got a glimpse of him a flight behind me when I reached the ninth floor. Coincidence, I figured. Speeding up would leave him behind and prove I was being paranoid. Besides, the hotel was a labyrinth. I've never been in one that formed such a maze. If I left the stairs on the wrong floor, I doubted I could find my way to the elevator again. If the man really was stalking me…" Her voice shook.

"I get it." He reached out, but she didn't take his hand. The waitress set the plates on the table. He pulled back and turned toward the Main Street sidewalk. Even her reflection in the glass looked pained.

Simple, one-time revenge wouldn't be enough to punish the rapist. What he had done hurt her over and over, and worse, isolated her. The man deserved something more painful than jail and more drawn-out than death.

"Caleb knows, doesn't he?" she asked.

"I'm sorry. I told him you were pregnant before I

knew what happened. He doesn't know about the dream or last night."

"Could you keep it that way? You're the only one who knows."

"It's your story to tell." Eventually, everyone would need to know, but for now, being the one she trusted almost made up for the fact that she wouldn't talk about their relationship.

After he prayed for the meal, she picked up her silverware. "So how's work?"

"I told Vanessa I wanted to try out some Internet sales by offering gift baskets on the site. The next time I went into the office, I found lists from her of what to put in five different kinds of baskets. She had everything priced out and dates the merchants could supply the goods. I left her alone for five minutes, she got bored, and she took over."

"Did she figure out who to sell them to?"

"No, she didn't."

"Then there's still something left for you to do."

"I'll have to get on it quick. She works again tomorrow."

The corners of her mouth tipped up. "Sounds like a good problem to have."

Twenty minutes later, Jake had just set down his fork when the waitress cleared their plates. The night would end, and their relationship had moved back miles overnight.

"Want to go for a walk?"

"Not really." Brooklyn slipped her wallet into her purse. "I've been really tired. We can stay here if you want."

If he wanted. Why did she want to leave when she'd let him so close last night? "I confess, I'm confused."

She tucked an escaped tendril of hair behind her ear and glanced at the door.

He pushed his chair back. There was no reason to stay if it meant ignoring whatever had settled between them.

"You know how you called me when your dad died?"

"Of course."

"I went right away. I was in your driveway for close to an hour so I wouldn't miss you."

She knew how to send a guy on a guilt trip. Especially considering he hadn't gone to her as soon as he'd had the dream. He'd waited two days. "Look, we don't have to do this. Forget it."

"No." She planted her palm on the table and leaned forward. "You don't get it. This is my apology. I'm sorry. I made you wait so much more than an hour. You've been waiting for me since you picked me up after New Wilshire. Even before that—years before that. At the same time I've been honored and thrilled at you waiting for me to be ready for more, I've always been scared I'd lose you, especially if we moved forward." She balled her hand into a fist. "That's sort of turned to terror these last few weeks."

"You're not losing me." He pulled his chair back up to the table. "Not over this."

"Even if you have to keep waiting? I feel safe with you. I wouldn't let anyone else as close, but when I let you that close...it's hard to describe how scary it is. I don't know what to think." She tucked her hands out of sight. "The assault left a block of fear and guilt. At the very least, I wonder what it was supposed to teach me. Those are the good days. Other times, I wonder if

God knew I'd mess up a marriage, so just when I was beginning to let down my barriers, he gave me new ones."

"You have to know that's not true."

She nodded but avoided eye contact.

"God will use this now that it's part of your life, but make no mistake: what happened was evil. That wasn't God trying to keep you from love. That was a fallen world wreaking havoc on innocence. If there's a voice in your head telling you that you can't get married or fall in love or be happy, you need to fight it."

She reached up to catch a tear.

"If I had a way to make him pay, I would. That's all I've been able to think since I found the dream was true. That criminal deserves Hell."

"We all do." She kept her eyes lowered and spoke softly. "That's why Christ died."

"Yeah, but real belief in Christ results in salvation, and it changes a person. Because you believe and it's changing you, your sins are forgiven. You're becoming more and more like Christ as you walk with him. Safe to say the rapist isn't."

"I don't think we're supposed to want anyone to go to Hell. Jesus can redeem anyone." She wiped her face as if each tear were an individual problem.

"Then you've got to believe redemption is possible for you, too. You've been redeemed. Even from this." He grabbed a napkin and handed it to her.

"I'm not in a position to date, and I'm not ready to tell more people. I don't want to go through another round of what happened with the doctor."

"Almost everyone who matters in either of our lives is pro-life. They will not say you made a stupid decision. They'll recognize you for the hero you are."

"I'm not a hero, and I'm not ready."

Below the table, he clenched his fist.

"Caleb's in town," she said. "Fishing for an explanation, and I couldn't give it to him. I haven't told Haley, either."

He measured his response. "I had that dream to show you what it will be like when you open up to people. Everyone will stand by you. If you don't tell them…"

"It'll be a scandal. But as hard as this decision was, to have it questioned at every turn would be unbearable."

For the sake of her reputation, he'd sacrifice being the only one in her confidence. "Practice on Caleb. See how it goes."

"I don't even know what I'd say. I don't know if I can sort everything in time. I've been at this for months now, and I don't…he's only here until Sunday."

He set his jaw against objecting to the way she kept saying "I" and never "we." "Start simple. It'll come from there." He could only hope the same held true for his relationship with her.

11

After dinner, Jake worked behind the counter until Caleb entered the side door, a duffle bag over his shoulder.

"You're missing a movie with the kids at church for this?" Caleb asked when Jake met him near the stairs.

Nights at Hillside tended to attract a rowdier demographic, partly thanks to the bars sprinkled throughout Main Street. Tonight's crowd, however, seemed as mellow as the guitarist on stage. With one exception, Jake's staff could've handled the shift without him. "The man with the newspaper by the stage? That's Harold Keen."

Caleb laughed once. "He even looks like a troll. He's the one who gave your band bad directions?"

"And to do it, he must've gotten into the office."

"That or he's hacked your e-mail."

Harold, who read the print version of the newspaper? "If that's what he's doing, my plan's not going to work."

Caleb rolled his shoulder, adjusting the duffle bag. "What's your plan?"

"Keep the office locked. Only managers get keys."

"Then e-mail's not your only weakness." He looked past Jake to the counter. "You sure your managers are on the up and up?"

The possibilities were so numerous. When he

figured out one of Harold's tricks, the man could simply change his strategy to stay ahead. Locking the office wasn't practical since the employees needed entry multiple times a day, and if it wouldn't stop Harold, there was no point doing it.

"Maybe it's time to put in cameras," Caleb said. "Put one behind the register, one in the office. Regardless of what a pain Harold is, you're lucky you've made it this long without a cashier ripping off the till."

They'd had ten or twenty dollars go missing from time to time, but no threat that justified the cost of a security system. Until now. He eyed Caleb's duffle. "Anyway, I heard you might be coming."

"She got to you first."

"You certainly took your time, if it was a race."

"You ought to be thanking me. I had dinner with my parents, who told me about the movie night, so I went to church. Guess who I happened to find making out in one of the classrooms."

Jake cringed. Devin and Lauren were headed for trouble. The leaders should've known better than to let them slip off together.

Caleb snickered. "I think I spooked him bad enough to keep him from trying again. Tonight, anyway."

Jake took his keys from his pocket and handed them over. "What happened to your date?"

"I rescheduled with Rosalie." He glanced toward Harold. "You waiting for your guest to leave?"

"Yeah."

Across the room, the man lowered the paper as Vanessa neared to give him a refill.

"Good luck with that."

Jake waited at the counter until Vanessa returned. "He doesn't have a mug." Policy promised free refills of regular coffee to anyone who brought a reusable mug.

"Kill with kindness. He finally bought something, so I figured we should reinforce good behavior." Her smile faded as she caught his expression.

"Now he's got an excuse to sit here another three hours."

She tilted her head to check the clock then shrugged. "He's not hurting anyone."

"He'd only be doing this if he were up to something."

"So kick him out."

"And let him sue over it? No, thanks."

She stooped to grab two empty syrup bottles from under the counter. "You don't have to stay because he's here. I've got it under control."

Harold turned a newspaper page and sipped his coffee. Separated by distance and dim lighting, Jake couldn't be sure, but he'd swear Harold smiled.

~*~

As Brooklyn rolled from one position to another, the quilt slid away. She pulled the blanket over her shoulder. Old questions crept back. Had she brought the attack on herself?

Jake's emotions blinded him to her faults, but Caleb's loyalty didn't go as deep. Even when Caleb tried to be gentle or careful, he spoke bluntly. He had seen her that night. Had the neckline of her sweater dropped too low or her pants hugged too tightly?

A rape crisis center's website said that rapists

didn't choose their victims based on any of that. But could it really be that she'd simply happened to be in the wrong place when a man just happened to be looking for a victim?

Her belief in God meant nothing could be coincidence. Instead, the question needed to be, had God allowed her to be in the stairwell when He knew she'd encounter a rapist? Why would He have done that if she hadn't deserved it? She drew a deep breath. Caleb already knew she was pregnant. How could telling him the rest of the story cast any more blame on her?

Her phone said it was 2:30 AM. The middle of the night, but if she didn't call now, she never would. As she dialed, her stomach turned to ice. With each ring, she hoped the call would go to voicemail. How much easier that would be.

12

Jake woke when Caleb's phone went off.

A call at this time of night resulted from alcohol, a misdial, or an emergency. The shadow of Caleb's voice drifted into the room. He spoke a couple more times, too many words for shooting down a drunk or hanging up on a misdial. No clunking accompanied his voice, no getting up to run off to the hospital.

Jake turned away, determined to fall back to sleep, but then a dull thud signaled Caleb rising. Jake rolled onto his back to listen.

His friend's shape—dark pants, white t-shirt—appeared in his door. "How have you justified this?"

So the call had come from Brooklyn. "Justified?"

"With your faith. If God is good, how did this happen to her?" He spat the words as if he didn't share the same faith. "Have you tried to find the rapist yet? She says you saw him."

"Only in a dream." Jake put his feet on the hardwood floor. "I don't justify it. That's God's job."

"His job was to protect her." Caleb jabbed his finger as if God were a visible presence in the doorway. "There's a rapist on the loose. We need to hunt him down. This can't just happen like this. Not on my watch."

That must be Caleb's real problem: Brooklyn had been attacked on his watch.

"You saw him," Caleb continued. "Together, we

could—"

"He was a guest at a hotel in a big city. He might not even live in the country, for all we know." The assailant spoke in a light southern accent in the dream. American. Possibly a New Wilshire local. "Scratch that. We don't even know he was a guest."

"How can you just sit there? I thought you felt something for her."

As if 'something' described the way he loved her. "What would you have me do, Caleb?"

"Go down there. Find him."

"If you're so sure it's possible to catch him, maybe you should try."

"I haven't seen him. You have. It's your responsibility."

"The dream wasn't some command to get revenge. God gave the dream so people could help her. Without intervention, she would've spent her life passing off the baby as if it was a lapse in judgment." He rubbed his arm. Caleb's initial question nagged him. How could he still believe in a God that let this happen? If God was good, how did he let Dad die? He debated applying the same answer to Brooklyn's situation, but Caleb continued to seethe in his doorway. "God's in charge. He doesn't owe us anything. Not even an explanation for bad things."

Caleb slammed his palm against the doorframe and let out a sound that landed between a growl and a roar. He disappeared. Minutes later, the door out of the apartment slammed.

At six, Jake woke to the shower hissing. Knowing Caleb, he'd been out running. The water shut off, and Caleb's footsteps went to the guest room. The bed creaked, and then the apartment went silent.

Jake got up and walked by the spare room. One of Caleb's arms hung over the edge of the bed, and his breathing was even. Asleep.

~*~

Brooklyn stumbled through her devotions, her cell phone nearby like an armed jack-in-the-box. Last night, she'd told Caleb he had to listen without asking questions. She'd stated as little as possible before hanging up. He'd call anytime now, demanding more details.

She went to the apartment complex's fitness room. Still no word from him.

Back in her living room, she scrolled through websites until she came across a pattern for a crochet scarf with a texture similar to Jake's hat. He didn't wear scarves. Still, she'd need something to work on at Closely Knit. Maybe she wouldn't give it to him, but she liked the idea of making something that could embrace him even when she couldn't. She worked on the project until lunch time.

As she ate, she skimmed a book on pregnancy from her doctor. At twelve thirty, her phone startled her. Finally.

"Want to take a drive?" Caleb asked.

"Sure. Are you here already?"

"Just pulled in."

"I'll be right there."

Outside, his car growled in idle. The stereo hit odd beats, but then the sound melted away. She took her seat as Caleb's hand dropped from the volume control. They'd gone for drives like these before, and Caleb's only set destination would be in conversation. An unpleasant one, judging by his hardened mouth and eyes.

Caleb soon cut into the countryside. A sign introduced an unincorporated village made up of three houses and a white church with a weathered cemetery. She could live in a place like this. It exuded peace and quiet. Maybe some of it would seep into her.

"Who called the police?"

Pressure built around her eyes. "A couple who was going into a room."

"Were you hurt?"

"I had to have stitches on the back of my head. I was bruised everywhere." When she'd gotten home and seen all the marks in her mirror, she'd broken down, sobbing.

"What about the police?"

"I spent hours answering questions. They searched the hotel and looked at the security footage."

"And no one saw him? The guy couldn't have just disappeared."

"There were a lot of people."

He'd been there and should understand, but he continued to scowl.

"The hotel hosted two other conferences the same week as ours, and the building's right near all the tourist spots and the stadiums. The lobby had two restaurants. Three, if you count the coffee place."

"That's why someone should've seen him. There's no way to explain how the police came up with nothing. It's their job to get results. What about security cameras?"

"They found footage of me and the man getting off the elevator, but there was no face shot of the man. Nothing to identify him by. They aren't even sure if they have footage of him leaving. The only cameras in the hotel are on the elevators and in the lobby. Nothing in the stairwells. I never should've been there."

Roadside trees flew by like the blades of a fan. What would she have done if they'd caught the rapist? How long would she have had to be in New Wilshire to testify? Who would've gone with her? Jake was the obvious answer, but she cringed to think of him listening to her testimony. The room would've been full of people, including a lawyer bent on discrediting her. She cracked open her window and breathed in the scent of earth, wet from melting snow. How could she have testified if she struggled with this conversation?

"You need to stay after them. If you don't, they won't follow through."

"There's nothing more they can do." A lie. A better victim wouldn't have been in the staircase. A better victim would've taken their pills. She would've stayed longer, helped with a sketch and looked at mug shots. But Brooklyn didn't want or deserve their best work. "I want to focus on the future, not the past."

"You don't have that choice when something like this happens. The guy's out there. He needs to be caught." Caleb let off the gas for a stop sign and looked at her. "I mean, is he a felon or not?"

Was the rapist's guilt questionable? Had she really not done enough? She needed space to breathe. The car neared the intersection, going less than five miles an hour. She pulled the door handle.

The car jerked as Caleb stomped the brake. "What are you doing?"

She pushed the door open, climbed out, and shut the door. She drank in a cool, deep breath and looked down the road. Home waited miles away, but a walk promised to gather her thoughts better than getting back in that car. She pulled her coat tighter and started on foot.

Caleb's door clunked open. "What are you doing?" His voice rang through the dampness of this no man's land between winter and spring.

"I'll walk home."

"It's freezing out. You can't do this. Get back in the car."

True, she couldn't walk away. Perhaps if she faced the truth about herself here, she could leave the ugliness of it in the country, buried in the graveyard of a small country church. "It was my fault, wasn't it?"

"Brooklyn, get in the car." Gravel ground as he followed her, but then his steps retreated and a door slammed. The engine rumbled as he put it in gear. The wheels rolled parallel to her on the far side of the road. "I don't know what you're so mad about. You can't walk all the way back."

"I'm not mad."

"I want to know they did their jobs. Why is that so wrong?"

"I told you. They did everything they could."

"They didn't catch him."

"No." She pulled her arms tighter. "They didn't."

"Exactly." He kept checking the road, but his shoulders angled toward her. "You should've come to me. This could've ended differently. I would've caught him and killed him."

A car came over the rise in front of them.

She stepped in the grass, and Caleb steered a tire onto the shoulder.

The car slowed to pass between them, and its breeze brushed her face.

"At least stay after them." The interruption faded into the background. "Make sure they don't forget about you."

Her breath caught. Was she really obligated to demand the police remember when she'd give anything to forget?

"Why didn't you come to me?" His voice tightened. Was he near tears? His face showed only frustration.

"Because I wanted to leave it all behind—my mistakes, the rape, the police, the doctor, the whole thing. And that's why they didn't catch him. I shouldn't have been in that staircase, that's for sure. I screwed up. Let's leave it at that. Any more people looking into it would've just added to the list of things I did wrong, so I didn't need anyone else investigating it. Least of all you, someone I would have to face from then on out."

Caleb stopped the car and jogged up next to her. "I'm sorry, Brook. You made your decisions, and they're good ones. OK?"

Nothing was OK.

"Even when I thought the baby had... come about the normal way, I didn't come to judge you. But I don't know what to do now. The father's not a decent guy you can fall back on."

What would that have been like, having a decent guy to fall back on? To regret the mistake of a physical relationship, instead of the mistake of taking the stairs?

"You're not to blame for anything. Nothing at all."

"Thank you." Now if only she could believe it.

Caleb drew a loud breath. "The baby's only half the reason I'm here. I started seeing Rosalie."

So he was letting her off the hook of this

conversation, changing the subject. She waited for the story of how he'd asked out their coworker, a Latina with gorgeous cascades of dark hair.

He scraped in another breath. "She's working on a project that I'm not supposed to know about, but she told me because of you." He stopped walking and touched her shoulder. "Brook, they're shutting down the North Adams office."

13

Brooklyn let her arms fall to her sides. Caleb would only scare her like this if he were certain. As project managers, he and Rosalie often knew what was in the pipeline for the company before word reached her.

When will the bad news stop, God? How much more do You think I can take?

"When Jake said you were having a kid, I had to know you had someone to fall back on. When I found out it was an assault, I…" His voice was heavy. "Trust me. Enough women have told me I'm terrible at communication. I wasn't trying to blame you for anything. Even not telling me, but…I can't tell you how I hate myself for not walking you to your room that night."

Her mouth trembled, and her eyes welled with tears.

Caleb squeezed her shoulder. "I won't make that mistake again, OK? I'll look out for you. Jake and I will make sure you have everything you need. It sounds like it'll be a couple of months yet. You can find something new before then."

She angled away and resumed her aimless walk into the countryside.

He kept pace. "I came to North Adams yesterday to test my boss. I didn't tell him I was coming to work from this office. It's never been a problem before, but I figured if they were cutting ties with North Adams, he'd call and question me on it. And he did. Before I even made it into the building. If I'm right, it'll be announced soon."

"And your job?"

"Secure, but once they announce it, I'm putting in my notice. Someone from this office can fill my spot, and I'll work with my aunt and uncle. They've been after me for years."

"Real estate?"

Caleb nodded. "They want someone they can train to take it over, and since they want to retire in the next year or two, it's time. Sounds like more fun than getting Terrence to accept new computer programs."

"Will you move back here?"

He pulled his hands from his pockets, keys jingling. "We'll see. I don't know how far off the announcement is, so it depends on what's available. Let me drive you home."

When he pulled to a halt outside her apartment, he didn't park or move to come in. "I'm sorry to add insult to injury like this."

"At least I have warning. I'll brush up my résumé."

"You shouldn't have to at a time like this."

Though she wanted to agree, she resisted. Caleb was already worried enough. "God's in control, right?"

Caleb's jaw pulsed, but he didn't argue. "You'll be OK. I'll make sure of it."

~*~

An afternoon rush landed Jake on the register. When the line died down, he lingered to cover a cashier's break. Vanessa had the day off, so he did a double take when he saw her pull open the Main Street door. Instead of giving him an order—something she took great joy in on other days off—she slid a sheet of paper toward him.

He picked it up. "This had better not be a resignation."

She scowled. "I'm not even going to honor that with an answer."

The page contained a message to her sent through a networking site. He glanced from the text to Vanessa. "This is from Harold."

She motioned him to keep reading, so he skimmed Harold's praises about her "exemplary demeanor." At the bottom, the man offered her a job.

"He says it would involve a raise." Jake didn't want to lose her, but she wouldn't have come in a huff if she'd planned to take the offer. He smiled. "I'm the one who told you to stop giving him refills. I knew he'd take it the wrong way."

"Did you even read it? Do you know what he's doing?"

A careful read would require more focus than Harold deserved.

"He's putting in a shop," Vanessa said. "That's why he wants me."

"A shop…" He forced himself to concentrate. *Venturing into food service by way of a remodel that will enable me and my team to address the lack of good coffee that exists in the downtown area…*

"He's recruiting."

Hillside was well-established. With the bookstore making up the majority of his business, Harold wouldn't be able to aim his full attention at competing in coffee. Jake read a few more lines. "Prematurely. He's talking about a remodel, which we both know he hasn't started yet."

Vanessa plucked the sheet from his hands. "He's offering me the chance to come on now so I can manage it. Help with design and equipment choices, hiring the baristas. Maybe I should go." She gave him a pointed look.

The offer involved a promotion, not just a raise. Enough messing around. He motioned her to follow him to the office. She sat at the desk, the e-mail in her hands, as he shut the door. "Would it be worth working for Harold?"

"What makes you so sure you're going to come out of this unscathed?"

"We've been here four years, and in that time, we've seen two other shops come and go. Neither of them had much effect on our bottom line once they got past their grand opening week."

She held up the e-mail. "Harold didn't open those other shops."

"What does he have that's so special?" Even as he asked, he remembered what his mom had said. Harold had dodged trouble with the law and the city before, compliments of his family ties.

"An insane jealous streak." She looked at the paper and then folded it into thirds and fit it into her purse. "And money."

"You think we should stop stocking the books?"

"No. But you have to do something. He can't get away with this. I mean, you didn't even do anything when he sent the band to the wrong place."

"I'm putting in cameras." He had a company scheduled to install one on the balcony, one behind the register, and another in the office. The two on the first floor would record both audio and video. He couldn't listen to or review it all, but if Harold pulled another stunt, he'd dig into the footage. Even the Keens would have a hard time sweeping away a crime if there was an incriminating recording.

"What if he tries to recruit someone else?" She motioned to the board that listed the names and numbers of Hillside employees.

"Let them go. It doesn't matter what he's selling, he's still the same man, and his business is going to reflect that. Just like this business reflects something about the people who run it." He read a few of the names on their list. Each represented a hire he had recruited, and he hated to think of any of them going to work for Harold. Except maybe Ronny.

"So you're not going to do anything?"

"There's nothing to do except to make those Easter baskets a hit. Expanding into online sales would diversify the business and give us a wider reach."

"You could recruit his people, if working for Harold's so bad."

"I wouldn't trust that. It might be just what he's counting on."

"You're not worried? Not even a little?"

"No." Annoyed and angry, yes, but Jake wasn't worried.

She'd work herself up again if he let her stew much longer.

He opened the door. "Go enjoy your day off."

14

On Good Friday, Jake, Devin, and Vanessa packed a load of gift baskets into the back of the SUV Jake borrowed from his sister. Days after Hillside had placed the first basket on display in the shop, they'd sold six despite the price tag. Then the manager of a Apple Bay office building saw the baskets on the site and sent an e-mail to order for each of the tenants in her building. Jake and Vanessa had to make thirty baskets before Easter.

When Jake picked up the SUV, Taylor begged to ride along. Vanessa kept up only a veneer of happiness—she wanted to make this delivery, too. Jake turned them both down. He had plans for this drive with Devin.

Vanessa stepped back from the tailgate. "That's it."

Thirty-two baskets, including extras in case the business wanted to add to their order. If not, Jake would give them as a thank you to the building manager.

"What's thirty times four?" Devin climbed into the passenger seat.

"Thirty-*two* times four." Jake turned the key. Thirty-two baskets, each with a four-pound chocolate egg. "One hundred twenty-eight."

Devin snorted as he connected his phone to the stereo. "The chocolate weighs more than Lauren."

"How is she?" Jake shot the question as he pulled onto the road.

He shrugged and started playing music. "Have you asked Brooklyn out yet?"

Brooklyn and Jake wandered in limbo. Every time he reached out to touch her—sometimes when he simply thought of it—she backed away. "When the time comes, I've got a strategy."

Devin laughed. "For what?"

"For how to stay out of trouble until I'm married."

He rolled his eyes. "Just don't. Right?"

"Strategy makes difficult things easier."

"I don't get why God made it like this. Why make it something people want and then command them not to do it? He should've made people hate it and then command them to do it when they're married. Only responsible people would have kids."

"That's probably it." Jake grinned. "The human race would die off for lack of responsible people."

"If it's good later, I don't get why it's got to be so bad now."

"STDs, pregnancies, bad breakups." Jake glanced over. "I want my wife to know she's my one and only. Plus, I want to honor God."

"I don't think Lauren and I are going to break up."

"She's the one?"

Devin put his foot on the dash and nodded, more confident than Jake had ever been about a high school girlfriend. Yet the odds favored him being wrong.

"One word of advice, then."

"What's that?"

"Wait. If you want it to last, you'll wait until you're married. From what you tell me, you've got the rest of your lives."

Devin bobbed his head. Either he'd heard the warning or had recognized the fastest way to end the subject.

~*~

At their Apple Bay destination, Jake asked Devin to wait in the car while he checked with the office. Devin nodded, busy with his music.

After a maze of carpeted hallways, Jake crossed the sparse reception area to the door with a name plaque that read Dorothy Trier. The narrow window revealed a woman at the desk. A soft knock drew her attention.

"How can I help you?"

"I'm here with the delivery from Hillside. The baskets."

"Baskets?"

He produced the print off of the e-mail from his back pocket.

Her eyebrows knit together as she read it.

"This is Fox Lake Center, right?"

"Yes, but..." She shook her head and held the paper toward him. "That's not my e-mail. See? The vowels in my last name are switched, and the domain is wrong. We use an abbreviation."

He hadn't had any run-ins with Harold since Hillside installed the cameras. If Harold sent the e-mails to place this bogus order—and what other possibilities were there?—he'd gotten Jake to invest hundreds in Easter-themed baskets. Now they had all this inventory with two days left before the holiday.

"That really is the strangest thing I've seen." A wary smile deepened the creases around her mouth.

"Is this some kind of prank?"

"No, not a prank from me if it's not a prank from you."

"No. No, certainly not."

Harold will pay for this. But first, he'd have to prove that Harold was behind the e-mails. And given the Keen family's power, he'd have to prove it beyond the shadow of a doubt.

"All right. I think I know what happened. Sorry to bother you." He left, calling Vanessa on the way out. "Bring up the e-mails with this order."

"Sure. Is something wrong?" The whine of the machines quieted as she presumably made her way toward the office. "Jake?"

"Just check, please."

"I thought they were in the order folder."

"Yeah."

"They're not here anymore. Let me check the—oh, the trash folder was emptied today. Why did you do that?"

He lowered the phone, quelling the temptation of saying something in anger. But Harold had made a mistake. He brought the phone back to his ear. "This office didn't place an order. I think Harold faked it, but if he went in and deleted the e-mails, we'll finally have proof."

"They didn't order? How...?" She let out a frustrated sigh. "He wouldn't do that. I worked so hard on this."

"I'll take care of it. He made a mistake this time."

But when he reviewed the security footage, only employees had used the computer. The camera didn't record the computer screen, so determining if one of them had deleted the e-mails or used the computer for some other, valid reason was impossible.

"What do we do now?" Vanessa's voice faltered. "We don't have proof, so we can't report it, can we?"

Harold must have one of Hillside's employees in on this. Or he'd hacked the computer, as Caleb had suggested.

"We'll sell what we can before Easter. After that, we'll remarket them as spring baskets." He left the office to find Ronny doing dishes for once. Brianne, another part-time employee, bustled behind the counter. Had one of them been involved? The cameras had shown others stopping in this morning, too. The doubt in his employees, the hit to sales, and the disappointment to Vanessa demanded he do more than sell the leftover baskets. He wouldn't sit idly by as Harold dismantled Hillside piece by piece.

15

Jake rested his hand on a bookcase. Made of real, new-looking boards, the shelf would serve his purpose of holding a free book exchange at Hillside. He'd stock the library with books from places like this thrift store, and customers could swap one book for another free of charge.

"Blond wood would glow in such a dark space," Brooklyn said, plunging her hands into the pouch on the front of her thick sweater.

"It'd be a beacon." Jake laughed.

Brooklyn pointed toward the end of the aisle. "That might work."

They wandered toward the case, pausing to consider other options along the way. Twenty baskets remained unsold with Easter a week behind them. Even with the draw of the book exchange, increasing traffic in the shop and selling all those baskets could take weeks. He'd have to discount them. Or, maybe, they'd break them apart. With smaller price tags, individual components would be an easier sell.

Brooklyn bumped his shoulder, and he held a breath of the musty thrift shop air, but she stepped away. "You and Devin came up with this together?"

"You say that like it's not going to work." Devin did approve of the book exchange, but Jake had come up with it on his own. He had a responsibility to make

Hillside as attractive as possible to customers. Online research yielded good reviews of other places that hosted similar exchanges. "It'll bring in customers."

"It'll upset Harold."

"Sometimes, you really can have it all."

Brooklyn raised her eyebrows.

"If you're concerned about his feelings…"

She shook her head before he had to finish.

They came to a stop at the end of the aisle, in front of the case.

"We have a winner," he said.

"It's still lighter."

"It doesn't glow."

She shrugged, conceding.

He purchased and loaded the case into the SUV. As he shifted into drive, she stared out the window, face set with a mindless frown.

"December called. It wants its sweater back." He grinned.

"I have to tell my parents." She folded her arms over her sweater. "Pretty soon, I won't be able to hide it anymore."

She needed a sweater to hide the baby already? They weren't even three months into this, and two days ago, her t-shirt and jeans hadn't revealed anything. But this was the first time since Caleb she'd volunteered to share her story with more people, and he had to encourage it. "How're you going to do it?"

"Do you think it would be cowardly to use e-mail?"

"They're not going to have a problem with it, Brook. You've got a career, a place of your own. It's not like you're dropping the baby off on their doorstep. Your mom will be thrilled. They all want to be grandmas." His mom, anyway, had been ecstatic when she'd found out Taylor was coming.

"The job won't last that much longer." Shortly after Brooklyn told him of Caleb's warning, Galley Paper had announced the North Adam's office would close in June. She'd told Jake she sent out a stack of résumés but had yet to garner any interest.

"I said career, not job. The skills you have go with you, and you have time to find something else. You're hirable."

The frown lessened as he spoke, but her shoulders remained rounded under her sweater. "If Mom didn't talk to people from around here, I'd have until July to mention the baby. Or not. I can't show up to Greg's birthday party looking like I've got a watermelon under my shirt."

Brooklyn's mom threw a party for her latest husband, Greg, each July. They lit fireworks, drank, and danced with all the ruckus of a college party.

"I can do it over the phone. Or webcam?"

"Sure." He couldn't advise her to tell her hypercritical mother in person.

"How long do you think it'll take to blow over?"

"However long it takes, it can't make things any worse between you, right?"

"I mean with everyone else. Will there be a big, scarlet R pinned to me and the baby forever?"

If she had taken the pills the nurse offered, she could have moved on. They both could have. But the idea of freedom came with a rush of shame. This was a human life.

"There is a middle option." He might not have a right to say this, but it was too late to stop now. "Between raising the baby and abortion. Have you thought about that?"

"I can't see going through with this and then letting go. I won't make this baby suffer for what happened to me." She twisted her fingers together.

"Being adopted isn't suffering."

"Being born unhealthy is." Her voice brimmed with determination. "If I put the work into making sure this baby is healthy, I have to love her. If I am called to love her for nine months, I can't see letting go at the end of it."

"You're getting ahead of yourself. You don't even know it'll be a girl."

"And you don't know that I wouldn't regret giving her up. Some people search for years and years to find family they lost through adoption."

"People search for years and years to get family through adoption. You have a lot of life to live yet, and you need to live it without regret."

"You think I should give her up?"

"I want you to be happy, Brook."

"If adoption would prevent this next part, the scandal, having to tell Mom and Greg, it would be tempting. But God's gone to a lot of trouble to give me this baby." She studied his face. "Once I'm through all of this, I can be a good mom, can't I? I don't want to let God down."

He'd always admired her determination to do the right thing, but each time she used "I" instead of "we" pricked him. He pulled to the curb and turned in his seat. His fingers hurt for how badly he longed to take her hands in his, but her gaze held question marks, not invitations. "This is your decision, but you should know I don't intend to let you handle the aftermath alone. If you love the baby and keep it, that's fine. I will fill whatever role you'll let me have in his or her life. And, yes, you'll be a great mom."

She broke eye contact. All the better. Looking into her lost expression had nearly strangled his composure.

"But if you're going to relive what happened every time you see the baby's face and ignore a valid option for a happy life for you and for the baby, know that it'll destroy me. This started with a nightmare, but it doesn't have to end that way."

The angle of her head distorted his view of her expression, but her sadness seemed to lessen.

"But, if you're in this," he continued, "I'm in it, too. We can handle anything. What matters is your own peace and joy and giving the baby the best life possible."

Her lashes shaded her eyes. "I'm keeping the baby."

"Well, then, good. The rapist took enough. Don't let him take your firstborn, too. I couldn't stand to not know such a big part of you." As he took his foot off the brake, he caught a glimpse of her smile. He'd be loyal to her and this baby forever.

~*~

Jake set up the book exchange before Vanessa's shift the next day. When she came in, they created a tally sheet to track how many people used it. They were talking behind the counter when Robyn Washburn came in.

She introduced her companion as Sylvia Monroe.

Vanessa started forward to ring the sale.

"I've got it." Jake stepped up to the register. Mom

had said Harold's ex-wife's name was Sylvia and that she helped with women's conferences, as did Robyn. Could this be her? Years of hunching away from Harold's insults could explain her rounded posture.

Robyn ordered like a pro, and Vanessa made her drink as he helped Sylvia through making a choice. Vanessa handed Robyn her iced latte and started the second drink.

Robyn swirled her cup. "You know, Jake, I've been wondering. Is everything all right with Brooklyn? After I saw you at the doctor, I kept an eye on prayer chain e-mails, but nothing came through."

He had been so busy searching for a way to ask about Harold that he hadn't seen this question brewing. He counted out Sylvia's change to hide his hesitation.

"She hasn't looked quite like herself in a while," Robyn continued. "If there's anything we can be praying about..."

"Everyone could use some prayer."

She nodded, her mouth tight.

Vanessa passed a cup to Sylvia, who took a sip and declared it delicious.

Jake held out a Hillside loyalty card. He couldn't ask about Harold, but he might be able to get her to return another time when he could. "We can start a card for you. Tenth drink is free."

She glanced toward Main Street and Harold's Books. "I don't make it down here often. Sorry."

She had to be Harold's ex. "No problem. Enjoy yourselves."

Once the women were at a table across the room, Vanessa giggled. "You have, like twenty mothers, don't you? Most people are lucky to have one, you know."

"Only because of church. You're welcome to start coming with me."

"Nah. How would that look? Me and the single boss being seen out together?"

Jake had never been less single. Brooklyn was all he wanted. Her happiness, her wholeness, her healing.

"What's that look?" Vanessa asked.

"That wasn't a look." He turned for the office, but she followed.

"You're keeping a lot of secrets these days. First, you didn't tell me you were installing a book exchange. Now this." She narrowed her eyes. "I better be the first to know."

"You bet."

She scoffed. "Anyway, just one thing. You don't plan to, like, leave at any point before Harold sees the books, right? Because he can be a handful on a good day, and today's not going to be so good."

"The farthest away I'll be is my apartment."

"And you'll have your cell phone on?"

"Scout's honor."

She nodded and then hurried back to work.

~*~

Two hours later, Jake was clearing tables when Robyn exited the side door, leaving Sylvia, who was still picking up her coat. He carried his plastic bin to the table next to hers and collected her now-empty mug.

"Good to the last drop?" he asked.

"Yes." She arranged her scarf around her neck.

"We've got some competition moving in soon, so I

like to know we're keeping our customers coming back." To hide the clumsy transition, he passed a rag over the table.

"Oh, it was wonderful. I'm sure you'll do just fine."

He dropped the rag into the bin with the mug. "It's Harold, actually. Across the street? He's getting into coffee, and it seems like it's because he's jealous of what we're doing over here."

She eyed the windows as if an army marched toward Hillside. "I heard once that ten percent of people just won't like you. Incompatible personalities." She offered a quick smile and pulled on her coat. "Robyn says you go to her church. You keep on trusting God, and you'll do all right, I'm sure."

"Good advice." Jake picked up the dish bin and headed for the counter. So much for finding out anything new about Harold's motives.

16

Jake set up his laptop between the register and the book exchange. He promised his growling stomach dinner once he finished the schedule, but he still hadn't taken time to eat when Brooklyn arrived at seven.

She eyed the books. "I was hoping we could go to a park."

It was a little cold for that, but how could he say no to her? "I haven't had dinner, and I promised Vanessa I would hang around in case Harold shows up. How about I make a sandwich, and we go sit on the fire escape?"

Once on the third floor, Brooklyn disappeared to the landing while he threw together his dinner. He tucked his Bible under his arm and found her seated against the railing.

"I read a verse this morning that made me think of you." He sat down balancing his food, water, and Bible. Once he settled, he passed her the book. "Deuteronomy 22:25 and 26."

The pages crackled as she searched.

The navy sky stretched over the buildings. Below, streetlights glowed at the perimeter of the parking lot.

Her fingers stilled as she read out loud. "But if in the open country a man meets a young woman who is betrothed, and the man seizes her and lies with her, then only the man who lay with her shall die. But you shall do nothing to the young woman; she has committed no offense punishable by death. For this case is like that of a man attacking and murdering his neighbor." Her voice steady and unaffected, Brooklyn folded the Bible shut.

"That means you're innocent, Brook."

"I figured that's what you were getting at."

"I like the part about the man dying, too."

Her laugh was dry. "Absalom got revenge on the man who raped his sister, and that didn't work out very well for him."

Jake's phone buzzed, and he took it out to check the text because of his promise to Vanessa.

Harold came, he saw, he left. All without a peep. What do you think that means?

It meant they'd finally gotten ahead of the man. He put the phone away. "Sorry."

"What Absalom did alienated him from his father, and it's not like Tamar was any better off. She lived the rest of her life in her brother's household as if she was ruined."

"You're not ruined."

"No, but..." She inhaled deeply. "I've been thinking about getting labeled with a big, red R. Outlasting that label will be a process."

"Why? Nobody's even applied it yet."

"I have." She folded her hands. "It's why we're sitting out here in the cold."

"I thought you wanted to be outside. We can go in."

"No. I..." She fidgeted with the Bible. "It's really important to me to stay pure. If it weren't, I would be curled up in my favorite chair in the world with my favorite afghan."

Possessions of his ranked as her world-wide

favorites. He smiled. "If you're afraid the chair will make some kind of move on you, I could go remind it of the house rules. It'll be on the curb in five minutes flat if it tries to pull anything."

Brooklyn remained unmoved. Since she was in control of her own actions, his actions must be the ones she doubted.

"I know how to keep my hands to myself."

"It's me. I feel guilty." Her gaze shifted toward the parking lot. "I'm slowly beginning to believe it's not my fault, what happened. That I was in the wrong place at the wrong time. But still, wanting simple things that I used to think were fine makes me feel so…" Her hands burrowed into the pockets of her coat.

"That's not God convicting you like that."

"He wants us to live pure lives."

"He does."

"I feel like…like I need to hold to a new standard of purity to prove to myself that I'm not who I think I am. Besides, if lusting in your heart is the same in God's eyes as committing adultery, then I have to believe God wants us to live up to a standard that keeps us from impure thoughts, right?"

He used to think he'd handled himself well in his relationships. Now, looking at her became as impossible as looking at the sun.

"I don't want you to think dating me would be normal," she said.

"You think the idea of a pure relationship would scare me off."

"More than pure. Above reproach." She paused on the phrase she'd borrowed from him, a phrase he'd picked up from his dad.

Jake lived by it. At least, he'd thought he had.

"It looks bad to be alone in each other's apartments."

He'd argue if she hadn't just mentioned dating. If he agreed to this, could they finally admit to being more than friends? What did he have to lose? "What else?"

She shifted, pulling her shoulders up.

"Let's start here. I don't know what you consider simple things, but for the right woman, if I could hold her hand, I could save our first kiss for our wedding day."

Brooklyn smiled and brushed her cheek, but it was too dark to see if she was crying. "Your wedding could be a long way off."

"That's not up to me."

She tugged her coat tighter. A pregnant woman shouldn't have to freeze out on a fire escape.

"Either way, Brook, I promise I'll control myself, even if we're in my living room, and if you're worried about how it looks to others...." He shrugged. "I doubt they'll notice in the first place. Besides, we'll obviously be alone at some point, whether it's in our apartments or in the car or any one of a hundred other places where we'd be together. No one is always in sight of someone else. It comes down to the integrity of the couple to stay pure. I have too much on the line to let things get carried away. I've already got firm boundaries of my own, but if yours are set differently, I'll follow those, too. I think I've proven that."

She sniffed. Definitely crying.

Her guilt locked him at a distance, as helpless to touch her as he'd been in his dream. He refused to repeat the mistake of giving up instead of fighting to break through. "Besides, last I checked, we're just friends, anyway. If the time comes and that changes, decide what's right based on prayer and study, not based on some lesson you imagine the rape was supposed to teach you. In fact, give up that idea completely—the one about what you're supposed to learn. This wasn't a punishment. You're as innocent as a murder victim."

"And as pregnant as a who—"

"Don't you dare." Where did these sudden rules and insults come from?

She tucked her chin and fell silent.

"You need to be angry at the attacker, not yourself."

"I am." Honesty rang in her tone. She climbed to her feet.

If she planned to leave angry, he'd follow to convince her of her innocence.

"There's nothing I can do about it." She splayed her hand, then raked her fingers into her tied-up hair. "If I concern myself with him, all I'm left with is nothing. He's got me over and over again. There's nothing I can do. I'm sick of him putting me in that position. In this position." She motioned at her belly. "So I try to focus on what I need to do, what I need to learn, what I can control. I'm trying to get ready to be a good mom. I'm trying to have faith in God when He said He has good plans for me. I want to live a pure life." She sucked in a breath, tears glinting on her face.

"No, you're attempting more than that. You're trying to be better than perfect, but you're human. Give yourself a break."

She frowned but didn't argue.

"God does have good plans for you. You're his daughter, and I will respect all the implications the status carries. I said I could wait until my wedding day to kiss the right woman. You're her, and this is a promise. Wherever our relationship goes, I won't cross that line until we're married. But we don't have to be married to sit in my living room on a cold night." He put his hand out. "Let's stop letting a rapist come between us. You can trust me."

She wiped her cheek on her shoulder then looked at his extended hand.

He waited. She must want more from their relationship like he did, or she would've walked away from him a long time ago. So they had to overcome this. Obeying her rules had only allowed her to make more of them, condemn herself further. Allowed to continue uncontested, her sense of shame would take away the little part of her she let him have.

When her fingers first touched his, the pressure was slight, but even that made his heartbeat race. He closed his hand around hers. In the living room, he picked up the blanket from the armchair. She slipped off her shoes and pulled her feet up, and then he draped the blanket over her. She needed something so much more powerful than anything he could offer.

He sat on the edge of his coffee table and clasped his hands together. "Father, You told us to cast our cares on You. I don't even know where to begin tonight. Brooklyn needs healing, and she needs to feel Your love. She needs to know she's safe with You and, frankly, I'd like to know she is, too. God, we're broken. I give this all to You."

He expected her to pray, but her cool, small hands surrounded his. "I love you."

Jake lifted his face.

She looked straight at him, her blue irises brilliant

from crying.

"I love you, too." He banished thoughts of kissing her and settled for touching her face. Even then, he didn't allow his fingers to linger on her skin. If she knew the self-control he exerted to lower his hand, would she trust him more, or less? "Always have."

17

Jake brought his Bible study to the alcove in Contact Point Billiards, two blocks from Hillside, because he'd hardly been away from the shop in days. At the end of the lesson, Sean challenged him to a game of pool. Devin and some of the others hung around to watch.

Jake's mom entered the room through the back door. She stopped to say hello to the guys she knew and then rubbed Jake's shoulder. "I have some news when you're free."

Jake sank two shots and glanced up in time to see Brooklyn step in off Main Street. The sign he'd left at Hillside for any boys who ran late must've steered her here.

She spotted him and smiled before dropping into conversation with his mom. Another bulky sweater blanketed her.

Snickering, Devin nudged him. "Your turn. Something distracting you?"

Jake laughed, but as soon as he won the game, he retreated to the counter.

Brooklyn shot him a glittering look unlike anything he'd seen from her in months.

His mom's grin matched.

"What're you two up to?" He stopped next to Brooklyn.

"I was just telling Brooklyn about some plans I'm

making." Mom clasped her hands. "I think it's time for the next step."

"What's that?"

"I think it's time for me to retire."

"Oh. Congratulations." He looked to Brooklyn, but she kept her eyes on Mom. "And?"

"I want to give you the business."

"Whoa. Now?"

She kept grinning.

"Mom." He shook his head. Problems already stretched him too thin. "Keep ownership a few more years. Bring on someone to manage it for you. I've got too much right now."

"Vanessa is capable of running Hillside, and you know it, Mister Easter Baskets. She's graduating in a couple of months, and you'll either have to make it worth her while to stay, or she's gone. Make her store manager."

"I'm not sure she's ready for that."

Mom waved off the concern. "Have faith."

"It's not that I don't want the pool hall." He strained to keep from checking Brooklyn's expression. One stray look and his mom would never stop pelting him with questions about her. He couldn't answer anything, not even the offer of Contact Point, until Brooklyn told her about the rape.

"What's the problem, then?" Mom asked.

"What about all this Harold stuff?" He hadn't told her he'd put in the book exchange. She'd disapprove. If he didn't take ownership of the pool hall, he wanted it to be for his reasons and not because she didn't trust his judgment. "And Vanessa hasn't even graduated yet."

"It's not like you wouldn't be around to help.

You'd work with her, not just walk away."

Four years ago, Mom had ordered him to do something with himself and the money Dad had left him. She'd claimed to have found a perfect location for a coffee shop, probably because he'd fallen into a rut after Dad died. Her options had been to put up with a grown child living in her house or inspire that child to greatness. Maybe this retirement announcement masked an effort to jumpstart him again.

Does she think I'm in a rut?

"You're so good with the youth, Jake." Mom lifted a hand toward the boys. "You could breathe new life into this place. Imagine. It might actually be profitable under you."

He risked a glance at Brooklyn.

"This fits with your dreams."

And that's why he couldn't give a flat-out no. He'd wanted Contact Point since his dad died. The outreach would be his chance to make a difference in the lives of more youth. He'd balance the workload the way his father had, keeping the day job for income and the hall for God. Mom could be right, though. The place should be capable of turning a profit. Owning it wouldn't have to be a pure charitable effort. "I'll think about it."

Mom smiled as if she could barely contain an all-out grin.

Brooklyn put her hand on his forearm as she rose.

"What are you two up to tonight?" The quickness of Mom's question meant she saw Brooklyn's touch and read into it.

"Nothing special." The pathetic answer sounded like something Devin would say. Jake whisked Brooklyn from the counter before Mom could get any more suspicious.

They passed onto the privacy of the deserted sidewalk.

"It's because of me, isn't it?"

If only Mom hadn't announced her news in front of Brooklyn.

He resisted reassuring her with touch because he could see Mom through Contact Point's windows. "This is her way of giving me a new challenge. She does this when she thinks I'm getting complacent."

"You don't believe she wants to retire?"

Rain had fallen most of the day, leaving the night air damp and the sidewalk full of wet shadows. He sidestepped a puddle. "I think once she knows what's going on, she'll suddenly feel like working a couple more years."

"What part of it? Harold? Or us? New Wilshire?"

"Us. If she knew you and I were..." They'd set relationship rules, held hands, and confessed to loving each other. Should he call it dating? Wasn't the tie between them so much more than that? Yet they'd never officially labeled it.

"Together?" Brooklyn asked.

"Yes." The windows of the pool hall were far enough behind them, so he took her hand. "If she knew we were together, she'd be satisfied."

"And you don't want to tell her about us because I'm pregnant."

"I want to tell her everything at once." They continued down Main. "Have you figured out how to tell your parents?"

"I'm waiting until after my twelve-week checkup because twenty percent of pregnancies end in miscarriages."

"Twenty percent?"

"Mostly in the first three months." She stubbed her foot on a crack in the sidewalk, and her fingers tightened around his hand.

"Are you worried?"

"What I said last night about being sick of the rapist putting me in this position...sometimes I want an easy out, but they say I'll be able to hear the heartbeat tomorrow. That's when the checkup is. When I think about that little heart, nothing about losing the baby sounds easy."

Jake glanced at the belly of her sweater. A little heart, along with little hands and a little nose, formed inside the woman he loved. He'd never think of miscarriage as an easy answer again, either. He cleared his throat.

"So...I might go see Mom and Greg right away on Saturday. Get it over with." Her voice dipped with uncertainty. "And we can maybe get into it with your mom, too."

He fixed his eyes on the shop at the end of the block. She'd said they were together, but she didn't invite him to hear the heartbeat. She seemed more hesitant to tell his mom than her own hypercritical mother.

"What're you doing Saturday? Can you come along?"

Progress. He'd take what he could get. "Of course."

18

On Saturday, Jake didn't intend to work, but Vanessa flagged him down. The phone was ringing, a customer waited, and the only employee up front with her had been hired days before. Vanessa handled the phone call while Jake walked Grace, a high school junior, through ringing up the order.

"He says the chairs are what we asked for," Vanessa said. "He wants to charge a sixty-dollar fee to switch them for the brown ones."

Jake pointed to the key Grace needed to hit. "Did you order the wrong ones?"

"No." Vanessa's voice hit with indignation.

"Then tell him so. It was done over the phone, so if the order says red, it's because his person entered the wrong color. We can't be responsible for their mistake."

"You want me to tell him that?"

"Yeah." He glanced at her as Grace counted the customer's change.

"What if this was Harold again? Because of the books."

The book exchange had been in place for almost a week, and their neighbor hadn't responded in any way. "Making me pay sixty dollars is way below his pattern of escalation. Tell them to figure it out."

Vanessa disappeared into the back again.

He instructed Grace to buzz the intercom—a

lesson she assured him Vanessa covered earlier—if another customer came.

He found Vanessa in the office, her forehead pressed to her palm, hair spilling through her fingers. "I don't think that's what I said. I can't pay the fine."

She wasn't getting anywhere. Hand extended, he stepped closer.

She gave up the receiver and her place at the desk without another word.

"Hey, this is Jake. What's happening with the chairs?"

The sales rep started over, explaining he could exchange the red chairs for brown ones, but he'd have to charge a fee.

"Sorry, but that doesn't work for us. We ordered brown."

"The last person said she wasn't sure."

"I'm sure. We ordered brown."

"It says right here on the order—"

"Which your associate entered by phone. We have no need for red. Come switch them out. We're good customers, and I don't want to have to find a new vendor."

The sales rep changed direction. Jake looked at Vanessa as he hung up. "You know you'll have to deal with this kind of thing as Internet sales manager." Even more so if he put her in charge of the entire location.

Grace buzzed the intercom.

"I'll go check on her." Vanessa turned away. "I'm sure I can do that right."

Jake sighed and checked the calendar. Today, the second Saturday in April, was just weeks before her graduation. That could explain her stress level, but taking on a new role at the shop would be at least as hard as the end of a semester. Considering the war with Harold and the situation with Brooklyn, he needed Vanessa to fill her role more than ever.

He and Brooklyn planned to leave for her parents' house as soon as he could get over there to pick her up. Vanessa's mood was no reason to be late.

~*~

Brooklyn motioned for Haley to sit on the couch.

Haley eyed her with a mischievous smile. "OK, shoot."

Over the last few weeks, Brooklyn had shared some details about Jake. She'd invited Haley over today to tell her the rest of the story as practice before talking to her mother.

"If you've decided to quit your job and become a nun, I cannot support that decision." Haley held down giggles as she cocked her head. Except for the laughter, the impersonation of Mom wasn't far off.

"OK." Brooklyn had heard the heartbeat yesterday. Her top showed a definite curve to her belly. She didn't want to wait until her mom or Haley or Closely Knit had to see it on their own, so she had to find a way past this burning fear. "I did make a decision, and I guess my faith has everything to do with it, so—"

The doorbell rang. An hour too early for Jake.

Haley bit the corner of a smile. "Going to get that?"

She ought to. Then she could come back up and blurt out the truth. *I was raped, and I'm keeping the baby.* Boldness would be key when she spoke with her mother, the only strategy that might keep Mom from ripping her decision to shreds. She jogged to the bottom of the stairs and opened the door, ready to dismiss whoever waited.

The sight of Jake jolted her nerves into a frenzy. She rubbed her palms together at the memory of his hand taking hers on the fire escape. "You're early."

"I thought we were going whenever I got over here."

"Didn't we say eleven?"

"Really?" He tucked his hands into his pockets. "I can wait if you're not ready."

"I have Haley upstairs. I was going to tell her, like practice for Mom."

"You want me to come back?"

Maybe telling Haley was more about letting her in than it was about practice. She had purposely surrounded herself with people who would never treat her the same as Mom did, even in role-play. She could talk with Haley another time. "No, come on up. We can go early."

Haley hopped to her feet when Jake appeared behind Brooklyn. "Is it about you two?"

"No. My news isn't about us." She glanced at Jake for help.

"Sorry, I'm early," he said. "Do you mind if I steal Brooklyn away?"

"No problem." Haley's smile turned into a full-blown grin. She must think Brooklyn and Jake were going to announce an engagement.

With a wave and a wish of good luck, Haley left before Brooklyn could set her straight.

~*~

The farther Jake drove toward her mother's house, the more Brooklyn fussed, tugging at her shirt and checking her reflection. She wore her hair in a fancier style than normal, one that must've taken forever to pin back.

A few miles from her mother's house, she leaned toward the mirror again and rubbed at the corner of her eye. She retrieved a makeup pencil from her purse, and redid her eyeliner. One bump in the road could cost her vision, but Jake kept his peace.

"I'm not going to say it until later," she said. "Maybe after dinner."

Great. An afternoon of skirting the subject. But he nodded. This was her choice.

When Gloria opened the door to them, the older woman, with thick makeup and puffed up hair, looked ready to anchor a news broadcast. Stretching a moment of silence, Gloria scanned her daughter.

He'd give Brooklyn a squeeze of reassurance, but she'd tucked away her hand when he tried to take it on their walk to the door.

"You look good, Mom." Brooklyn offered a smile.

Gloria smiled, a taut, plastic movement. "You've put on weight."

19

Brooklyn chopped tomatoes for the salad that would be served with dinner. She'd soon have to break the news about the rape and the baby.

Jake reached for a second knife to help, but his phone rang before he grasped it.

Her mom didn't acknowledge him when he excused himself to take the call.

Left alone with her mother, Brooklyn's pulse kicked up.

Mom selected a cucumber and ran a blade along its sides, separating long swaths of the peel. "You'll be forced to tell me why you're here eventually. Perhaps we could cut to the chase."

Brooklyn continued with her work. She'd determined this morning that she needed to make her announcement quickly, concisely. The same way Mom was chopping up that cucumber. "I'm having a baby."

Jake finished his call and returned.

"With him?" Gloria tilted her head in his direction, but her eyes bored into Brooklyn.

She should've said something about the rape immediately, but the concerned look on Jake's face derailed her. Why had she decided to do this in person, and then let her mom choose the timing? "No. Maybe we should bring Greg in for this. I'd like to say it just once."

"You want to give him a heart attack by springing

this on him?" She motioned with her knife. "Do you know how hard it is to be a single mom?"

"It wasn't a choice."

"There are so many methods of birth control. You couldn't find one to work?"

Brooklyn locked eyes with Jake.

He nodded. She had to speak up.

She let the words fly. "It was an assault."

Mom sucked a breath as if she'd been slapped.

"A rape, and I don't believe in morning after pills."

"You worried about that at a time like this?"

Brooklyn blinked toward the red mess of seeds on the cutting board. "My priorities haven't changed."

"Is the chicken ready?" Greg asked.

Mom scraped her knife across the cutting board. "Brooklyn says she was raped, is pregnant, and has decided to raise the baby."

So much for not wanting to spring the news on him.

Greg stared, and then his body folded into a kitchen chair, eyes glazed. "When did this happen?" His question was soft, his look pensive with some emotion. Pity?

She hadn't expected him to be so affected. "January."

"North Adams must have changed tremendously." Mom's voice rang with accusation.

"I was in New Wilshire on a business trip. I took the stairs at the hotel one night."

Mom clanked the tongs against the glass bowl to toss the salad. "Greg, the chicken is ready to go on. Jake, why don't you help him?"

Alone with Mom, she could talk this through.

Their relationship might take a turn. Mom might come to respect Brooklyn's decisions and look forward to the promise of a grandchild.

Jake stood firm, one hand clenched, green eyes on her as if he awaited an order. He shot a glare at her mom.

Brooklyn nodded to him to leave. Knowing he was just outside would be enough. Hearing the rough part of this conversation would only make him dislike her mom more, adding a barrier to any hope of restoration. She mouthed the word *go*. She had survived the stairwell. She could survive a few minutes with her mother.

Greg slid open the door to the patio.

Jake took the platter of raw chicken from the counter and followed him out.

~*~

The time at the grill passed in silence. When he and Greg returned to the kitchen, Jake couldn't guess what had happened between Brooklyn and Gloria.

Dinner conversation lagged, but as Gloria stood to collect dishes, she announced they had a new board game to play.

Jake longed to sweep Brooklyn away, but she nodded again, forever surrendering.

Gloria's wedding ring clicked against the dinner plates as she stacked them. "Set up the game in the living room. I haven't looked at the directions yet."

Jake rallied the little enthusiasm he could muster. "We'll figure it out then." The time alone would allow a few minutes to build Brooklyn up. Maybe it'd be enough to help her through the evening.

Brooklyn trailed her hand along the hallway, drawing an invisible line below the family portraits. None contained all three of them, since Greg joined the family as Brooklyn moved out. No evidence of the former husbands remained. In middle school, she'd smuggled a picture of her biological father to Jake for safekeeping. Gloria had purged all other evidence of the man. Jake gave the photo back to her the day he left for college, when she was moving into the dorms.

In the living room, she broke the plastic that protected the game. "She said I should terminate the pregnancy and that I'm throwing my life away to indulge a passing religious phase. It takes eighteen years to raise a child, and it'll get old long before the kid does. Her words. I asked what that says about her experience raising me. She said my birth was a different world, whatever that means."

"It means you have eighteen years to prove her wrong."

"She asked what my intentions toward you are, as if I'm a predator."

He laughed. "What are your intentions toward me?"

Her cheeks turned pink, and her eyes watered. She'd kept herself together through her mom's words, yet the mention of their future brought her to tears? He'd have to wait until he could take her home to fix this. And he'd have to keep Gloria from plunging the knife deeper in the meantime.

~*~

Greg clunked his marker across the spaces as if to clear up doubt he hated the game. "How could this happen?"

Jake looked up. Greg focused on his stepdaughter.

Brooklyn looked as if she expected a slap. "What?"

"You couldn't fight him off or get away? Did he have a gun?"

"He was stronger."

Gloria's shoulders squared. "You're not fighting his baby."

Brooklyn put down the game card and twisted her bracelet. "I'm trying to do the right thing."

"It's not right to bear the child of a rapist, and it's even worse to raise it as your own."

Brooklyn took a long, slow breath.

Jake stood. "What kind of mother are you?"

"Evidently, I'm the kind who raises a fool." She sipped her wine, eyes on her daughter.

He put a hand on Brooklyn's shoulder. He had to get her out of there. "We're here as a courtesy to you. This was your shot at coming through for your daughter, and you blew it. She's not looking for your help or your opinions. We have this handled."

"Jake." Brooklyn's voice had lost its meekness.

Gloria swirled her wineglass. "That's awfully involved for a man who's not the father."

Brooklyn's shoulder stiffened under his touch. "Mom."

"I think I know exactly what happened here," Gloria said.

"We're leaving." He moved his hand to help Brooklyn up.

She wouldn't budge. "Mom, don't do this."

"You're too embarrassed to admit all that Jesus garbage didn't work. What a story to tell. I believed you for a while. I really did."

"Brooklyn." Why wouldn't she get up? Why take this?

Gloria's gaze fixed on Jake. "Whatever does your mother think?"

Brooklyn stood. "You're wrong." She looked to Greg, but he shook his head. She lowered her face. This was where her self-condemnation came from, the root of her insecurity. She nudged up against Jake.

"If you want to believe this is my child, you go right ahead. I'll show you how being a parent is supposed to look." He put his arm around Brooklyn and led her to the front door. In the driveway, he opened the car for her.

She remained standing. "I'm sorry."

"Don't be. That's on her."

"I hate that she tried to put it on you."

"If she's the kind of person who'd treat her own daughter the way she treated you, then I don't care what she says or thinks about me. It's you I'm worried about."

"Your reputation…"

"With your mother? My reputation's the last thing I'm worried about." He motioned for her to get in, and once she did, he closed the door. How good it would feel to leave this house miles behind.

Three blocks down the road, Brooklyn touched his forearm. For her to reach out, especially at a time like this, was precious. He tried to enclose her hand in his, but she shrank away. "Will other people think the same thing?"

"No one's as crazy as your mother. Wait until you see how my mom reacts. It'll be different."

"No one's as loyal to you as your mother." Sadness poisoned her words. "You can't assume other people will react the way she does."

"It won't be an issue. I promise."

"Maybe we're on the wrong track with all of this."

"With all of what?"

She shook her head, paused, then shook it again. "Nothing."

20

Haley stood outside the door of Brooklyn's Sunday school classroom. When class ended, she dodged in between exiting kids. "So how'd it go with your visit to your mom?"

"Worse than I could've imagined." Brooklyn had expected the disapproval, but she'd never guessed her mother could steal her peace about her relationship with Jake.

"This day and age, you don't need your parents' approval to marry, anyway."

"That wasn't it, but..."

Elizabeth walked by the door of the classroom and smiled. Brooklyn lifted her hand in return. Brooklyn had read stories in rape survivor forums about women whose friends couldn't endure supporting them through healing after such a traumatic event. If friendships years in the making died at the news, what chance did she have with Haley or the women in Closely Knit, or anyone?

"Can I tell you half the story? There's more to it, but there's only so much I can get into today."

"I have a strict no-patience rule regarding learning all the dirt on my friends, but I will make one exception for you." She winked. "Use it wisely."

"I've never felt like I was supposed to get married, and we weren't there to make any big announcements like that, but Mom said some things that have me thinking maybe I have no business dating him."

"Your mother is evil."

Despite the despair, Brooklyn laughed.

"Seriously. If that guy walked into my life and asked me on a date, I would not take a moment to think that maybe I wasn't good enough. If he thinks you're good enough, voila, you're good enough." Haley shook her head. "You cannot second guess a good thing. Especially not a good thing like that. If you end it, some other girl's going to snatch him up."

Maybe that'd be for the best.

~*~

"Jake to the front register. Jake to the register." Ronny laughed before the intercom cut out. The kid should know better than to page him for the fun of it, so Jake walked to the counter.

"What'd you need?"

Ronny pointed toward the Main Street windows. Pastor Simeon Weismann, from Jake's church, sat on the mezzanine holding a small cup of coffee.

"He wants to see you or something."

They shook hands when Jake approached, and the older man motioned Jake to sit. "I'll cut right to the chase. I'm here for a reason. Your mother tells me she's looking to retire."

Jake groaned and laughed. So Mom had sent the pastor after him. "Why do you think she's looking to do that?"

Pastor's smile brought out well-worn lines. "You're very important to the youth. They listen to you in ways they'd never listen to me. Too old, you know? But you. The kids listen to you. To some of them…You're enjoying your freedom, and maybe this'll sound too old to you, but to some of them, you're the best father figure they've got."

He'd wondered what it'd be like to help Brooklyn raise her baby, but it never occurred to him that he'd had practice. Pastor had one son leading a church in Texas and another at seminary. From such a successful father, the observation carried weight. "If I'm already in that role, I don't need to run Contact Point. Why put something new on my plate?"

"The decision needs to be made with prayer and godly counsel, but when we've talked about this before, you've always indicated an interest in the outreach."

"Yeah." Jake took in the floor of the coffee shop. "It's not a great time. Mom isn't exactly retirement age. I thought it'd be another ten years."

"The things God brings into our lives often don't seem to be at a great time. I'm not saying this is definitely something you should do, but—"

"But God's brought it into my life right now?" Jake chuckled.

The joy didn't leave Pastor's eyes. "Your dad once said the pool hall was the second most important work in his life. Do you know what he said came first?"

"His work in the church?"

"No. He said raising you right was his most important job because your reach would go far beyond that of a pool hall."

"No pressure or anything."

"You could've turned down the pressure. You didn't have to take the place you've taken with the youth, but you did, and he would be very proud of you."

"It felt right." Doing anything less with his time would've meant turning his back on his dad. And his God.

"Sometimes, the right choice doesn't feel right." Pastor pushed back his chair, a full smile on his face. "I'm excited to see what God will do, whatever you decide."

~*~

Brooklyn came to Hillside after work. Jake longed to take her to his mom for the talk. If they didn't have it soon, Mom would send in the whole elder board about Contact Point, but tonight, he'd scheduled himself as manager to give others time off. He fixed Brooklyn a hot cider.

"Are you working all night?"

Many of the tables were taken, but only one person still waited in line. Amy could cover his break. "I can spare a little time. Come on back." In the office, he related his conversation with Pastor Simeon.

When he finished, she stared at the screensaver on the computer. "What's keeping you from agreeing?"

"We talked about this. We already have enough going on."

She frowned and looked toward him, but her eyes didn't meet his. "I think we're moving too fast."

"I don't think we could move slower if we tried."

"At first, it was kind of nice, thinking I'm not alone in this, but the truth is, I am. I'm having a baby. We're not married or engaged. I mean, how do we even categorize what we are?" She lifted her gaze, a sad challenge.

"I thought you said we were moving too fast. We

could do those things, be more public, get engaged, but that'd be moving faster."

"You talk like we are, though. Like you're planning to be a dad." She curled her fingers around her cider. "I'm not sure this is what God wants for us."

"Then how do you explain everything that's happened?"

"Having open doors in front of us doesn't mean we should keep moving forward. You have an open door at the pool hall, too, and I'm not so sure you should ignore that because of me and a baby."

"The pool hall isn't a once-in-a-lifetime opportunity. But you. This baby...how could you even suggest that's not supposed to be my priority right now?"

"I'm starting to see the effect my having a baby is going to have on you, and it's for the worse. You'd be better off walking away from this and taking the pool hall. Four months ago, you would've jumped at this chance."

"No, you were my priority four months ago, too."

Brooklyn glanced at the door, reminding Jake to quiet down or be overheard by his employees. "Look. It's busy tonight. I shouldn't have started this now. We can talk another time. Just...let me give you this." She reached into her purse and pulled out a wad of yarn the color of the hat she'd given him. "It's a scarf."

A scarf in April? Yarn must be her preferred way of letting him down easy. Couldn't she see life hadn't been great four months ago? So convinced by her upbringing that she had no chance at lifelong love, she'd prevented any possibility of them being more than friends. Now, he wouldn't trade what they had for a scarf. "You want me to take on the outreach, fine.

I'll call her right now."

She stood, pressing a hand on the desk for support. "That's not what I'm saying. I want you to make the decision God's calling you to, the one that's right for you, not for me."

He touched her forearm, the most he dared when she was in this mood. "I made the right decision for me. Don't you see that? It's you. The rest is secondary."

"I want nothing to do with the work of God coming in second place. You've been called to minister to those boys. The pool hall will give you a better channel for that."

"Supporting you is the work of God, too."

She opened the door to leave.

"You're worth it, you know. He brings people into your life to minister to you, too, but you have to let us."

She didn't glance back as she stepped away. "We'll talk another time, Jake."

The next day, she didn't come by the shop. He gave it until nine then called her, but she didn't call back.

21

Jake grabbed the phone because Vanessa was handing a customer a coffee. He wasn't on the schedule today, and she'd ordered him to stop hovering a few times. He brushed off the complaints. Brooklyn hadn't spoken to him in days, and he needed a distraction at least until her workday ended at five. "Hillside Coffee. This is Jake." He grinned at Vanessa, rubbing in that he'd found a way to make himself useful.

"Jake Davidson?"

"In the flesh. What can I do for you?"

Vanessa pointed to move him away from the blender so she could wipe it down. A chore she'd probably chosen to show him he was in the way. Still smiling, he moved aside.

"I'm calling from Carter Group," the woman on the phone said. "Vanessa Richards listed you as her employer. Would you be willing to answer a few questions regarding her employment?"

Jake's smile faded. Carter Group designed some of Hillside's signs and ads. Vanessa's marketing degree fit their niche. "Sure. Go ahead."

"How long has she worked for you?"

"Two and a half years. It will be three in September."

"What kind of employee would you say she's been?"

The first answer that came to mind was "full of surprises," but if she wanted to leave, he wouldn't sabotage her into having to stay. "She runs the shop when I go to trade shows. She also came up with some pretty popular promotions."

Vanessa froze for a moment, her rag on the handle of a coffeepot.

Jake described the flower giveaways, the Easter baskets, and Vanessa's attendance.

"Are there any other impressions you'd like to share?"

He ended the call. He'd done her enough favors without gushing about her status as his best manager. Carter Group probably paid more than anything Hillside could offer a manager. Unless, possibly, he promoted her to location manager. The only way to open that position was for him to leave it and take on Contact Point. Agreeing to the deal his mom offered would quiet Brooklyn's fear that she and the baby kept him from reaching his potential. The responsibility would be added to a list that already daunted him, but it looked as if he'd lose all around if he didn't try. He took out his cell and called his mom. "I'm in."

He climbed the stairs to his apartment, listening as his mom gushed about what a good decision he'd made, admiration he didn't deserve. This was nothing more than a reaction to being backed into a corner.

He grabbed a scrap of paper and a pen and jotted down things he'd need to do to get the deal rolling. The more he wrote, the more tasks that came to mind. He switched to a full sheet. When he made it back down to Hillside to collect his laptop, Vanessa's shift was over. He found a note from her in the bin with the mail.

Sorry, I didn't mean for you to find out like that. The jumble of a scribble suggested she'd considered writing more before ending with a sad face and signing her name.

He dropped the note in the garbage and started down the street. A contractor friend had agreed to stop by Contact Point to start an estimate on improvements.

He called Brooklyn but ended up talking to her voicemail. "I'm moving on Contact Point. I'll ask Vanessa to manage Hillside. You promised me a talk. I'm still waiting." He'd have to convince her he hadn't accepted the pool hall in order to keep her. Had he? Mostly, but she, Pastor, and Mom all seemed to think it was the right choice.

But the list of votes in favor of the pool hall was short one important name: Jesus. He hadn't spent time praying about it.

God, I can't lose Brooklyn.

If Devin said something like that to him, Jake would reply he needed to have faith and put God first. What he couldn't afford to lose was God's favor.

Guide these decisions. Show me what You want me to do. Give Brooklyn peace and joy and bless our relationship. Show me Your will for Contact Point.

~*~

Brooklyn texted Jake from the boardwalk along the lake. *Sunset's beautiful over the lake.*

Behind her, tall grass and cattails spiked through the water, providing shelter for a heron. In front of her, ducks and geese dotted the smooth water, which turned neon blue as the sun neared the horizon. She smiled with giddy satisfaction when Jake replied that he'd come watch the sunset with her. She was blessed to have a friend who knew where to find her from such a vague message.

A friend.

His title was at least boyfriend, and at most fiancé, since he'd made it clear he had every intention of making her his wife. To have someone who never seemed to doubt her value flattered and confounded her.

She boosted herself onto the railing and glanced down the trail toward the nearest parking lot. A lone form approached, still a football field away, yet unmistakable. Jake.

Sometime after he'd returned from college, she'd realized he dressed up to see her. If he expected to see Caleb or Devin, he wore hoodies instead of jackets and left his hair soft and unstyled. But nights like this, when she was part of his plans, he wore a fleece and crisply tousled his hair, the way his stylist left it after a haircut. Her pulse ticked faster. She turned back toward the lake and the orange, burning sun.

"How's your day been?" she asked.

"Busy." He leaned against the railing next to her.

A duck skidded to a landing on the water twenty feet away. Ripples washed against the bridge pilings.

"I don't want you to worry about me," Jake said. "You have enough to worry about. Have you thought about how hard it's going to be to have a baby? Especially if you don't let me help?"

He had to ask if she'd thought this through? She could do whatever God asked her to do. He needed to know she could get through this alone if this fiasco interfered with his ministries. "I told my mom I don't have intentions toward you."

He stepped away from the railing. His dark lashes

sloped toward the planks of the bridge. After a few seconds, he lifted his face again.

His gaze fixed on the scenery.

She studied his face, the single day's progress of beard that he'd shave off in the morning, the pulse of his jaw as he clenched it, the skin that creased when he squinted.

"Is that true?"

Such pain, and she'd caused it. She eased down, leaned her forearms on the railing, and gazed toward the dying sun. "Someday you're going to get a more complete offer than me."

"You are complete, Brook."

The baby had grown. Her jeans were held as close to buttoned as possible by a belt. *Complete women can button their pants.* But Jake would crucify such a simplistic response. "I'm screwed up. I've got this baby growing inside me when…" The idea of sex scared her. How could she explain the war between the attraction that pulled her toward him and the guilt and fear that pushed her away? "The thought of kissing a man closes up my throat. I can hardly breathe." She stared at a stone wedged between the planks of the bridge. "Frankly, I've never been sure I could hold up my end of a marriage. I'll have enough of a challenge being a mom, let alone being a wife. Look at my mom. What does that mean about me?"

"Nothing." He ducked his face to look into hers. His hand moved her direction then stopped. "If you think any of that matters, you're seriously underestimating my commitment to you. God can heal anything, Brook. We can do this, and we can be happy. We can help each other."

What if they couldn't? What if she pulled him

down? She looked to the pink remains of the sunset. *God, I need help.*

"Your input helped me make an important decision about Contact Point." He touched her shoulder, oblivious to or ignoring the emotion he sent through her. "Let me help you with one. My mom's going to see for herself pretty soon. I think we should get her in on this. You need someone besides me and Caleb, and she'd take awesome care of you."

She laughed.

He dropped his hand, forehead furrowed.

"I'm not a puppy."

He gave a short-lived smile. "Like it or not, you can't do this alone. Before you decide you're bad for me, you ought to discuss it with someone else."

She laughed, this time letting skepticism replace the joy. "You think your mother will be unbiased?"

"Absolutely not. She is biased. She doesn't want me marrying the wrong person." He winced, as if regretting the marriage reference.

As if she didn't know his intentions. What was she getting into?

"We can tell her?"

"She'll find out sooner or later." Within a week or two, Brooklyn would need maternity clothes. "Sooner."

"Tonight?"

Her gaze settled on the spot where the sun fell. This mood would pass and, with it, the courage to tell Jake's mom, Margaret.

"It'll help everything," Jake said.

Their versions of "everything" differed. He believed Margaret would help them stay together by helping Brooklyn. She believed Margaret would help them both find God's will in this, even if that meant encouraging them to go separate ways.

22

When Mom swung open the door, suspicion played in her eyes. "What brings you here?"

Jake forced a laugh. He had to get Brooklyn through the door before they could answer.

"I'm not letting you back out of our deal," Mom said as they headed for the kitchen.

"I'm not letting you out of it," he countered. "But once you see what Contact Point turns into, you'll wish you still ran it."

"Then what's wrong?" She eyed him and cleared documents off the table. "Anyone want a drink?"

"Water, please." Brooklyn took a seat.

"Nothing for me, thanks." Jake leaned down to Brooklyn's ear. "Should I do the talking?"

She moistened her lips. "I will."

"Look at you two. Still whispering secrets like you did when you were thirteen."

"This is one we're letting you in on." Jake pulled out a chair and sat.

Mom set down the water and took a seat. "You didn't go and elope behind my back, did you?" A smile bubbled to her face. "Because Carol's wedding was too stressful to enjoy. I'm expecting to enjoy my son's wedding. Which means there has to be a ceremony."

"It's not like that, Mom." Talking as if they were engaged might spook Brooklyn right out of here. He waited for her to speak up.

Mom laughed nervously. "Tell me you're not pregnant."

"Mom, please."

Brooklyn tilted her head. "It's not Jake's. We're not involved."

Involved was a funny word for her to choose. In all but about one way, it defined them perfectly.

Mom looked back and forth between them again, all the joy replaced by confusion.

"I went on that business trip in January and made the mistake of taking the stairs at the hotel late one night. Alone." She paused to press her lips together. "A man followed me."

Mom reached for Brooklyn's hands then paused and withdrew again. She looked at Jake as if to be sure she understood. Even when his dad had been diagnosed with cancer, shock and dismay hadn't painted her this white.

"Remember when I asked you about a dream I had? Brooklyn didn't tell me herself. They never caught the man."

"Oh, honey." Mom pulled her chair around and wrapped an arm across Brooklyn's shoulders.

Brooklyn leaned her head on his mom and sobbed.

~*~

Jake's Bible study students interacted more than the groups he'd led other years. Devin played a big role in that, a ringleader in everything from pranks to frank discussion. Tonight, however, he'd said little. As the others bounded down from Hillside's balcony to the first floor of the coffee shop, where the girls' study had met, Jake called him back.

Devin caught a chair like he needed the weight to slow him down. "What's up?"

Jake motioned to a table, and Devin trudged over.

"What's going on?" Jake asked.

Devin's gaze shot down to the girls. Lauren stood among them.

"Are you two doing all right?"

A twinge crossed Devin's face, tightening his eyes and mouth. "We're good."

"Fighting again?"

"No." He met Jake's eyes on that answer, so it was probably true.

Below, the kids grew louder. Lauren smacked a guy's shoulder.

Devin chewed his lip. Not being down there was killing him.

"Did you ever come up with that strategy we talked about?"

"What strategy?" Devin asked.

"For staying out of trouble. With Lauren."

The boy's face seemed to redden, but night had fallen, and the shop was dimly lit. Hard to tell for sure if it was a blush.

"Am I already too late for this?" Even to Jake's ears the question sounded way too much like one that should come from a parent. If Devin told him to mind his own business, he would feel bad, but, of course, he'd also have an answer.

"No." He shook his head without making eye contact. "No."

A lie. He didn't know how far Devin had gone, but he had to stop it from going further without making the kid any more uncomfortable or Jake wouldn't see him again until Lauren was history. "Imagine her dad's standing there, watching whenever you're together."

Devin laughed. "That's what you do?"

"Her Heavenly Father's there. There've been a few times when remembering that has helped me leave when I needed to."

"You leave?"

"Sometimes. Set boundaries. When you can't stick to them, leave. It's what Joseph did with Potiphar's wife."

"It didn't work out very well for him."

"Sure, it did. He ended up being second in command behind Pharaoh. The trick is to think long-term. Long-term, your wife is going to appreciate you keeping your hands off other women. Even if you end up marrying Lauren, she'll trust you all the more for it."

"Do you think..." Devin clamped his lip between his teeth.

"What?"

"Everybody says we'll break up when we go to college."

Ah. Maybe Jake had read him wrong. Devin's problem might be as simple as worry over losing Lauren. "That's up to you. Some people marry their high school sweethearts. Or you might change, break up, and find someone better for you. God's got a plan. We just have to stay the course. And play by His rules."

"Got it." Devin raised his eyebrows, silently asking if Jake was done.

"Yeah, go on."

Devin jumped up and flew down the stairs.

With no one to hurry down to, Jake lingered on the balcony. Mom and Brooklyn had been spending evenings together, talking and shopping for maternity clothes. Over the weekends, Brooklyn had been tied up reading books Mom found for her. This might be the only therapy Brooklyn would get, so Jake had kept his distance.

Tonight, he busied himself praying for Devin and Lauren and Brooklyn. And himself.

Justice

23

Jake shook his accountant's hand before leaving the man's office. His phone had vibrated every couple of minutes since he took a seat in the meeting, so he dialed voicemail as he stepped outside.

"It's Vanessa. Harold's up to something. You need to call me as soon as you get this." Her voice grated with agitation.

Perhaps "up to something" meant they had time before it developed.

In the second message, Mom asked how the meeting had gone.

He glanced over the missed calls. Four from Vanessa, one from Mom, and three from Devin. Just one text message, and it was from Devin. Jake fumbled with his keys, trying to unlock the car while he read the text.

What's going on?????

Combined with all the calls from Vanessa, the text could be related to Harold.

He opted to call Vanessa.

Her tense voice answered in seconds. "Jake. Are you having a baby?"

"What? Why?"

"So you're not. I mean, Brooklyn's not. You and Brooklyn?"

Adrenaline shot through his body. How could this be related to Harold? He'd never talked to Brooklyn

139

about how to handle questions when people started noticing. He had to stall. "What are you talking about?"

"A kid was out on the corner, handing out flyers for a band playing at Hillside called Symbiotic Relationship. That's not who I booked for tonight—a weird name for a band, right?—so I thought maybe we accidentally double booked. I pulled up the band's demo—there was a URL on the flyer—but it turned out to be a video about you and Brooklyn. It was...I'm sorry. Maybe I shouldn't have watched it, but..."

The way she talked, it was a sex tape. Impossible. But hadn't Harold mentioned a symbiotic relationship the first day he complained about Hillside's gift books? "Take a deep breath. What's on this video?"

"It's from the security cameras. It's this montage of you and her coming and going from your place, and then there's this conversation in the office where you're talking about having a baby together. Half the customers in the shop had the flyers—the kid was out there for, like, half an hour before I figured it out and took them all away. Plus, I think he handed them out other places around town. But Brooklyn and you...how would he have gotten all this? Did he make it up?"

"I don't know what he did. Send me the link."

Silence met the order. Jake lowered his phone. She hadn't hung up. He raised it back to his ear.

"You never answered."

"Vanessa, this needs to stay between us."

She took the deep breath he had ordered a few minutes ago, but it caught in a shudder. "So it's true."

Was she crying? He'd witnessed to her over the years, but he never thought she cared this much about his morals.

"If it were true, I would deserve for the world to know. But the way it is, the truth is none of the world's business." He pressed his fist to his forehead. "She and I do spend a lot of time together, but we're not sleeping together."

"You guys were talking about you being a dad."

He hated Harold for forcing his hand. "Brooklyn is pregnant. She was raped."

She gasped.

"Send the video."

"OK. Yeah. Right away."

"I need you to hold things down there. Stay until I get back."

"Matt starts in ten minutes."

"Stay on," he said. "If anyone brings up the video, I need you to handle it."

"How?"

"Tell them it's not what it looks like, that it's a prank."

"Where are you going?" she asked.

"To see Brooklyn."

He checked his e-mail for the link. It took a couple of minutes. Vanessa may have overreacted, but experience assured him Harold would make it as bad as possible.

When it loaded, music started. An image of Hillside's balcony came into focus. Harold had somehow gotten his hands on the feed from the second-floor security camera. Based on the date and time stamp, this was from a couple of months ago.

There were two people in the shot, sitting at a booth, talking. But then a couple came on screen. Him and Brooklyn. They crossed the balcony and disappeared through the door that led up to his apartment. The timestamp flashed ahead three hours, and the door opened again. Brooklyn left, oblivious to the fact that she was being recorded.

The next minute showcased a sequence of more. Brooklyn came up alone, Jake let her in, and then she left two hours later. The footage sped up through at least a half of a dozen visits covering the course of a couple of months. When it returned to normal speed, the door opened, and they were the only people on the balcony. They talked for a bit, though their conversation was muted beneath the song.

Jake put a hand on Brooklyn's shoulder, and his mouth moved as he spoke. She looked sad, but she nodded. He pulled her into a hug. The time stamp ticked off a new minute. She left, and he shut the door. That had been the first night they'd held hands, the night she'd said she loved him. That was also the night he'd convinced her they didn't have to worry about staying out of each other's apartments to appear above reproach.

Thank God the upstairs camera didn't have sound. They hadn't said anything incriminating, but Brooklyn had been violated enough. She didn't need a private conversation handed out on the sidewalk or published on the Internet.

His gut soured at the sight of the next shot, one showcasing him and Brooklyn entering the office. That camera recorded sound as well as video. It was supposed to be insurance against Harold, and here it was being used against Jake. But how? Harold couldn't have the knowledge to access files on a computer remotely.

The screen went blank, and the song ended.

Words scrolled across.

Someone's been hiding a secret.

There was a second of black silence, and then the image cut back to Jake and Brooklyn in the office.

"At first, it was kind of nice, thinking I'm not alone in this, but the truth is, I am," Brooklyn said. "I'm having a baby. We're not married or engaged. I mean, how do we even categorize what we are?"

Jake's back was to the camera. "I thought you said we were moving too fast. We could do those things, be more public, get engaged, but that'd be moving faster."

"You talk like we are, though. Like you're planning to be a dad. I'm not sure this is what God wants for us."

"Then how do you explain everything that's happened?" At the time, he hadn't realized how desperate he'd sounded. Or how determined she'd been.

"Having open doors in front of us doesn't mean we should keep moving forward. You have an open door at the pool hall, too, and I'm not so sure you should ignore that because of me and a baby."

So they'd talked about Contact Point in the video, too. Vanessa must have questions about that. He'd been waiting to tell her on the chance that the purchase fell through, but following today's meeting, the deal seemed solid.

"The pool hall isn't a once-in-a-lifetime opportunity. But you. This baby…how could you even suggest that's not supposed to be my priority right now?" Jake's voice rang with frustration.

"I'm starting to see what kind of effect my having a baby is going to have on you, and it's for the worse. You'd be better off walking away from this and taking the pool hall. Four months ago, you would've jumped at this chance."

Jake winced on hearing it again. She definitely had intended to break it off.

"No. You were my priority four months ago, too."

"Look." On the tiny screen, Brooklyn's face smoothed, and her voice was quiet. "It's busy tonight. I shouldn't have started this now. We can talk another time."

The video went silent and words appeared on the screen, white letters on a black background.

This is the youth leader who credits his success to Jesus?

The screen came to life. Brooklyn left the office, and Jake sat at the desk, rubbing his forehead. Then, the video ended.

Harold had cut out the part where she gave him the scarf. Only she and Jake knew that was her way of softening the worst blows.

His anger tore him in different directions. Should he prepare Brooklyn or call the police? This was an invasion of privacy and defamation of character.

His laptop was in his car. But the office computer had all the security footage on it, too. If Harold had found a way into their system, he needed to unplug it so no one could access it before Jake could deliver everything to the police.

~*~

Jake passed through the door of the coffee shop.

Devin shot up from a table. "You owe me an explanation." The kid held up a postcard-sized advertisement.

Jake slipped it from his grasp. The card even had the Hillside logo on it. "It's Harold. What more do you need?" He brushed past. He had to hurry if he wanted to gather the computer and get to Brooklyn before she heard from someone else.

"So all that about Joseph and leaving and honoring God was just a charade."

"This isn't the time or the place." He reached the sales counter.

"Lauren was right. You are a hypocrite. That's what she said when I told her about your book exchange. I never should've defended you." Devin's voice hushed most other conversations in the shop. "I don't know why I ever listened to you."

Grace, who stood at the register, diverted her gaze.

"It's not what it looks like, but we're not having this out here and now." He was careful to speak so only Devin could hear. "If this is all the faith you've got, you're in for a lifetime of trouble."

"I'm supposed to have faith in you? Who do you think you are? God?"

"That's not what I meant." This conversation needed to wait. "Consider your source. It's not how it looks. I'll catch up with you later."

"Whatever." Devin stomped out.

Vanessa rushed from the back. "I heard someone yelling. What're you doing here?"

"What do you think?" He reached the office.

"I covered the camera. I didn't know what else to do."

She'd done more than cover the lens. The camera in the corner of the office had been encased in some kind of foam, probably an attempt to stop it from recording sound. Fair enough. He was the only one—

besides Harold, apparently—with access to turn it off. He yanked out the computer's power cord and Internet cable and then moved on to the wires for the mouse and keyboard. He slid the computer tower toward the edge of the desk to take it with him. First stop, Brooklyn. Second, police station.

His phone rang, and Pastor Simeon's name appeared on the display.

Jake rubbed his face. The man had to be calling about the video. He grabbed the tower and started for the door. He could not allow Brooklyn to find out about this from anyone else.

Vanessa followed. "Harold started his remodel today."

He froze.

"There's a building permit and a crew going in and out with supplies and stuff."

"If he's trying to take Hillside's customers by slandering me, he started way too early. No one will care about this by the time he manages to open in a couple of months."

But the man hadn't miscalculated a blow yet, so maybe Jake didn't understand something about his motivation. Maybe Harold was after Jake personally and not professionally. Jake's weak spot had always been Brooklyn. He had to get to her before the video did. "Hold down the fort."

24

"I'm done in forty-five minutes. Does this have to be now?" Brooklyn looked at her computer screen, where an angry e-mail awaited a response. Galley Paper was hiring in Madison to replace some of the North Adams staff that would be cut. She had been asked to screen candidates and perform initial interviews, a job that put her at odds with most of her North Adams coworkers.

"It's nothing that'll change much in forty-five minutes, but I want it to come from me. I'll be by your car."

"What's going on? You're scaring me."

"Please just trust me, Brook."

She'd finally taken some steps toward healing with Margaret's help and now they had to suffer something new? *Lord, I can't take more. Please let this be nothing.* "OK. I'll see you at five."

She replaced the phone and went back to the angry e-mail. If she didn't take the time to reply, she would have no excuse not to skip out early and let Jake shatter her further with more bad news.

~*~

Jake listened to the voicemail from Pastor Simeon as he waited in the parking lot. "Something's come to light. I need to meet with you before Sunday. I'll be in the office tomorrow from nine to one. Otherwise, call and we can set something up. The sooner, the better."

That wouldn't be a fun talk, but he couldn't keep brushing people off the way he'd dismissed Devin. He'd call Pastor later. For now, he texted Devin to meet at Hillside at eight thirty. By then, he and Brooklyn should be done talking and the police notified.

At quarter to five, she met him in the parking lot. Her loose cardigan was layered over a ruffled top, hiding any sign of her pregnancy. "All right. What is it?"

"You're early."

"What're they going to do? Fire me?"

He opened the video on his phone, hit play, and handed it to her.

"What's this?"

"Harold's mastermind attempt to be a thorn in my side."

"All this over Harold?" A line formed between her eyebrows as she focused on the small screen. Horror popped her mouth ajar as the clip ended. "This is on the Internet?"

He hated Harold for doing this to her.

"We'll have to explain. I told Vanessa, and Devin and Pastor are already asking." He'd hoped to put off telling people until their relationship was more solid. At least the pool hall deal was in motion. He could point to that as proof that she wasn't coming between him and his dreams.

"Your mom planned to start telling people." Brooklyn handed the phone back. "Who are they going to believe now?"

Why was Mom in charge of breaking the news? Tears rimmed Brooklyn's eyes, preventing him from asking.

"They'll believe us." He shoved the phone into his pocket.

"You watched that, right?"

"It's not a sex tape."

"Have you read Ephesians? There's not supposed to be a hint of sexual immorality among believers. Whether I'm pregnant or not, that tape is a hint." Her fingers clenched the bottom edge of her sweater. "Combine the two…"

"We're innocent, Brooklyn. Vanessa believed me on the spot. Everyone knows we're innocent."

"Then why's everybody calling you?"

"Pastor and Devin? The problem would be if they weren't calling. They know us well enough to recognize it's time to ask more questions. They're asking because they see they've got a twisted story in that clip. They trust there's a better explanation."

"I knew we shouldn't be spending time alone together." She pressed her lips together.

"He's been looking for anything he could get on me. If not this, it'd be something else. But he's got nothing. We have the truth. We haven't made mistakes. Even Harold knows there's no story here."

She unlocked her car. "The truth doesn't mean as much as a scandal does."

"Brooklyn, we're innocent."

"People don't know that." She tugged open her door. "It's our word against a video, and I can tell you which one people will believe."

"I'll prove it to you. Come with me to talk to Pastor tomorrow. You'll see. Everyone who matters will believe us."

She studied him. "If you don't think this is a big

deal, why did you call me like you did? Why did you wait out here?"

"Because he's forcing our hand, making us tell everyone sooner. They'll believe us. I just didn't think you were ready for everyone to know, and I hate that he put you in this position. Going after me is one thing, but you...Harold's insane. That's criminal, hacking a computer or whatever he did to get the surveillance footage. And it's slander. I'm going to the police right after this. Come with me. You've been through enough. You don't deserve this."

Brooklyn shook her head. "I have to think." And then she left.

25

Jake returned to Hillside after the police station.

Vanessa was on the balcony with an army of cleaning supplies. She sat on the ground below one of the wrought-iron tables near the railing, scraping at the underside.

"Couldn't find any other way to keep busy?" Jake asked.

"Why do people think this is a good place for gum? I thought coffee shop customers were supposed to be environmentally conscious hipsters. This is an environment. Why can't they respect it?" She worked her putty knife as if the gum threatened to bring down the whole store.

Jake rummaged through her tote of supplies, found a second putty knife, and took it to one of the booths. He lay on his back and scanned for something to attack, too.

"So what happened?" Vanessa asked.

"I reported it. Things got weird when I mentioned Harold."

"Weird like how?"

"I've been told the last name Keen carries some weight. I'm beginning to believe it. I get the feeling we're on our own with this one."

"How would he do something like this? I can't even get into that program to see the footage. He hired someone, didn't he?"

"I don't know."

Maybe the police would get somewhere despite their doubts about tracing the video back to anything but Jake's own system. All this over gift books. It'd be laughable if it weren't for the harm it did to Brooklyn.

"Can I tell you something?" Vanessa asked.

"Sure, let's hear it." Couldn't be worse than anything else he'd heard today.

"Carter Group found someone else."

His knife wedged under a wad of gum, which stuck to the blade. Jake propped himself up on an elbow. Vanessa's expression offered an apology.

"I don't blame you for wanting to advance."

Her frown drooped with misery.

He sat up. "Contact Point. You heard us talking about it on the clip."

She nodded.

"If it goes through, I want to make you store manager here. I didn't want to get your hopes up before everything was final, but...any chance you'll stop job hunting?"

"Carter Group was the only place that interviewed me. I don't know if you've heard, but Galley Paper is laying off over a hundred people. All of them are experienced and looking for work."

Jake moved to a new booth and leaned back, checking under the table again. "Yeah, I heard something about that."

"You're doing a really good thing. Loving her anyway, you know? Despite the scandal."

As if his love for Brooklyn was a choice. Even when he'd thought the baby was Caleb's, he couldn't walk away. "It'll blow over. He'll have to try harder if he wants to break us up."

"Be careful how loud you say that." She sighed. "What will you do if the police don't find anything?"

"Maybe there's a better way to deal with Harold."

"A better way? Like revenge?" She'd traded her putty knife for a rag, but stood without using it.

"I don't know. You can head home."

"The kid handing out flyers saw him. If there's no trail online but they find the kid, I could ID him, and he could tie Harold to it."

"They'd have to care enough to find the kid, and he'd have to cooperate. Even then, I'm not sure impersonating a Hillside employee would land Harold in jail." And if all Harold got was a slap on the wrist, he'd just gloat because they'd tried. If nothing came of reporting the crime, Jake would bide his time until he had something to wipe the smile off Harold's face.

Vanessa gathered the cleaning supplies and left.

Jake climbed the stairs to the third floor.

It was already past eight thirty, and there'd been no sign of Devin. If Jake had screwed this up with Devin, who thought the world of him, how would it go with everyone else? Each hour the teen didn't show, proved Brooklyn more right.

~*~

Brooklyn clutched her phone to her ear.

"Hey." Caleb's voice had never been so welcome.

He had never steered her wrong before, and if anyone would help her keep the right perspective now, it was him. "Are you free?"

"I hear there's some trouble."

The acknowledgement that all wasn't as it should be and that news had already reached Madison began a tremor in her hands. "Jake called?"

"Devin, actually. Sounds like quite a story. I told him to call Jake."

Caleb didn't interact with the teen regularly. Devin's call was just one more surreal detail.

"Jake says everyone will believe us. Do you think that's true? Because if it's not, I'm completely ruining his chances at ministry. I can't do that. I can't be responsible for that."

"How about I call you back a little later?"

"Oh. You're busy?"

"I'm at dinner."

"With Rosalie?" As if she wasn't about to be unpopular enough, now she was infringing on a date. "Tell her I'm sorry."

"Don't worry about it. I'll catch you back, all right?"

"Yes. All right." She hit the button to disconnect, trying to draw reassurance from his concerned tone. She couldn't think straight or even say a decent prayer.

She could only cling to the phone and wait.

26

On Saturday morning, Brooklyn parked her car at Elizabeth Stein's house, a two-story with outdated siding. The bushes grew a bit out of control, but overall, the house and yard were orderly and well-kept. Brooklyn gathered the books from the passenger seat of her car, her arms tight with nervous, tired energy.

She'd stayed up late talking to Caleb, and even then, she couldn't sleep until the early hours of the morning. Her ringing phone had woken her an hour ago, and Elizabeth's voicemail, though kind, meant the video had made its way to the elderly of the church. If only she'd told the ladies of Closely Knit about the rape.

She'd try to explain now, but Elizabeth might draw the same conclusion Mom had. In that case, she had to return the books of crochet patterns. One of the pamphlets fluttered to the ground. She scooped it up and brushed off the dirt. She couldn't catch a break. The books had been pristine when Elizabeth lent them to her. She rang the bell and waited.

The lace curtain shuttered as the door opened. Elizabeth's face wrinkled with a smile. "Come on in, dear."

Maybe Elizabeth didn't know about the video. She led the way to the kitchen. On the table sat a fabric-covered storage box. "I have something for you."

Brooklyn bit her lip. The box was large enough to hold an afghan, but before she could accept such a precious gift, she had to confess the truth. "There's something you need to know."

Elizabeth lifted the lid off the box. "On March first, I woke up and asked God what I should do with my day. He told me to start making these. And I thought it meant I got to be a great grandma again, but none of my granddaughters are having little ones. So I just kept working, making the baby clothes, wondering where God was going to find a baby who could use them."

The box was full of sweaters, hats, and socks so perfectly made they might as well have been professional. Brooklyn had meant to make things like these, but the only two projects that had turned out had been the hat and scarf for Jake. And he probably didn't even realize half the feelings the gifts were meant to convey.

"A parka only hides so much, dear."

"You started March first?"

Elizabeth straightened the top row of clothing. "March first, yes."

"That's the day I found out I was pregnant."

Elizabeth laid a hand on her shoulder. "'The Lord within her is righteous; he does no injustice: every morning he shows forth his justice; each dawn he does not fail.' Even on the morning of March first, he was busy."

She tried to memorize the first phrase of the verse so she could look it up when she got home. *The Lord within her is righteous.* "I was attacked. Assaulted. But some people think Jake's the dad. They even made a video about it and put it on the Internet." Tears hit her eyes. "And I am so ashamed. So embarrassed."

Elizabeth's face pulled into a scowl. "Nothing good will ever come of the Internet. People can't even recognize a hurting girl anymore."

"I'm afraid it'll ruin his ministries. I can't be the one who pulls him down. I need him to live the life God has for him, making a difference, no matter what happens to me. I think I need to break up with him to show people the truth."

Caleb had flatly disagreed with her, but her conviction hadn't faded.

"Sounds like love." Elizabeth smiled. "But, dear, you can't assume you know what life God has for him. It's not so farfetched that God would give you a partner in this. You can break that boy's heart if you feel called to something else, but do him the favor of waiting until you get your orders from God."

"You don't think all of this is an order from God? I don't know how else to right this. And I'm...I'm mortified that people think it about us."

"Whenever fear and insecurity are your leading reasons for something, those aren't orders. At least not from God. Jesus loves you, and that ought to be enough for the whole world. This is the Davidson boy we're talking about?"

The Davidson boy. Jake. The godly son of an elder paired with her, and she was supposed to believe God did that on purpose? But Elizabeth had a point about fear. The Bible was filled with verses about not fearing.

Elizabeth ran shaking fingers over her work. "Do you like them? Maybe they're old-fashioned, but I just did what I was told."

A blue and tan sweater topped one of the stacks, and Brooklyn lifted it. Each knot of the yarn represented a movement Elizabeth had made with her unsteady hands. Brooklyn didn't deserve Elizabeth or Jake, yet God had given her both. She placed the sweater back in the box and looked around for a tissue.

"None of that. Take a seat. Why don't you try talking for once? You do know that's the whole reason for a knitting club in the first place, don't you?" Elizabeth pulled out two chairs, sat down, and waited expectantly.

~*~

The church lot was deserted except for Pastor Simeon's sensible sedan. Jake parked and headed into the building. His call to Brooklyn had gone to voicemail, and he was too anxious to put this off, waiting on the chance that she'd join him. Since she'd asked his mom to tell people about the rape for her, she'd probably be more comfortable with him taking care of this, anyway.

Sunlight streamed through the windows down the hall to Pastor Simeon's office. The door stood ajar, and Pastor sat behind his desk. Jake knocked, his stomach knotted.

"Jake." Pastor came around the desk and rested a hand on his shoulder. "I hope you can appreciate why I called you here." He motioned him to the couch and took a seat in the armchair. "It's with the best intentions for you and for the youth you lead."

The man must be as uncomfortable as Jake.

"It's really not what it looks like, Pastor."

"Brooklyn is going to have a child." He hesitated like he wanted Jake to correct him. "Are you the father?"

He should've secured Brooklyn's permission to

reveal the whole truth. "No." Maybe that'd be enough.

"You and Brooklyn are famously close friends. I doubt you'd be surprised there's been speculation about when the wedding would be."

"Because of the video?"

"No, no. For years now. You've been friends for so long. It was widely predicted that we'd have a wedding on our hands, especially when you moved back from college."

Back then, Jake saw nothing but the loss of his father, and here, the church had been planning his wedding. He rubbed his forehead, waiting for Pastor's advice. The community would misinterpret his relationship with Brooklyn now if they had been this whole time.

"I've been in ministry for over thirty years. I've seen elders steal from the offering plate. I've seen married couples with grown children divorce because of affairs. I've seen solid church kids succumb to drugs. Frankly, this would be one of the least surprising disappointments."

Jake may as well have been pushed from a moving car. What had he done to deserve this kind of suspicion? "I wouldn't throw my morals to the wind just because it wouldn't surprise you."

Pastor waited.

He wouldn't be forced to tell Brooklyn's story for her. A good reputation should be enough. "I'd prefer to be a good surprise than a bad one. I've told the guys a million times to wait for marriage, and I won't be a hypocrite."

"When I heard of the video, I couldn't help recalling that Robyn Washburn saw you with Brooklyn when she got what looked like difficult news from the doctor."

"I was there when she found out, but not when she conceived. If you want the whole story, it's hers to tell, not mine."

Pastor's lips formed a couple of words, but he didn't put his voice behind them, probably a silent prayer. "Jake, I'm afraid there's a problem."

"It's not what it looks like."

Pastor held up a hand in a request for silence.

Brooklyn was right. This would be a battle every step of the way.

"Have you heard about Lauren Mulvey?"

"What does she have to do with any of this?"

"She's in the same…situation as Brooklyn."

Jake sat back into the couch. He'd warned Devin again and again.

"The entire congregation will know shortly. Rumors have a way of going viral." Pastor Simeon scooted closer. "You're a big influence in the lives of the high school boys. They look up to you. In their eyes, you can do no wrong. Mrs. Mulvey is aware that you have been mentoring Devin. They got the news about Lauren a couple of days ago, and then, yesterday, learned of the movie about you and Brooklyn. She says she had noticed that Brooklyn was looking…" He glanced toward the books on the shelves.

Not only was he being blamed for Brooklyn's baby, but they'd found a way to blame him for Devin and Lauren, too. "Brooklyn and I are innocent, Pastor."

"I confess I've seen the movie."

"That proves we're friends, not that we had sex."

"I'm aware. However, appearances…the Mulveys assert that you're a bad influence over the youth. They want you to step down from your work with the kids."

"Because I'm friends with a pregnant woman."

"You're more than friends, aren't you?"

Jake got to his feet. "Do you know how ridiculous this is? We've held hands! That doesn't make me the one to blame for all the sins of the high schoolers any more than you're to blame for the sins of your congregation. You have to believe that."

"I would like to, Jake, but there's a reasonable appearance of sin here and until that can be cleared up—"

"Pastor."

The man held out his hands helplessly. "I wish there were another way. Letting you stay on when all the evidence points to the contrary would make us look like a group of easily conned old men."

"Ask your congregation to trust you. To extend grace."

He shook his head. "You're in a leadership role. If it looks like you've fallen, and we leave you in charge of a ministry before your name is cleared, it undermines the entire belief system we stand for."

"So I'm a disgrace for standing by a hurting friend. I'm a bad role model for that."

Something clunked at the door.

Jake turned, but the visible slice of hall was empty and still.

"This isn't necessarily a permanent or even a long-term decision. This is just for now, until whatever this is can be cleared up."

"And until then, I'm not welcome in my own church? Because people have runaway imaginations?"

"You are welcome here, Jake. You always will be."

But he wasn't. Not the way he should be. He

couldn't stand it any longer. "She was raped, Pastor."

Another noise from the hall drew Jake's attention. No one stood at the door, but he went and swung it open.

Deanna Mulvey, Lauren's mom, lingered there, her mouth drawn into a thin line. He'd encountered her over-involvement in Lauren's life before when she'd complained to the elders that the youth leaders had the nerve to require Lauren to participate in game time like everybody else. Jake glanced back into the office.

Pastor Simeon was trying to get his footing on the word rape.

Deanna stepped in from the hall. "There is no way that is true." Each word punched Jake's direction.

"He's a respected member of our congregation," Pastor said.

"It's too convenient for him to claim something like that now." She whipped around to face Jake. "What an insult to all the women who have been through that horror. You should be ashamed of yourself."

"Convenient? It's anything but."

"Deanna, let's sit down and talk about this." Pastor Simeon looked at him, too. "Sit down."

No reasonable conversation would take place with someone who called rape convenient.

"Pastor, do you believe me?" he asked.

"Sit down so we can talk."

Which meant he didn't. The hot metal brand of the word *hypocrite* had been pressed into his skin, and the mark couldn't be undone. "You can fill our positions. I won't subject Brooklyn to this. It was hard enough when she thought she had the support of the church. If she doesn't have that, we're done."

Deanna's expression turned triumphant.

Jake stepped her way. "As for Lauren and Devin, instead of blaming the rest of the world, look at your own parenting."

She hissed some words in his direction as he exited to the hall.

Pastor called after him, but Jake didn't slow.

27

Jake threw wooden pallets from Contact Point's basement into the alley. Technically, the clutter in the pool hall still belonged to Mom, but she wouldn't be able to take care of all of this, and he boiled with too much anger to do desk work. If the project didn't take all day, he'd head over to Hillside and see if there was something he could throw around there, too. He returned to the basement for another load.

"Are these going, too?"

He turned.

Caleb stood behind him, peering into a box.

Jake hadn't heard of plans for him to be in town this weekend, which hinted that he knew about the video.

"Brook called last night," Caleb said.

Brook. How close were those two? But Caleb had come to help, and Jake was short on allies. "It's all got to go."

Caleb grabbed the box, and they climbed back upstairs.

"I don't know why people think I'm the next best thing to you. But when they want to talk about you, they call me." He hefted the box into the dumpster. "So keep it together. I'm not qualified to take over all your people."

"People?" Jake led the way back inside.

"Devin." The old stairs creaked beneath their feet.

"Brook."

"What'd they say?" Jake grabbed the next box.

"Devin mostly had questions."

"I bet."

Devin had only met Caleb a handful of times. He must've been desperate for help.

"He's going to be a dad. He tell you that?"

Caleb sucked in a breath. "No, he asked about you and Brooklyn. I told him to call you."

"What about Brooklyn?"

"She's embarrassed. And worried."

They pounded back up the steps.

"About?" Jake asked.

"She thinks you don't know what you're up against. She said something about dragging you into this and how she's interfering with God's plan for your life. She thinks it's her fault."

"Harold dragged us into this."

They lifted the boxes into the dumpster.

Caleb turned his head from the dust cloud that rose and swiped a hand over his hair. "What about you?"

Jake sat on the cement stairs. The blue sky overhead stretched pale and clear. A nice day, wasted in an alley with a dumpster. "I quit church today."

"What's that mean?" Caleb folded his arms. "It's not a job."

What little peace he'd retained scattered. "I went to talk to Pastor Simeon this morning."

"With Brooklyn?"

"She didn't answer when I invited her. I told Pastor I'm not the father. He said if he let me keep leading the high schoolers, he'd look like a gullible old man. Then he said Devin and Lauren are having a kid.

Her mom came storming in, said I was lying about Brooklyn being raped and my example is why Devin and Lauren slept together. She wanted someone to blame, and I'm that scapegoat. I resigned and left."

"So you're letting Harold win."

Jake scowled.

Caleb splayed his hands. "This is exactly what he was going for, right?"

"This isn't Harold. This is church. Deanna probably would've believed me over Harold, if it weren't for Lauren being pregnant. To get this from the church after all the work I've done is a slap in the face. That's what I can't stand."

"But you know how that'll look to Harold." Caleb sat next to Jake. "Besides, you've got a million other reasons you need to clear your name, not the least of which is Brooklyn. If you clear your name, you clear hers, and she deserves that. Plus, she's already talking about how she'll walk away before she ruins your opportunity to carry on your dad's legacy."

"What?"

"She said she's not letting you sacrifice your calling. Said she'd break ties with you to prove you don't have that kind of relationship, if she had to."

"She's always ready to run, isn't she?"

Caleb's shoulder hit Jake's. "That's only a problem if you're suddenly tired of chasing."

He had to believe someday they'd be side-by-side, no one running, no one chasing. "She doesn't have to worry about Contact Point. Mom won't change her mind over this. *She* knows the truth."

"Yeah, but what'll that look like if none of the good Christians think you're a good Christian? Who would the pool hall be for?"

"Christ came to save the lost. Seems logical that's where I should focus, too."

"How're you going to get the lost teens in if the found ones aren't bringing them? If you lose your reputation, you lose the outreach. You'd lose Brooklyn. And don't act like acceptance from the Christian community doesn't help Hillside, too. How many Bible studies meet there? How many people from church go there just because it's yours? If he wins this, he's got you in checkmate. You can't just roll over."

"Leaving wasn't rolling over."

"Yeah. You're angry, and I get that. But the church has to be careful with its leaders. There's accountability. Aim that anger at Harold, and get justice there. But don't throw your life away. Don't quit."

Jake stood. "How do you get justice for what he's done? Especially when his family's in a position to make problems go away."

"Put him out of business." Caleb laughed.

"You let me know when you figure out how to do that."

They each claimed another box for the dumpster.

"As long as you don't let him ruin your life in the meantime."

"Deal."

~*~

Brooklyn wore a short-sleeved top in her favorite shade of emerald green. The thin fabric didn't hide her pregnancy, but it was modest. If her time with Elizabeth this morning was any indication, the truth, once out, would bring relief. And support. She didn't need to break up with Jake, and she didn't need to cook under sweaters that were never intended for May.

She heard the bell and went to open the door.

Jake's neat, damp hair suggested he'd just showered. His gaze brushed the shirt. "You look nice."

She stepped out to join him in the sunlight. The temperature hovered in the mid-sixties. She could do this, face telling Pastor Simeon her story. "Are we meeting him at church?"

"We should talk first."

The grass stretched away from the parking lot. The weathered wood of a picnic table beckoned in the sunshine. She sat on the bench.

"I need to know you're not going to give up on this." Jake stood in front of her.

Caleb must have talked with him.

"I'm not going to give up on you, but it's important to me that you get to do the things you're meant to do, too."

"You have to let go of this idea of what you think I'm meant to do." He paced. "If it turns out that I don't work with the youth anymore, is that it? Is that the only thing you think I'm good for? I'm not going to be in that role for the rest of my life. What about then?"

Thank God for Elizabeth's advice. Without it, she wouldn't have answers for him. "When God gives us orders, we have to follow. That's what our relationship depends on, not what ministry you're involved in at any given time."

"I'm sick of being underestimated."

"Who's underestimating you?"

His chest broadened with a deep breath. "Lauren's pregnant."

Oh. Oh, no wonder. She stood and placed her hand

on his shoulder. The tensed muscles didn't relax under her touch. "That doesn't mean it's time to give up. You make a difference. And Devin needs you now more than ever."

His eyes, a mossy green, focused on her abdomen for a moment. The anger that drew his eyebrows together lessened. In its place, either regret or worry drew his mouth down. "You were right. It's going to be more of a battle than I thought. Deanna Mulvey's demanding that I step down from the youth group. Which I did. This morning."

"Jake. Devin needs you."

"I called you so we could go set things right. I'll apologize for being rash." His voice lowered, tired. "I just don't want to worry about losing you, too, if this doesn't work out."

"When you say you stepped down, you mean you already met with Pastor?"

"Yeah. I told him and Deanna that you were raped. I was trying not to, but...I got frustrated, and I'm sorry. I didn't mean to go behind your back."

He shouldn't have taken matters into his own hands like that, but at least Pastor was primed with the news.

"Deanna said I was lying about you. I lost my temper. That's why we have to talk to him. Together. We can explain the truth. He'll listen."

She'd have to believe Jake's words and ignore his defeated tone. It was the only way to maintain her courage.

28

Brooklyn fiddled with her papers as she waited at Haley's door. Though Pastor Simeon had believed her and Jake yesterday, he needed to discuss the situation with the elders before he would have an action plan. At church this morning, the stares had nearly driven her to run before the service started. She needed to talk to anyone she cared about before they could judge.

Haley's silky hair swung as she opened the door. "Brooklyn, what brings you here?"

She held out the papers.

Uncertainty creased Haley's forehead as she accepted the packet and scanned the paper. "What's this?"

"Remember the day I asked to only tell you half of a story? You've seen the video?"

"Brooklyn, this is a police report." Haley's gaze lifted, expression still drawn. "You were raped?"

"And now I'm pregnant. I thought everyone knew and would blame Jake, so…"

"Oh." Haley kept looking at the papers and then at Brooklyn. "Oh. Oh." She pulled Brooklyn into the house.

~*~

"Do you still think the book exchange was worth it?" Mom's lecture voice rang through the phone.

It was bad enough Jake had to sit out youth group because Pastor Simeon wouldn't reinstate him until after the elder's meeting tomorrow night. "It's a business, Mom. Businesses compete."

"You sell coffee. He sells books. Why cross the line?"

He got up to pace his living room. "Because he crossed the line. The Easter baskets. And the band. Why should I back off a good idea just because he happens to sell books? I have to make up the ground he's taken. I'm not just going to sit there and let him mess with the business."

"How much did you spend to put the books in? A hundred dollars?"

More.

"Did it bring in one extra dollar in sales?"

"People use it all the time." They'd received tons of positive feedback. Someone browsed the shelves every time he passed.

"A hundred dollars' worth of sales?"

Sales beat this time last year, but crediting the increase to one particular cause defied the complexity of the economy, the growing downtown business sector, and Hillside's promotions. "The exchange is popular. It'll pay for itself, if it hasn't already. Besides, if you don't think it's brought in a hundred dollars, then it couldn't have taken that much away from Harold." A firm knock sounded at his door. "You can't blame the book exchange for his insanity."

"You sound really angry, Jake."

"I am. Have you even noticed the things he's done? He needs to pay for all that, and if I can see that happen, I'm going to."

"That sounds an awful lot like malice and seeking

revenge. You represent Christ to the community. That includes to Harold. You need to be above reproach."

Everyone thought they needed to quote Dad to him. "Didn't Jesus say we needed to be as wise as serpents? Doesn't that mean with people like Harold?"

"You ought to look up that passage."

Whoever waited at the door pounded again.

"Fine. I have to go, anyway." He disconnected and went to the door.

Rain streaked Devin's hair and shirt, and his chin bunched up toward his mouth. The boy shuddered and lifted a hand to cover his face. "I'm sorry I lied."

Jake had been furious with Devin for contributing to Deanna Mulvey's quest against him. Seeing him now, the anger sank away. Devin had bigger things to worry about than someone else's reputation. Jake had struggled to accept news of Brooklyn's baby. Devin had it worse as a teen and the father. He put a hand on the boy's shoulder and let him in. Devin stumbled to the couch, put his face in his hands, and sobbed.

Jake sat next to him, rested a hand on his shoulder, and waited.

Devin finally pulled himself together. He leaned back, and they both stared toward the coffee table. Jake could explain Harold's video, but Devin hadn't come about that. He came in spite of it.

"How's Lauren holding up?" Jake asked.

"How long have you known?" His voice was ragged.

"Since yesterday morning."

"That Kelley guy they subbed in for you just told me. After youth group."

"Kelley? You didn't know?"

Devin's frown intensified. "She hasn't talked to me

in three weeks. Then tonight Kelley said something about knowing about Lauren like there was some big secret. And something about being a dad. I said there was no way, but I lied. Like I lied to you. So I went over there, and she wouldn't come to the door, but her mom said I have to make this right. I think we're supposed to get married, but she won't even talk to me. She didn't even tell me."

"You just found out." No wonder he was a wreck.

Devin put his head down and pressed his palms against his eyes. "Am I supposed to marry her?"

"I think she'd have to be talking to you for that to be a possibility."

Devin's hands covered his eyes as if he could hold his tears in. "What about you and Brooklyn? Are you marrying her?"

"Her baby isn't mine."

Devin stared at him.

"She was raped. Back in January. In New Wilshire."

"She's been…this whole time?"

"Yeah." They should've told everyone before Harold had the chance to twist the story.

"So when you were talking about Joseph and leaving…"

"I meant it. I wanted to spare you this."

"Then why weren't you at youth group?"

Deanna Mulvey hadn't helped, but Jake's initial reaction to Pastor Simeon was the reason. He paced away from the couch and paused by the desk. Bills peppered the work surface. He'd meant to take care of those this weekend. Instead, the basement of the pool hall was spotless. "I was asked to step down because the video looked bad. Brooklyn and I tried to explain, but the elders want to meet about it before I can go back."

"They don't believe you?"

"Supposedly, they do. But they're having a meeting about it tomorrow."

"I hope they're considering how much you need to be at youth group."

So did he. But for now, they had more immediate problems. "Have you told your parents yet?"

"I went straight from church to Lauren's to here." Devin met his gaze. "If I'm getting married, I want you to stand up."

"Stand up for what?"

"Be my best man."

Jake gaped at him. "Even if that's what Deanna meant, they can't force you to get married."

"If she says yes, I'm marrying her. If Brooklyn needed you, you'd be there, wouldn't you?"

"Lauren needs a lot more than a wedding. She needs shelter and food and emotional support. How will that work if she won't even talk to you?"

"It couldn't be worse than any other arranged marriage."

"Who do you know in an arranged marriage?"

"I thought you'd agree." His chin knotted again. "You talk about being above reproach and doing the right thing."

"You were supposed to be above reproach instead of sleeping with her."

"It was only once, and it wasn't...it wasn't worth all this." His shoulders rounded. "I don't mind marrying her. I guess I wanted to, even before. That's why sex wasn't supposed to be a big deal."

"I tried to warn you, Devin."

He slumped again.

"Look. I'll study it in the Bible. Marriage. What to do. There's got to be a better answer."

Devin nodded and stood without eye contact.

"Give me a couple of days." Jake walked him to the door. "We'll meet up, figure it out. For now, go on home. Talk to your parents."

"Like they'll fix anything." Devin started down the stairs. "It wasn't supposed to turn into this."

No, it wasn't. And something told Jake they hadn't seen the worst of it yet.

29

On Tuesday morning, Jake reviewed the notes he'd taken as he'd searched the Scriptures for Devin's answers. Too distracted by his own wait for answers from the elder meeting, he hadn't found anything helpful. He finished his coffee and went down to the shop.

His mom approached from the side door, but Pastor Simeon sat at his usual table.

Jake pointed toward Pastor. "I'm a little busy."

"Oh. Mind if I come along?" Mom would find out the elders' decision by attending church, and if her concern over his dealings with Harold was serious, she'd eventually talk to Pastor about it.

He'd prefer to be there to defend himself when she tried it. "Might as well."

They took seats next to a window that framed a view of Harold's Books. Pastor Simeon gripped his coffee cup. "I've received a number of concerned calls. Eight or so." He frowned out the window. "We haven't responded, given the sensitivity of the issue."

Mom nodded her approval.

"We feel we have two options. Either we can defend you and reinstate you immediately, or we can let the truth of what happened spread through Brooklyn's interactions and communication with members of the church at whatever pace she chooses. We'd like to set up a time with you and Brooklyn to talk about it."

"What does publically defending us entail?"

"We could either clear your name alone or both of your names. But one way suggests Brooklyn isn't innocent, and the other means informing the congregation she was assaulted."

Jake couldn't allow them to defend his name without also defending hers. Brooklyn would probably let them give a specific explanation, but what kind of pain would that expose her to, given the animosity of Deanna Mulvey and Harold Keen? Her mom had already hurt her deeply enough. "She doesn't deserve to be put on public display. I won't ask her for that."

They sat in silence.

"I'd rather do what you said. Let people find out from her."

Pastor lifted his cup but set it back down before drinking. "Unfortunately, that means people will learn about the circumstances gradually, and, in the meantime, there's room for misunderstanding."

"But you believe us."

"Yes, but we can't deal with the shadow over your ministry unless we're as public with your defense as the video was with the lie. That's why we'd like to meet with you and Brooklyn together. If we go this route, the gradual one, you'll need to stay on break for weeks or possibly months."

Brooklyn would feel as if she had no choice but to tell everyone everything. She'd never let him put his ministries on hold, no matter the personal cost to her.

"No. I won't add to what she's going through. I resign." The words burned on the way out, a flame escaping the bonfire of his anger at the situation. At the rapist. At Harold. At Deanna for calling him a liar, and toward Pastor for not finding an acceptable solution.

"Let's call it a sabbatical." Pastor sighed. "Kelley has offered to assume your role. If it's sorted out over the course of the summer, we'd like to have you back in the fall."

"You have other things to focus on." Mom turned to Jake. "This dispute with Harold is not benefitting you in any way."

"I have a right to defend myself from slander." He glanced at Pastor. "The owner of Harold's Books has been harassing Hillside. I put in a free book exchange and, suddenly, I'm the bad guy."

Pastor frowned but refrained from commenting.

"Defend yourself by following up with the police. Nothing more. Seeking revenge is not above reproach, and that's exactly what you're trying to do by giving out free books." Mom stabbed her finger into the table. "Wise as serpents and innocent as doves. That's how that passage goes."

He needed to be what she claimed he wasn't—above reproach. He'd advised Devin to walk away from temptation, so he had to do the same, walk away from the temptation to lose his cool. He pushed his chair back. "Thanks for the follow up."

"Jake."

Mom thought she could smooth this over with more explanations.

Only his respect for her tethered him to the table.

"About the pool hall."

"What about it?"

"I don't think I gave the matter enough prayer. I'm so sorry for that. You tried to tell me you had too much going on."

His hands tightened into fists. "You're taking that

away, too."

"Delaying, not taking it away. It'll wait for this all to get sorted out. You don't want to start it under the shadow of sin."

"Whose sin? Harold's? The rapist's? An outreach shouldn't wait on the world to be sinless. That's why there're outreaches in the first place."

"Yours, too, Jake," Mom spoke quietly. "You're losing your perspective. You have some serious obligations in your life right now, and you need to spend some time considering where you are in your walk if you hope to succeed. This isn't the best place you've been."

They'd come here, sat at his table, drank his coffee, and acted as if he was in the wrong for standing up to Harold. As if he wasn't Christian enough to work with kids like Devin. "You realize this'll kill my relationship with Brooklyn."

"Jake." Mom touched his arm.

He left the table and exited the Main Street door.

Harold pulled his luxury sedan to the curb in front of the bookstore and popped the trunk. Jake used his phone to snap a picture of him carrying the box from the car.

If Harold twisted innocent footage, Jake would find a way to twist some photos himself. He'd wait for the right moment, and he would see Harold pay for what he'd done.

~*~

Brooklyn walked into her ultrasound appointment numb. She hadn't mentioned the appointment to Jake because today was just another day, following through on the task God had assigned her.

The gel was cold, and the wand, an invasion of privacy. But the image onscreen was unmistakable. The fist balled in front of the baby's face, right below the perfect nose. The baby was sucking on a thumb.

Her discomfort faded, taking the numbness with it. Emotions long-suppressed stepped forward and then flew away. The man and the stairwell and the shame disappeared. The guilt. Gone. Replaced by life as she'd never felt it before. Life and joy and awesome responsibility.

The baby grew safe inside her, knitted by God, and together, they had a future the past couldn't touch. God had picked her and this baby to be together, and He'd gone to great and painful lengths to bring it to pass. Much like He went to great and painful lengths to bring humanity into communion with Himself. So, for her and this baby, there was hope.

And hope does not put us to shame, because God's love has been poured into our hearts through the Holy Spirit, who has been given to us.

Romans 5:5 echoed in her mind from a memorization kick in high school. She wasn't certain the words were right, but her spirit attested to the truth of them. Somehow, against all odds, she loved this baby, and that had to be the hallmark of the Holy Spirit in her heart.

"Do you want to know the sex?"

"Yes." She'd spent so much time hoping for a girl. But that sweet, sweet face. Would it matter if the baby were a boy at this point?

"You're having a boy. Congratulations."

After the appointment ended, she sat behind the wheel of her car without turning the key. She laid her hand on her stomach. "You will not have the experience your father had. You won't have the experience I had, either."

Fathers coming and going from her life. Learning that there was no such thing as happily ever after. Her child would know none of that. The keys to succeeding started with God, first and foremost. Second, she would not raise this baby alone. He needed a new father to step in where his first left off, to heal the wounds, to train up the kind of man who could change the world for the better, the way this little boy was meant to do.

She called Jake.

It was Tuesday. He should've heard from the elders by now. His silence meant they'd told him to keep his distance from the youth group. Whatever decision the elders and Pastor Simeon made, it wasn't for doubting Jake and Brooklyn. Pastor believed them.

This little boy needed Jake. She needed him. And there was no one she wanted to show these pictures to more than him. Her stomach fluttered at the timbre of his voice in the recorded greeting.

"I had an appointment. It's a boy. I have to go back to work, but we should get together."

~*~

Jake sat at the desk in the office. Devin had already called twice, but Jake had no advice for him, so he hadn't answered. Now, the phone rang with a third call, then beeped, signaling new voicemail. He played the message.

Brooklyn was having a boy? She was right, they did need to talk, but how could he tell her he'd lost

Contact Point without also losing her?

The office door opened. Vanessa squeezed behind his chair to the employee cubbies. "What's eating you?"

He'd have to tell her also the pool hall was a lost cause. It wouldn't be long before other companies started to call for references again. He could only handle one conversation that risky in a day. "Harold's been quiet."

"He got you good." She grabbed her apron from a hook. "You don't think he has anything else up his sleeve?"

"I figured we'd see him for a victory lap." The police had been in touch to say there were no ties to an individual that could be followed up on. Either it was true and Harold had hired a professional hacker, or they were lying because of the Keen family. Whatever the case, Harold had won.

"If he has any sense, he knows to steer clear of you now."

"What's that mean?"

"It means whatever plan you come up with, I know it's worth waiting for. I'll leave you to it."

As satisfying as plotting revenge would be, Brooklyn needed to take priority. He texted her, asking if she'd like to have a picnic dinner. When she agreed, he invited her to meet at the park after work.

30

From the picnic table, Jake kept an eye on Brooklyn, who'd parked on the far side of a soccer field. The noise of her car door sent a flock of seagulls soaring, and she started across the grass. She smiled hello as she sat on the bench.

"A boy?"

"Yeah. I'm thinking Gabriel. Is that too girly?" Her warm tone matched her expression, and she'd come up with a name.

He'd expected her to be upset it wasn't a girl. She wasn't, but her mood would certainly fall when she heard his news. He dug sandwiches out of his grocery bag. "It's good."

"You could sound more enthusiastic."

"It's good enough for an angel."

"Angels have a girly reputation." She glanced toward the fluffy clouds with another smile. "No offense."

He set out paper plates. "Angels are warriors and God's messengers. Whenever they appeared in the Bible, they had to lead with the line, 'Do not fear.' That's not girly."

She tugged her shirt, sobering. "I thought a girl would be more likely to take after me. A boy, though...the name means devoted to God. Considering the heritage he has to overcome, I figure being devoted to God is his best chance."

"He'll have you. He'll be all right."

"He'll have you, too." The corners of her mouth perked up.

He stared. Was she inviting him to the family? How could he risk alienating her now by telling her what he'd lost?

"They asked you to quit the youth group."

He focused on the seagulls in the field. "Did you know we've been expected to get married since high school?"

"No." Her voice curved with her smile.

He'd brought up Pastor's comment to foster indignation, a little common ground to stand on. They had the best chance of coming out of this together if she shared his anger. "Pastor said they were all expecting it when I gave up on school."

"You didn't give up."

Funny that was the part she argued with. He'd call her bluff. "Maybe we should."

"Should what?"

"Get married. It'd seem like an admission of guilt. The scandal would come and go. If we keep up like we have been, it lives on forever." This idea, the idea of admitting guilt when there was none, repulsed him. It ought to upset her, too.

She laughed. "Surely, we could come up with a better reason to get married."

Maybe she wasn't bluffing. If she was that committed to their relationship, he wouldn't lose her over what had happened. "The police say they can't tie it to Harold, and I'm out of youth group because I don't think we should just publish a report saying to the church that you were raped."

"Publish a report?"

"The elders are offering to clear our names, but that basically means telling everyone what happened in a service or at a meeting or in an e-mail."

"If it saves your ministries, it'd be worth it."

"No. You're not going through that. You didn't even tell me for weeks. There must've been a reason for that."

"God's brought me a long way since then. Look at the damage I did by staying quiet. One way or the other, everyone's going to need to know, right? And it's my decision."

"Do what you want, then, but I won't have you do it for my sake. I resigned. It's done. You have a right to control who finds out and when on your own terms, not because Harold and Deanna are forcing it from you. And the church. Giving us just those two choices—expose everything or step down. This isn't justice. I'm sick of it. Why are we paying when we're not to blame?"

Her expression remained clear, but she lowered her eyes. "I think I'm finally forgiving—the rapist and myself. I'm leaving the blame and moving forward. It's part of having faith."

She didn't get it. Harold continued to cause problems. Forgiving him wouldn't solve this. But then, she didn't yet know how bad the problem was. "I don't get Contact Point, either."

"What? Why?" Her voice dripped with indignation. Finally.

"Because Mom says there's a shadow of sin."

"She knows the truth."

"She's up in arms that I shouldn't have put in the book exchange, but I have to run the business. He posts videos and scares off my customers and gets me banned from the youth group, and I'm the one who has to pay for it all? No. It's time for justice."

Brooklyn blinked at him.

"Everyone is dropping the ball here. Police. Church. Mom. I don't know what to do about the cops, but we need to start going somewhere else for church. Somewhere you'll get support instead of doubt."

Her answering silence overshadowed the entire meal.

After eating, she rose to throw out her plate then eased down next to him. "Justice." The word rolled off her tongue like a stone. He could practically hear the thud of it hit the grass. "You think it would be just to let you work with the youth group without any explanation?"

"I think they owe us an apology at this point. We're the victims here."

"Churches split over sillier things than rumors. Remember the rummage sale?"

Some members wanted to host a rummage sale in the church basement. Others said it was turning the church into a marketplace. Leadership decided the sale would be held in the parking lot, but then it rained and the people running it moved the merchandise inside. The offense took weeks to work through.

"Letting the truth come out and the rumors die...it makes sense."

"And Harold? You'd have me just ignore him?"

"Forgiving isn't ignoring." She twisted her ring. "It's leaving it to God."

"God works through people."

"Not every time. If he did, the rapist would've been caught. Sometimes, God works on His own. I did what you did. I reported a crime. And then I let the police do their work like you need to."

"But they're not doing anything for either of us."

"Here's a question, Jake. If Harold were fined or spent a couple of days in jail or whatever they do for something like posting a video, would that be enough? Or are you looking for a punishment that's greater than the crime? I get the feeling you're looking for revenge, not justice."

"I expected a lot of things from you, but not this." He grabbed his plate, an excuse to pace to the trash can.

"What did you expect?" Offense echoed in her voice.

He dropped his plate in the metal cylinder. Brooklyn faced him from the bench. Her belly looked as if a phone book had been strapped to her. Another man did this to her. He hated that.

"What did you expect?" she repeated.

"Don't you wish you didn't have to pay for it anymore?"

"That's why I'm learning to forgive."

"Forgive, sure, but you won't stop paying for it until you also get justice. The blame has to go somewhere. That's what justice is for."

She gave her ring another twist. "That's a pretty small view of justice."

"And your view of forgiveness is too all-encompassing."

"I guess time will tell." The sad slant of her voice implied the time she spoke of would be spent apart. She pushed up from the table. "If you feel called to go to a different church, you should go."

"Come." He swallowed. "Come with me."

She shook her head.

"And us?" His voice went hoarse.

"We both need to do what we're called to do. I don't know how that looks. I never thought it would look like this." She touched her belly. "But since it does, and I don't know the next step, the only thing I can do is follow the One who does. Any deviation from that will be disaster."

Mom really was killing his relationship with Brooklyn by taking back the pool hall. After everything they'd been through and how far they'd come, he was losing her. "Brooklyn."

She wouldn't look at him. "I thought you were solid, but you've changed. You're letting anger control your decisions."

She'd take his protests as a sign he wasn't as interested in God's will as she was. "What do you want, Brooklyn? What do you think is fair?"

"What happened to me was worse, wasn't it?" She searched his face, her eyes collecting tears. "It was worse, but I'm called to forgive and you're not?"

"I want justice for you, too."

"I don't want your kind of justice. What I want is to heal. I want to be whole. I want to find the treasures God has for me here. Those are the things you need, too, but you're going to miss it all if you're chasing after Harold and apologies from church. You can't even see the ways you brought this on yourself by doing it. How much worse is it going to have to get to break through to you?"

"You blame me for the video."

"Stop thinking in terms of blame. I had to start telling people, and I'll have to be grateful that the video broke the ice. But I need you to see the way this is affecting everyone. You said you had too much on the line to get into a sinful physical relationship, but somehow, you're not seeing that you've got the same things on the line with Harold. The youth group, the pool hall, me, even the future of this baby, and things I'm sure neither of us could dream of. You need to let this whole thing go. Until then, everyone in their right minds is going to minimize the damage you can do by protecting what's important the way your mom and Pastor Simeon are doing."

"You're on their side."

"Think, Jake. The only safe way to go here is forgiveness. You're playing a game with factors you can't control, and I can't subject myself or a baby to that kind of danger. He and I both need a man in our lives, and I want that to be you more than I can say. But we need God more, and God demands forgiveness." She hesitated a moment, then started across the field.

"You're going to give up on this that easy," he called.

She turned back. "If you think anything I've done in the last four months is easy, you've never known me at all."

"Then at least fight with me before you spend your whole life giving up."

Her expression flashed to clear anger. "I'm not going to fight to keep this version of you, Jake. And you know what? Maybe you're right. Maybe this is easy."

He worked through their conversation again. She hadn't balked at talk of marriage or left over the pool hall. Could she finally be tired of running away? And now, he was losing her. "I'll take it down," he shouted. "The book exchange. All of it."

"For the wrong reasons." At least, that could've been what she said. She marched on. The seagulls rose in a cloud as she got close. She drove away, and they settled back over the field like ash.

31

Jake spotted the card on the table and stopped short. The small flyer resembled the ones dispersed to tell the world he and Brooklyn were having a baby. Harold's red logo screamed across the voucher for a free drink at the new "coffee bar," which was scheduled to open in two weeks. He stuffed the card into his pocket and got back to work clearing tables.

He'd hired computer experts of his own to install extra security on his laptop and the desktop in the office. He took down the book exchange and even stopped selling the gift books. The actions had changed nothing with Brooklyn, who hadn't spoken to him since a month ago. He must've left her a dozen voicemails. Harold deserved to be put out of business for coming between them. Better yet, run out of town the way he'd run Jake out of his church and away from Brooklyn.

He took the ad to the office. Maybe the police could match these new coffee bar cards to the ones about the video. Or not. Even if he could get someone to care, the Keens would squash an effort like that. Ruining Harold would take something more than a postcard. Mold or rodents or termites. Building condemned. Public outrage.

Vanessa rushed into the office. She knew the pool hall was on hold, but he hadn't explained what the problem was or how long it would go on. Eventually, she'd get impatient, and he'd have her resignation in hand. Maybe Harold would still hire her.

Humming, she strung on her apron.

A book languished upstairs, half-read. He had little desire to rescue it, but his options were the biography or the office, and sitting here only deepened his frustration. "I'm punching out."

Vanessa laughed. "That's allowed?"

"Only when you're here to take over." Flattery couldn't hurt.

A sign at the bottom of the stairs announced the balcony was closed for a meeting, so he took pains to be quiet on the stairs.

"You know running away makes you look guilty." Devin stood at the balcony railing. His graduation party, which Jake had promised to attend months ago, had been earlier today. Skipping must've prompted this visit.

"I'm sorry I missed your party."

Devin's forehead knotted. "No, you're not. And anyway, this isn't about that."

"I'm not guilty of what the video said. My understanding is that people are learning the truth." Jake hadn't been a part of sharing the story because he was now attending a big church north of town. "So what do I look guilty of?"

"A bad attitude. Why not hang around and let them clear it up? Pastor didn't send you away from everything. Just leading youth group for a bit. There's a difference."

Jake hadn't found insight from God or the Bible into the question of Devin's desire to marry Lauren. But Devin wasn't asking why Jake had lost touch with him. He was asking why he'd left the church. "I left because they're more willing to bow to false accusations than to assume the best in people who have solid histories. That's not the kind of church I want to be a part of. Anyway, Brooklyn wants space."

"So she got the church in the divorce? She actually told you to stop coming?"

No, but he wouldn't go to a church where the likes of Deanna Mulvey wandered the halls. And Pastor Simeon. There must've been a better way to handle the video than giving him just two options—publish news of the rape or take a sabbatical.

"I trusted you," Devin said. "They're telling me you were a bad influence. They're talking about adoption and me and Lauren getting married, but their advice is crap. The one person who could help me can't even face a little gossip."

"I can't help you, Devin. There are factors in play here that I—" No. He couldn't admit God had asked him to step down, too, by not giving him any insight for the teen's situation. "You want advice? Pray. Talk to your parents. Try Kelley and see if he's got anything for you. But find someone else to send on this guilt trip. I don't need it."

"Who do you think is telling me all this? It is my parents. And Kelley and the Mulveys, but Lauren's not talking to me. So who're these nameless people who're bowing to false accusations that you just can't face? 'Cause I don't believe for a minute that Brooklyn told you she wanted that much space, and things aren't right without you."

He almost named Deanna and Pastor, but caught himself. "I can't help you, Devin." He stepped past to his apartment.

Despite locking himself in, Jake could still see

Devin's face, knotted with worry and anger. Instead of being the mentor he'd always aspired to be, Jake had gone after Harold, and now he was angry with Pastor Simeon for a situation that couldn't be helped? And in front of Devin? He'd hit a new low.

32

Brooklyn's car door echoed Caleb's.

The pistachio siding of the duplex before them was unfortunate but standard for the decade the house had been built. Through the narrow space between the garage and the building, the blue lake glittered under the June sun.

Caleb frowned, as he had at most of the places they'd looked. "At least it's close to the water."

"The inside's newly remodeled."

He wandered away from her, around the outside of the duplex. She had two more days at Galley Paper—Monday and Tuesday. Her severance ought to carry her for months, but baby expenses loomed, and the job hunt was dismal. Downgrading seemed like the only prudent option. Caleb had claimed the task of apartment shopping with her. "To keep you from getting into some place you'll regret," he'd said.

But according to him, every place in her budget would come with regret. If he didn't approve of one soon, she'd have to pick against his recommendation. He rejoined her by the car.

"What do you think?"

"Nice lot. Fresh paint and new windows. Still. It's old. A remodel can't get rid of all the creaks."

"I can handle creaks. And I like being near water."

"Sure. Have fun with those stairs."

The vacancy was on the second floor. "It would be

good exercise."

"Easy to say now when you're how far along?"

"Five months. But I can't afford to be picky like you."

He now worked real estate with his aunt and uncle. The offer he'd accepted on his house in Madison meant he needed to find a new place, but with equity, savings, and a solid job, he'd brought her along as he toured a few nice houses.

The duplex's owner came out and led them up the stairs to the apartment. After giving them the basic details, she let them wander through the empty rooms. The washer and dryer were in a closet in the bathroom. Every other place they'd toured had relegated the machines to the basement.

"What do you think?" Even he would have to admit this was nice.

"I don't like that you can't pull into a garage and get up to the apartment without going outside. You'd be going up those stairs at night."

Her heart sped up, but the whole staircase was in sight from the ground. She could see to the top that no one was there.

"If you're going to move, you might as well go someplace safer."

She no longer felt completely safe anywhere when she was alone. Was the detached garage really that big of a risk? North Adams' crime rates were extremely low, and though the duplex was old, this was a nice neighborhood.

"Hillside's stairs are all interior."

So this wasn't about the stairs or danger at all. Caleb wanted her to marry Jake. He swore Jake was changing, giving up on Harold and revenge, but an external show was different than a heart-level change.

She made her way down the hall. "This place fits the budget and has a view of the lake."

The landlord waited in the kitchen. "Would you like to fill out an application?"

A tree blocked the view of the water, but it was still there. Like the baby, who shifted in Brooklyn's belly. And the pending unemployment. And the fact that Caleb wouldn't approve of anywhere for her other than Jake's arms. "Sure."

Once she finished the application, they trooped out.

Brooklyn turned to look back up at the stairs they'd just descended. She'd have to walk about twenty feet to get to them from the garage. *Lord, I'm going to need Your help to do this.* She pulled open the passenger door. "I can't live the rest of my life in fear of something as common as stairs."

"You still might get a good job that'll let you stay where you are."

"It'd have to pay a lot more than my last one. If it's the same salary, it'd put me right over the line where assistance kicks in, and I'd have to find someplace less expensive to afford daycare. A place like this."

Caleb tossed her a grin.

"What?"

"Jake could watch him. He could work nights, watch the kid days while you work."

"Easy for you to say." Even if Jake did want her back, he wouldn't want to play nanny forty hours a week on top of working full-time. Come to think of it, she'd never seen him hold a baby, let alone feed or care for one.

"It can't be that hard to change a diaper. He'd do

it."

Caleb had probably never cared for a baby, either. Gabriel shifted as if to promise he'd be too much for either Jake or Caleb to handle. "You should tell him you volunteered him for that."

"He volunteered."

Caleb was playing matchmaker at Jake's request?

"Look. I saw the video like everybody else. He clearly wants a place in Gabriel's life."

So Jake hadn't sent him. "Him wanting to help isn't a good reason."

"Then what is?"

"I want him to follow God, not me. And, frankly, I want to be longing for God, not Jake. Besides, using him as a babysitter doesn't seem wrong to you?"

"He'd do it." If he balked at the job, Caleb would probably knock him upside the head.

Gabriel kicked. She put her hand over the spot. "He doesn't usually move this much in the middle of the day."

Caleb didn't reply.

"No matter what, I have to relocate. With no job, the realistic options are a cheap apartment or living with Mom and Greg. I've been thinking I should work on that relationship, but living in their house would make it worse."

Caleb rested his wrist on top of the steering wheel, fingers tapping the dash. "When I told you the North Adams office was closing, I promised I'd look out for you."

"You are looking out for me. You're helping me find a place to live."

"My aunt and uncle own an apartment complex in Bethel. It has a few openings. They offered me one for almost nothing until I find a house. I'm sure they can do the same for you until you find a job. Without one, there's nothing holding you here, anyway, and that's halfway to your parents' house, if you're serious about them. There are a few companies out there that might be hiring. Since Bethel's an hour away, the others from Galley Paper probably aren't applying there."

"We would be neighbors?"

He hesitated before nodding. "Yes. I could arrange that."

~*~

Jake hiked to the bridge where he'd met up with Brooklyn in April. This seemed like the place she'd come to get her head together after her last shift at Galley Paper. Caleb had been pretty ominous when he'd told Jake to "get it together and talk to her." She might read a chance meeting on the bridge as a sign she ought to forgive him.

Too bad all the bridge held was a couple of men fishing.

He resorted to texting her, trying to quote what she'd sent him all those weeks ago. *Sunset's going to be beautiful over the lake.*

Her response took a few minutes. *OK.*

Did that mean she was coming or not? And when? His hand tightened on the phone with the urge to chuck it into the water.

The wait to find out what she meant would be long; the sun dawdled at least an hour from the horizon. They used to understand each other, but then, they used to say more than *OK*. He played on his phone. The fishermen started packing up, and he went online to find the official time of sunset for the day.

"It'll be hard to enjoy the sunset like that," Brooklyn said.

He hadn't noticed her approach.

Her pregnancy had progressed. If they couldn't fix their disagreement, he wouldn't meet Gabriel. The child and Brooklyn would grow older in the black spaces between chance meetings. How had he allowed so much distance between himself and her? Why hadn't he pounded down her door when she'd stopped returning his calls?

"How are you doing?" He eyed the plastic grocery bag she carried. It looked like another yarn creation, but the plastic swelled as if it were stuffed full. She only gave him gifts she'd made when she wanted to end or postpone a part of their relationship, so he had to believe whatever it was wasn't for him.

She set the bag on the ground. "Healthy, at least."

True to his expectations, Harold continued to work toward opening his coffee bar though Jake had taken down the book exchange and returned the gift books to the vendor. Now, Hillside's sales were down. But being right wasn't worth the price he'd paid. He ached for all the times over the last weeks when he could've held her if he hadn't alienated her. Regret over losing her would drop him to his knees if he dwelled on it. "Any job leads?"

"I have a couple of interviews next week." She studied him. "How have you been?"

"Fine. Working a lot, as always. Going to church at North Adams Living Water."

"Sounds nice."

"You should try it with me."

"I do have to change churches."

"Because of the video?"

"No, if anything's left, it's just a couple of people here and there, and they're pretty quiet about it." She touched her fingers to the nape of her neck. "I came tonight because I'm moving. Caleb offered me a nearly free place to stay until I find a job, and I couldn't turn it down. Plus, it's closer to Mom, and I've been praying a lot about her. I need to find a way to mend that relationship and maybe even live close enough to let her see her grandson regularly."

So the new apartment wasn't in North Adams. What was Caleb thinking? "She wanted you to abort him."

"I've been praying about it a lot."

As if that would dampen the blow. His gaze hit on the bag again.

"Besides." A tear collected on her lower eyelashes. "I don't have a job. I need to expand my search somehow, so either I start competing for entry-level jobs with high schoolers, or I broaden the area. I think this is God's leading. There are things here that I hang on to that I shouldn't, and He's calling me away from that."

"Where does that leave us?"

She shook her head.

"It was one fight," he said. "And it wasn't even about us."

"It's only an hour away. Caleb's staying in the apartment next door, so if you visit him, maybe we'll run into each other."

"And you're not coming back."

"It depends on where I get a job and what happens with Mom." She gave him the same look she'd given him the time he caught the flu. "My cell phone number is staying the same, so…" She lifted the bag. "Consider not keeping this one in a box, even if I'm not around to appreciate it."

He separated the handles of the bag for a look inside. An afghan. He'd never stay sane, facing a blanket from her every time he came home. What good was it without her? He'd already packed away the one from his grandmother. "Brook."

Tears coated her cheeks. "I spent a lot of time on it. You don't want to know how much. And I did it because you might not get it, but walking away from you…" She shook her head and stared at the water. "It takes all my faith."

"You don't have to go through all this, Brooklyn. You don't have to end this."

She retreated toward the trail. "I wish you all the best things, Jake. More than you could ever know." She clipped her words as if she was breaking her heart by leaving, but if that was the case, why do it?

He didn't understand her. Maybe he never had.

33

Jake was in no mood to talk or work, but Vanessa waved her hand. He approached the counter and set down the bag from Brooklyn.

"Do you have five minutes?"

He might be able to keep himself together that long. "If it's literally only that."

"Is everything OK?"

"Fine. What'd you need?"

"OK. Don't move." She ran into the back of the shop and returned with a binder and a French press.

Jake waited, drumming his fingers over the pocket of his jeans and refusing to look down at the bag. Four minutes left.

"Since we'll have such direct competition soon, Hillside needs something to set it apart."

The glass and metal carafe she set between them was pretty tame for an adversary like Harold.

"We're starting to use French presses?"

"I thought about that, but this is better." She fiddled with the press and grabbed a mug from the stack behind the counter. "When people are walking through the mall and they pass a coffee place, what makes them stop?"

"They need caffeine."

She glowered at him. "The smell."

"You stopped me for smelly coffee."

She pointed at him, the struggle to not snap back

evident before she plastered on a smile. "Better. Our walls contain the smell of coffee brewing, right? But if we roast our own, it'll give us some powerful sidewalk marketing because it's aromatic."

"North Adams doesn't have much foot traffic."

"Think of market days or the gallery walks. It would pay off. Plus, Harold won't roast his own. He's already advertising the brand he's serving." She pushed down on the knob. After pouring him a mug, she gripped the binder. "In fact, you have to drive about an hour to find a coffee roaster."

Jake sipped the drink. Not bad. "You're telling me you roasted this."

She bit her lips together.

"Finish the pitch."

"I did a lot of research. A market analysis and everything. I won't lie; it'd be an investment. Commercial roasters are expensive. But we could get a return on it." She pushed the binder across the counter. "Look it over. I tried to think of everything. And as for flavor, this is what a home roaster and Internet videos can do. I brought the roaster here, if you want to see it. It wouldn't even take half an hour to make a batch."

"Not right now." He set the mug down, looked toward Harold's Books, and stepped back. If she was warning him this was expensive, the venture might not make a big enough difference to justify the cost.

"Do you like it?"

He picked up the binder and the bag. "Not bad."

"So you'll seriously look into it?"

Roasting coffee was an OK idea, but he liked another plan better—converting Hillside's second floor into a bookshop. "This might not be the time for it."

"I have a dark roast, too."

As if that would be the deciding factor. He raised the binder, which easily held a textbook's worth of paper. "It'll take a while to get through all this."

He had to get someplace he could be alone. A bookshop was a bad idea, but only a blanket from Brooklyn would be around to care. And Caleb, who'd promised to help find a way to even the score with Harold, was the one escorting her away.

~*~

Brooklyn packed her belongings until her feet and back ached. By moving day, boxes crowded the top of the stairs, yet as Caleb and some of the men from church hauled everything out, the emptying rooms seemed to be a better representation of her life than her possessions. She had so little left.

Elizabeth stopped by to drop off a casserole, and Brooklyn met her in the garage because of all the stairs inside. Brooklyn had already heard Caleb and the others talking about going for pizza for lunch, but baking this for dinner, at the apartment in Bethel, might be the perfect way to make the new place feel like home.

"God is proud of you, dear," Elizabeth said. "Not everyone has the gumption to up and leave when God says His best for them isn't where they are."

"It's not like I have a lot of choices."

"There's always a choice. But I won't keep you to argue about it." Elizabeth opened her arms. "All I want is a hug before you run off."

Elizabeth's embrace was stronger than her shaky hands had led Brooklyn to expect.

"You take care." Elizabeth stepped back. "The

girls and I will always save a spot for you."

Brooklyn nodded, her throat a knot.

"Make some friends there. And not just old folks. Open up once in a while." Elizabeth winked at her. "Now, go find a place to keep the casserole cool until you're ready to bake it."

A swell of gratitude left Brooklyn searching for words. Elizabeth, however, had already gone out of the garage and down the sidewalk.

34

Jake sipped his coffee and scrolled through another of Devin's cryptic online statuses. A few days ago, the kid had changed his profile to say he was in a relationship with Lauren again, but his status updates weren't the ecstatic kind he would've expected.

I'd tell you, but you'd just be happy.

Then another.

Lacie Jeremiah told me to ask.

Today's was just as cryptic.

I'm still waiting. You know what you need to say.

Jake found the view out the Main Street window equally annoying. Maybe Harold wouldn't pass inspection to serve food. Unlikely, if his family could fix everything else for him.

"I take it your talk with Brooklyn didn't go well?" Caleb took the seat across from him.

"Someone's talked her into moving away, so that was doomed from the start, wasn't it? You could've given me a heads up."

"I let her down once. I'm not going to do it again."

Traffic backed up at a red light, and the people in the cars looked around at the buildings. They'd notice the gigantic advertisement in Harold's window about the grand opening of his new venture.

"I think we'll start painting on the windows again." Hillside used to have something on two of the Main Street-facing windows at all times. He'd stopped, unsure if they were drawing business or ruining the view. But people needed something to look at other than Harold's ads. "And maybe turn the second floor into a mini bookstore."

"Tell me you're joking."

He hadn't done anything with his bookstore idea, but it kept coming back to mind.

"You're obsessed, aren't you?"

"With running a good business? Yeah. It's my job to be."

"No," Caleb said. "Pretty sure your problem is Harold."

Jake drank more coffee. He should've chosen a roast with more caffeine. "Why'd you come?"

"Brooklyn's never changed her mind about you before."

"Sure, she has."

"Nah." His gaze roved over Harold's storefront.

"What?"

"If she did change her mind about you, it must mean something else changed, right? Your focus." He tipped his head toward Harold's Books. "Maybe you should let him be. Forget about it all and go about your business."

"He's making his business my business. Literally."

"God claimed vengeance for Himself," Caleb said. "This painting windows and starting bookstores and who knows what else you're considering isn't leaving it to Him."

"You sound like Mom."

Instead of taking that like the insult it was meant to be, Caleb nodded. "She's been telling you the same thing, huh?"

"No." She and Jake no longer talked shop. "This is

what businesses do. They watch the competition, and they respond. It's the only way to compete."

"With Harold? He's crazy. Let him go for it. He'll shoot himself in the foot. Think about it. What was that video supposed to do? You think he cared about you leading in youth group? Not a chance. He was going after your customer base. He thought your only customers were the church crowd. But that didn't work because you've got a store full of customers. So that was his first failure. It'll happen again—and worse.

"Just don't push your customers too far in the meantime. They don't want to get involved in some weird war. They want a shop they know and love. I promised you a way to get even with Harold after he posted that video, so here it is: Ignore him. Give him enough rope to hang himself. He won't make enough to justify what he's already poured into this remodel, but he'll take you under with him if you go spending money and alienating customers by changing a good thing."

"And if you're wrong and the shop starts to lose more money when he opens? It'll be too late to turn it around."

Caleb reached across the table, pressed the button on Jake's phone, and angled his head to read the time. He pushed back from the table. "You've got a succession plan here, right? Put that person in place now, and walk away. Get completely out of town if you have to. Let someone with a clear head run it until Harold does himself in." He stood. "She's all packed. We're leaving." Caleb took out his phone and sent a text. He lifted his chin toward Jake's cell as the screen lit up. "That's my new address. See you when you're ready to move on with your life."

~*~

"Is everything OK?" Vanessa held a carafe in each hand. "You've been sitting here for hours."

The table was clear except for his phone and empty coffee cup. Normally, if he sat at a table this long, he was working on a month's worth of schedules, writing a radio commercial, or looking through résumés. He and Caleb had never come down on opposite sides of a decision. But how could any good come from walking away from a direct challenge to his livelihood? His employees, from underachieving Ronny to Vanessa with her generous refills, needed him to be making money as much as he needed income to live on.

A bookstore was a bad idea, but joking about it shouldn't have set Caleb off. To suggest Jake let someone else run the shop, Caleb must've sensed it wasn't as much of a joke as it should've been. Such a radical suggestion meant Caleb thought Jake was seriously off course.

And maybe he was. He'd lost his position with the youth, left his church, let Brooklyn walk away, and now he wanted to gamble with a bookstore.

Lord, help me turn this around.

Caleb was right. He needed to give up on games with Harold, but he didn't have to walk away from the shop to do it.

Vanessa stood there fidgeting. He should've answered her question by now. Was everything OK? "I read your binder about coffee roasting."

Joy transformed her face. "That's what you're mulling over?" She set the carafes on the table and slid into a seat.

Letting her run with the roasting idea would count as taking Caleb's advice, wouldn't it? A desire for experience and accolades fueled her more than a hunger for revenge did. "I've got some funds set aside that'll cover start up. I'll give you a budget, and then I want you to manage the project."

Vanessa hopped to her feet. "You won't regret this."

"I know." Peace settled over him. More than he'd felt when he considered putting in a bookstore, anyway.

35

Jake swiveled toward the door of the office.

Vanessa had appeared there a minute ago, silently waiting for his attention.

In the month since Brooklyn had moved away, Vanessa had travelled to Seattle for training to roast coffee. The day she got back, she and Jake drove to Illinois to look at a used roaster, which he'd purchased.

Once the machine was set up in the basement—a goliath task, given the size and weight of the roaster—they started with small batches. The first bags of the finished product went up for sale in the shop a week ago, and they'd already sold out twice. Between roasting ever-larger batches and developing wholesale accounts, the project consumed most of Vanessa's time at work.

Meanwhile, Harold hired a woman named Ashley to run his coffee bar. She and Vanessa had met in a class, so Ashley shared information. She insisted Harold didn't hate Hillside. He hated Jake.

The whole thing—running a special project, the success of her roast sales, and the secret information on Harold—had boosted Vanessa to cloud nine. But now, her bottom lip shook. "Ashley says Harold just got a roaster. The exact same model I got to make that test batch for you."

"Of course he did." Jake crossed his arms, covering the fury that singed his lungs. He had reimbursed Vanessa for the home roaster, and it sat in the basement of the shop, dwarfed by the gigantic commercial one. They never used it on roasts for customers because regulations only allowed them to use commercial-grade equipment.

The same law would apply to Harold, assuming he'd be held accountable, but his purchasing the small model could signal he was preparing to follow them into roasting. Next, he'd go to Seattle for training, and he'd buy a commercial roaster to match Hillside's. He could probably afford a new one, skipping all the time Jake had spent dismantling and cleaning their used model.

"How can you be so calm?" Vanessa wiped her eyes, despite the absence of tears. "We're going to do something back, right? What can we do? We should post that we'll honor all competitor coupons."

"No. Then Harold could print a ton of free drink coupons, and Hillside would end up giving out more product than he would."

"Give Ashley a raise to come over here. She says he has no idea how to run her department."

Tempting. The time had come to replace Vanessa as a manager since she couldn't manage a regular shift on top of her new responsibilities. The other employees had taken to calling her Roast Master. He'd love to make it her official title.

"Harold's not paying her very well."

"I'm not going to walk over there and ask for her résumé."

"Just list the position online. That's all it would take. She's always watching postings."

Over the intercom, an employee called Jake to the front. "Fine. Take care of it. I want a new manager. But you can't just hand it to a friend. We're not doing this to steal an employee from Harold."

"Another manager?"

"Yeah, to replace you."

Her face faded from pink to white. "What?"

"You're the coffee manager now. Roast Master. Replace yourself." He started for the front.

"Does this involve a raise?"

It would have to, but he wouldn't shout confirmation when other employees were in earshot.

The cashier pointed Jake toward the mezzanine.

Devin. Did he still want Jake to be his best man?

"Long time no see." Jake fought against staring at Harold's Books.

"You heard Lauren lost the baby?" Devin's face held steady. So this wasn't new.

Jake sat down. Those statuses made more sense now. "No. I'm sorry."

"She still won't marry me. Something about not having a place to live. But she's at least talking to me again. I guess people don't usually do this for miscarriages since she wasn't real far along, but Pastor's doing a memorial for LJ. I came to invite you."

"LJ?"

"We liked Lacie and Jeremiah for names. Since we don't know boy or girl, we went with both. Lacie first, though, because we usually called her a girl."

Guilt ate at his stomach. He shouldn't have ignored Devin for so long. "I'm sorry."

Devin inhaled. "The memorial's Thursday at five. It'd be good if you came."

Attending would mean he'd have to face Pastor Simeon. Yet the change in Devin convicted him. The boy had matured years since he'd last seen him. Jake should've been there to help. "Sure. Where?"

Devin named a park and then paused again. "We should hang out. Like old times." He smiled. "I'd actually take your advice this time around."

"Yeah, maybe we should."

He nodded, and then stood. "See you Thursday."

~*~

On Wednesday, Brooklyn stepped from her bedroom when a key scraped in the lock of the apartment. Caleb carried the only spare, and she expected him because they'd settled into a routine. To stretch out her severance pay, she cooked for them both, and he footed the grocery bill. He declared the deal worth the expense because he hated cooking and liked eating. Most nights, he hung around after dinner for a few hours, working or watching movies.

The companionship worked for Brooklyn because her mother was holding her at bay. Mom was convinced Brooklyn wanted to use her to support Gabriel. Brooklyn didn't argue. What proof did she have that she could support herself? Maybe even Caleb resented this arrangement. About a week ago, she'd risked questioning him. "Do you wish you hadn't agreed to come here?"

A baseball game had played on TV, and he didn't turn from it. "I'm exactly where I want to be."

"Wouldn't you rather be closer to Rosalie? Or your family? Instead, you're here."

"I see Rosalie once or twice a week, my rent is almost nothing, and I've got a personal chef. I'm exactly where I want to be."

All that, and he hadn't looked away from the

screen.

At the sound of him entering the apartment, she made her way down the hall.

In one hand, Caleb held a bag from a local restaurant. Because of her out-of-town interview this afternoon, he'd insisted on picking up dinner. In his other hand, he gripped a shopping bag and his laptop. "How'd the interview go?" He set the food on the table.

She laid out plates. "I stopped on the way home to get applications at a couple of stores."

"For what? A cashier job?"

"I can't let you buy my groceries forever."

He poured a glass of milk. "What makes you think you won't get the job you interviewed for today?"

"Same reason I won't get the one tomorrow." She set down the silverware and sat. "Gabriel."

"It's illegal to not hire you because of a pregnancy."

"I'd have to prove that's what they're doing." She paused while he prayed for the meal then transferred her food to a plate.

Eating directly from his to-go box, Caleb stabbed his fork into his steak. "Do you think it would help if you were married?"

A husband would support her emotionally and even financially if she couldn't get a job. Mom wouldn't accuse her of wanting money. Gabriel would have a dad. Yet God hadn't provided her with the right man, and if He was telling her to wait, she wouldn't complain. "I suppose a husband could make me look more stable to employers, but either way, one look at me, and I'm obviously going to need maternity leave. Most of them are hiring because they need someone who'll actually be able to work."

"So you don't think it would help?"

"I'm trying to operate within the realm of possibility."

"Why are you making this so complicated?"

She laughed. He'd better not be building up to a proposal. "Yes, it would help."

"I made a stop today." He circled the table to dig in the shopping bag. Yesterday, he complained about needing new dress pants, but whatever he pulled from the bag was much smaller. "And I saw this." He lifted a tiny black box.

"Caleb."

"Relax." With a smirk, he tossed her the box.

A ring sparkled on black velvet, but a small sticker identified the gem as cubic zirconia.

"Looking like you're hitched might solve some of those problems, huh?"

"Yeah, until they find out I'm faking." The ring fit loosely, but given that her fingers kept swelling more, the extra space would come in handy. Was wearing it the same as lying about her situation? But maybe it would help her get a job, and Gabriel needed her to do that. She wouldn't tell anyone she was married or put it on any forms. She slipped the ring on and lifted her fingers for him.

"Hey, congratulations. Why didn't you invite me to the wedding?"

Caleb would be at her wedding. She wouldn't let Greg give her away. Unless God didn't intend for her to get married at all. How lonely would life be? More pressing, how long would Rosalie tolerate Caleb's care for her? Tomorrow's interview needed to go better than all the others. Maybe this ring had come at just this time to help. Maybe it was God's doing.

"I found a property in downtown Bethel that I want to flip. I've got a meeting with some investors tomorrow." He forked in another mouthful.

She nodded. The company where she'd interview tomorrow was five minutes away. The job was in her field though she'd never intended to stay in Bethel. Maybe right here, away from both her Mom and Jake, was the best place for her. The fake wedding ring glinted. She caught Caleb smiling at her.

"Buck up. I've got a good feeling about this one tomorrow."

She bit her tongue and smiled.

36

On Thursday afternoon, Jake used a fan to prop open the door to the alley behind Hillside. Vanessa had crossed the line between roasted and burnt coffee beans. He should've made her come in for her trial batches between midnight and six, when customers wouldn't be around to smell the failure. If Harold got a whiff of this, he'd find a way to use the error against them.

Before Lacie Jeremiah's memorial, he and Vanessa were scheduled to conduct two interviews for the manager opening. She'd picked Ashley, and he'd picked the résumé of a new college grad with some coffeehouse experience.

He'd never allowed anyone to help with interviews, but Caleb's questions about his succession plan rang in his head. He ought to train Vanessa. Someday, for one reason or another, he'd need to trust Hillside to someone.

~*~

Brooklyn hurried around the apartment, straightening up.

Caleb massaged his neck, closed the laptop, and took his feet from the edge of her coffee table, making way for Haley's visit. He'd come here for lunch after his meeting about the property this morning, but she'd been too distracted to ask how it'd gone.

She sat on the arm of the couch. "Is this property a house, or…?"

"Business. Should be the same concept." He jimmied the laptop into its case. "A few things have to fall into place first. I need an investor, the owner would have to take my offer, and I need to find a buyer. I have one in mind, but something tells me he's going to be a tough sell. But if the deal does get going, it should move fast."

There was a knock, and she opened the door to Haley.

Her friend looked as if she were about to let out a flood of words, but then her expression turned sheepish.

Caleb rested a hand on Brooklyn's shoulder. "See you tomorrow." He nodded to Haley and let himself into the apartment next door.

Haley pried off her shoes and drew a loud breath. "I'm so sorry it's taken me this long to visit. Your place is really cute. And look at you!"

"Come on in."

Haley sat, but her gaze fastened on Brooklyn's ring. "What is that? Don't tell me you've got both of those guys' hearts. Leave some cute guys for the rest of us."

"We're only friends. It's not an engagement ring, but the idea was for it to look like one, since I'm having so much trouble finding a job. Caleb gave it to me, thinking it'd make me look like I had a more stable life so they'd be more likely to hire me."

Haley picked at the pillow she held. "Does that seem dishonest?"

Brooklyn's cheeks stung as she slid the ring from

her finger. "I haven't worn it to any interviews yet."

"I'm sorry."

"You're right." Pressure built in her eyes.

"But now you're kicking yourself over it. You're going to cry, aren't you? Come on, this isn't the end of the world. You'll get a job."

Brooklyn nodded, careful to contain her tears. "You're right. God's in control, and He's looking out for me. Look at this apartment, nearly free. And Caleb, keeping me company."

"Are you sure you want to act like this is easy?"

Brooklyn fixed her gaze on the ring, a couple of tears escaping. She wiped them away. "Do you think it's OK for me to wear it on my right hand? Just to symbolize the friendship? Because sometimes, it feels like that's all I've got."

Haley scooted closer and wrapped her arms around her. "Of course, it's OK. And you've got more friends than you know."

~*~

When the manager interviews ended, Jake and Vanessa sat at a table under the second-floor overhang.

"So can I offer it to Ashley?" she asked.

"I think she was a last-minute stop gap for Harold. He could've hired someone better."

Her mouth popped open. They'd had plenty of frank discussions about employees' performance and potential, and she'd never seemed offended, but then none of her friends had interviewed before.

"Gareth thinks in the long term, and he has more leadership experience." Ashley had floundered when Jake asked for an example of a time she'd resolved a conflict with a direct report. He'd tried to help her by asking if she had resolved one with a coworker. When she continued to stare, he asked if she'd solved a conflict with a boss. She'd shrugged and claimed to get along with everyone.

"She could do the job."

"So could Gareth." More than that, Gareth could give Vanessa a run for her money, and competition would only make her a stronger employee. Maybe she was intimidated by the idea? Or maybe this was about helping a friend. Or bugging Harold.

She glared at her notes. She had to see it. Gareth was the man for the job.

"Look at it this way," he said. "The better the people you hire, the better they'll make you look. If you make decisions just to bother Harold, it'll be the wrong one every time."

She tapped her stack of papers on the table, as if threatening to walk away from the conversation.

"Let's just leave it for a couple of days," he said. She'd come around. "We can regroup. If we don't go with Ashley, I'll take care of calling her to let her know."

"Why wait if you've already decided?"

She needed time, whether she wanted it or not. Jake stood to turn off the fan and leave for the memorial. "To let the decision settle. See if a couple of days doesn't help." He left her scowling at the résumés.

He shut off the fan and glanced at his watch. How did it get so late? The memorial had started ten minutes ago, and he lived about ten minutes away. So much for changing into something nicer. He whipped the cord around his arm, rounding it up with the intention of piling it on the fan and jogging out to his car.

A shadow moved in the normally empty alley.

Haley held up some paper. "Have you seen this?"

He froze. Her tone echoed the same kind of offense that had been aimed his way after Harold posted the video. Had Harold found out Hillside interviewed Ashley and managed to retaliate this fast? "What'd he do now?"

She held out the papers. "She needs us."

The only possible *she* was Brooklyn. He unfolded the papers. A police report. If something had happened to her, he would—what? Seek revenge? Hate himself for pushing her away? He had to focus. The paper was dated January from New Wilshire. "Thank God. I thought something new happened."

"You've seen it before?"

He folded the paper, which was peppered with words hinting the details were personal. Brooklyn wouldn't want him reading them. "I really have to run."

"Look, I realize I've only gotten to know her well these last couple of months, while you've known her for years, but we need to talk. I went to see her today. She's wearing a ring from Caleb."

What about Rosalie? And all Caleb's efforts to get Jake to go after her again?

The memorial must be almost over, and he couldn't turn away this kind of news about Brooklyn. He motioned her to sit with him on the steps in the alley and tried to give the report back, but she refused to accept it.

"She says she's wearing it to stop people from judging her and that Caleb has a girlfriend, but it's just weird." She looked at him. "What got between you?"

"She thought I was too fixed on revenge against the guy who posted that video of us."

Haley shifted. "She says you're in a bad place spiritually."

"She's always had a problem with being in a relationship. That's what that video really proved. She looks for an excuse to get out. I knew it all along."

"That's why you dated that Sarah girl I've heard about." Haley folded her hands. "Brooklyn's the kind of woman that the rest of us look at and think she has everything we want. Up until I really got to know her, she was the pretty blonde with the hot guy following her around. A good job, an apartment in a nice place, and a really sweet person. She's still the pretty, sweet woman, but as much as she'd like to act like she has it together, she doesn't, and she's not the type who knows how to ask for the help she needs. She's been through a lot. Whatever went wrong between you, I hope you fix it, because she shouldn't have to go through anything else alone."

"She's got Caleb with her. She's only as alone as she's chosen to be."

"She's been hurt, though. Isn't there a way to win her over?"

Caleb had suggested Jake walk away from Hillside and leave town. Between them, Gareth and Vanessa could run the shop. Jake could go live in Bethel. But Brooklyn deemed him spiritually lacking and insisted he needed to chase God, not her. Moving close to her would definitely be the latter.

Haley rose and dusted off her jeans. "You'll think of something."

Jake ran his fingers along the fold of the papers,

tightening the crease. If he could've thought of something to restore his broken relationship with Brooklyn, he would've done it long ago.

37

When Jake turned around during his Saturday morning shift, Pastor Simeon stood at the counter, studying the menu board, his short-sleeve t-shirt and the perspiration on his forehead a testament to the heat of the July morning.

Jake struggled to smile. "What can I get for you?"

"A black coffee and some company?"

Another man stood in line. Ronny hadn't shown up, so they were shorthanded for the Saturday morning onslaught of customers. "It's crazy today."

Pastor dropped his change in the tip jar. "I have time. I'll be at my usual table when it slows down."

"It'll be a while."

The next customer stepped up to the counter as Pastor waved off the warning.

~*~

At ten, the kid Jake had called in showed up, but the line stood four people deep.

Pastor Simeon continued to sit on the mezzanine, flipping through a book and jotting notes. The man would wait all day. The time had come to face him.

Pastor's face brightened when Jake sat, and he flipped the book shut. "We've missed you at church."

"I've been attending North Adams Living Water." It felt like a weak cover up.

"Devin, especially, missed you at the memorial."

He should've watched the time more closely that day. Showing up for Devin should've been a simple, important task. If he couldn't do that, how could he get his life back on track? "How is he doing?"

"He says life isn't what he thought it was, which leads me to believe he's grieving more than the loss of the baby. So far, he's chosen to turn toward God, not away."

Could the same be said of Jake? That he was turning toward God rather than away?

Pastor Simeon sighed. "The tide has turned. I've had a couple of people talk to me about reinstating you. Shortly after our last conversation, Devin showed up at an elders' meeting to tell us that you're the reason he waited as long as he did before getting over-involved with Lauren. And the spirit he's shown in this, particularly the things he credits you with instilling in him, are good fruit. Dead trees don't bear fruit."

"What about Lauren's parents?"

"They've stopped attending since the miscarriage."

Jake stared at his hands.

"Kelley's work schedule has become more demanding. He can't continue with the ministry next year. Are you at all interested in coming back?"

Leading had always been a motivation to delve deeper with God. He could use that. "I'm interested."

"You've been gone a while."

The lacquer in the grooves of the hardwood shone with the morning sun. What did God want from him? Did he have to confess he'd let bitterness get the best of him or could he just change?

"How's your personal walk with Christ?"

He had kept up with daily devotions, but what used to feel like a relationship became a one-sided conversation with Jake doing all the talking. Somewhere along the line, he had stopped trying. How could he help anyone with their walk when his own relationship with God needed life support? He'd never confessed anything to Pastor that had such a choke hold on him as this. "Quiet."

A Hillside employee stopped at the table. "Would you like a refill?"

Pastor Simeon slid his mug to the edge, and she filled it. He circled his hand around the ceramic. "Did you know it's not a sin to be angry? Psalm 4 tells us to be angry and not sin. It wouldn't say that if it weren't possible."

Jake nodded.

Pastor had shared the same verse after Dad died.

"But Psalm 66 says, 'If I had cherished iniquity in my heart, the Lord would not have listened.' If he's not listening, he's not speaking back, and that could lead to quietness."

This was the opportunity to lay it all out. Jake cleared his throat, but it only tightened. "It started with Harold, but my anger tainted everything. The worse things got, the more I sacrificed relationships and kept the anger. To say I cherished iniquity...seems accurate. I even resented you and the elders for your decision, but you didn't have any better options."

The older man's expression stayed steady.

Jake heaved a breath. "I'm sorry for my anger and the things I did because of it."

"I forgive you, and God is willing to, as well."

At the counter, the team had begun to fall behind.

The phone rang over the whir of a blender. The boy on register answered the call and held the receiver against his shoulder as he made someone's change.

"Youth group and the Bible studies don't start up again until the first weekend in September. I'd like you to be in prayer about who the best leader for the boys will be." Pastor stacked his notebook and Bible.

"OK."

"And, between now and September, it would be nice to see more of you." Pastor scooted his chair back.

Jake stood. "I'll come back."

"That would be nice, too, but it's not what I had in mind. I'd like to stop in more often. Maybe not on a Saturday morning."

"Try a Wednesday or Thursday."

Pastor reached out as if to shake on it, but when Jake gripped his hand, the older man latched on with both hands. "I'm not the only one who's been worried about you, and we've all missed you." Pastor released his arm and scooped up the coffee mug. "I'll visit again on Thursday."

~*~

On Sunday morning, Jake parked in the lot of his home church for the first time since May. His plan was to attend the service and then find Mom to repeat the same apology he'd given Pastor Simeon. An old hymn rang from the sanctuary. He entered through a side door and had to go up five rows from the back because the aisle seats were taken. So much for being inconspicuous.

Devin pushed past Jake and plopped down next to him.

"Where'd you come from?" Thankfully, the music covered his shocked question.

Devin lifted his phone, grinning. "I was late. Sean texted that you were here."

~*~

After the sermon, Jake faced Devin. "We should talk this week."

"Whenever you're free."

"I'm sorry for everything."

"Save it." He slugged Jake's shoulder.

Why was he so ready to stand by him? Jake had no time to get into it now if he hoped to catch Mom. Since she wasn't in the sanctuary, she'd probably been assigned to the nursery. "I'll be in touch." He jogged to the nursery, where he found his mom shutting off the lights.

She gave him a half-hug. "I didn't expect to see you here."

"Want to go to lunch? My treat. I'd say I owe you that and more."

With a smile, she squeezed his arm. "Let me just get my purse."

~*~

Sunday and Monday were a blur of customers, employees, and performers. On Tuesday, Jake texted Devin, asking when he'd be free, then made some calls for Hillside and ran a couple of errands. When he got back, he went to his apartment to study the subject of marriage, hoping to come up with some wisdom before he faced Devin.

But the teen sat at the top of the stairs just outside Jake's door, pecking at his phone.

"How long have you been here?"

All through high school youth group, Devin hid the cell phone so he could keep using it, but today he packed it away. The kid really had grown up. "How long ago did you text me?"

"An hour ago." Jake climbed the stairs.

"And I live about eight minutes from here." Devin moved aside to let him unlock the apartment. "Lauren won't say yes, no matter what I do. I even got a job."

"What about college?"

He rolled his whole head, not just his eyes. "You sound like everyone else."

In the living room, Devin fell to the couch.

"Can we get something straight first?" Jake crossed his arms.

Devin scowled and sat up.

"I was a bad example."

The scowl deepened. "What are you talking about? You didn't—"

"The things I said when you came to see me. The fact that I quit attending. How angry I got. Video or not, I needed to stop leading for a while. I was off course."

Devin slumped back into the couch. "You had a right to be mad."

"No. Not like that. Even where Brooklyn's concerned, I made mistakes. She felt pretty strongly that we were called to a different level of purity, not spending time alone together. If I had been as sensitive to the Spirit as she was, Harold would've had a harder time making that video."

Devin sighed. He didn't care about anything but

Lauren. If only Jake had prepared before texting him. *God, this will have to be all You.*

He took his Bible from one of the end tables. The leather was smooth and soft under his fingers. Familiar. "You want to get married."

Devin shrugged. "It's not crazy. It's in the Bible."

Jake studied the book in his hands.

"Exodus 22:16," Devin said. "'If a man seduces a virgin who is not betrothed and lies with her, he shall give the bride price for her and make her his wife.' Some other verse says he can't divorce her, either. It's the only option I've got that's above reproach, and that's what you always told me to be."

Jake opened the Bible and double checked the verse.

Devin had taken this seriously. Transparency might be the answer. Pretending to have all the answers would get them nowhere. Devin had grown a lot since he'd last studied with Jake. He needed a mentor, not an outright leader.

Jake opened the Bible to First Thessalonians and passed it to Devin. "Where I get stuck is whether or not the old law still applies. The world is a lot different than it used to be. We're under a covenant of grace. But purity is more of a gauge of our commitment than we'd like to think it is. I've done talks and led Bible studies on the subject, but somehow, I never noticed First Thessalonians 4:8 until I found out about you and Lauren. It says that sexual sin is a rejection of God. People talk about how kids shouldn't be cursed for the rest of their lives by having to marry someone because they got caught up in the moment, but in the Bible, we're told sin determines the course of generations. And a rejection of God is a serious sin. I'm not sure we take it as seriously as we're meant to."

Devin read the verse. "So you think we should get married."

He took the Bible back, thumbing the markers he'd left in other passages. *Help the right one to stand out to me now.* "You can't pressure Lauren into it. Even if she comes around, husbands have a lot of commands in the Bible. Marriage represents Christ's relationship with the church. That's a tall order. If you're not prepared to live up to it, I don't think I can support you going from one sin—sex outside of marriage—to another—an ungodly marriage."

"Kelley lectured me on all the stuff about what husbands and fathers are supposed to do. I think I've got it."

There. *Thank You, Lord.* "You'd die for her."

"That's pretty much what I'm doing. Not to be dramatic, or anything, but I'm skipping college. I found a full-time job."

"That's not dying." Jake paged to a passage in Judges. "This is the account of a man who let a mob take his wife in order to save himself from them. He had a choice. His safety, or hers. He chose his own. After the mob finished with her, she died on the doorstep of the house where he'd spent the night, safe. She ran away from him at the start of the story. That's the whole reason they were traveling through the town where this happened.

"Flash forward, and the same thing happens again, only instead of a wife running away, it was all of us. We ran away from God by sinning, so He sent Jesus after us. Jesus's choice was either He could have His comfort, or He could have us. He chose us even when it meant the cross. With that image in mind, if you tell me that you'll honor your marriage to Lauren no matter what, I'll stand with you."

Devin's eyes locked on the page in Judges. "I can't believe anyone would do that."

"Sin takes us shockingly far from where we ought to be."

"How could anyone hand over his own wife?" He looked up from the Bible.

"We don't usually face mobs here, but marriage is supposed to be an example of Christ's love for the church. It's about sacrificial love when it'd be easier to walk away."

Devin's mouth tugged down with determination. "I understand what I'm getting into."

Maybe, maybe not. Jake wasn't even sure he understood. He'd let Brooklyn walk away when he could've kept her. Still, happy marriages were possible because he'd seen them modeled. "Stay committed to God, and you'll be OK."

"And you'll be in the wedding?"

"Yes. I'll stand by you." One way or the other.

38

Brooklyn folded laundry on the bed until the apartment door rattled open.

Caleb paused and smiled when she met him in the living room. "What's got you all excited?"

"I got an offer in Greenly today." She grinned.

A frown hijacked his expression for a moment before he nodded encouragement. "The ring worked."

"No, the Greenly interview happened before you gave it to me. Besides." She held up her right hand, where the ring sparkled. "I like it as a reminder that I have a friend who'll stand by me, but I can't pretend to be married. I have to trust God, not a lie."

He wandered past and lifted the lid on the pot of potatoes that boiled on the stove then cracked open the oven to see the chicken. "Looks good."

"Why aren't you happy for me?"

He locked his fingers behind his head. "I've been praying for something pretty specific. The job in Greenly isn't it. Did you take it already?"

"No. They're e-mailing the offer so I can review the benefits package. It was less than I wanted, and I haven't heard from the place in Bethel yet. What were you praying for?"

"Nothing short of a miracle." His arms fell, and he turned toward her. "I think you'll get a better offer. Can you wait a few days before you say one way or the other?"

"Is there something I should know?"

He shook his head. "Just give the miracle a couple of days."

Back in March, she'd experienced her first miracle: Jake's dream. If one miracle could happen, another could, as well. But since when had Caleb had that kind of faith? "What miracle are we talking about?"

His expression soured.

That could only mean one thing. She set a strainer in the sink. "I thought you understood when I said Jake's not where he needs to be." Billows of steam swept her face as she dumped out the water and potatoes.

"He's human, Brook. He got rid of the exchange. He stopped selling books altogether." He unbuttoned his cuffs and rolled them. "Pastor Simeon asked him back to help with the guys again. He must be doing something right."

She gave the strainer a shake before transferring the potatoes to a bowl. "He does a lot of things right, but what's his motivation? Just trying to earn me back isn't enough. He still can't get past Harold. He's locked on him. Jesus said hate is the same as murder."

"He doesn't hate Harold."

"He's not trusting God with him, either."

"There have been times in my life where I knew what the right thing was so I did it, even though I didn't feel like it."

"If you obey in the middle of not feeling like it to honor God, that's one thing. He's obeying to win back his reputation, and maybe, me."

"He thinks you're a lost cause."

She plunged the potato masher down until it clicked on the glass of the bowl. She was a lost cause.

"I'm not praying for him to come here and sweep you off your feet. Not exactly, anyway. I'm praying he'll buy the space from me and start a second Hillside location. And that you'll still be here when it happens. So give it a few more days, OK?"

The idea of a miracle, the idea of hope, drew her.

Caleb started toward the living room only to turn abruptly. "If he were after his reputation, why do you think he didn't accept?"

"Accept what?"

"His old responsibilities back. He and Pastor started meeting. Pastor asked if he wanted back in, and he didn't jump at it. He's not after his reputation. For a while there, maybe you're right that he was, but not anymore."

Either Jake was changing, or Caleb, once again, colored him in favorable light. How could she know the truth from Bethel?

Caleb stopped at her elbow. "I think they're dead."

The potatoes had turned smooth, almost whipped. She reached for the salt shaker. "Grab the milk and butter."

When he didn't, she turned and found herself the subject of his scrutiny.

She went to the fridge to grab the dairy products. "I'm not sure how to tell if his priorities are right. He's so tied up in this thing with Harold. He has a responsibility to his business, so how do you separate that out?"

"If it's meant to be and he's changed, it'll be clear. Your skepticism is why I'm leaving it up to God to bring him here. I haven't tried to talk him into coming since the day you moved. He doesn't know about the space I bought, doesn't know I want to sell it to him."

He offered a tight smile. "If he shows up, it'll be a miracle."

~*~

"Vanessa." Jake shook his head and searched for tact.

Nearly a week had passed since they'd conducted the interviews, and Wednesday had arrived. She refused to recognize Gareth as the better candidate, but Jake overrode her by giving him the job. Next, he had to call Ashley.

"At least offer her Ronny's old job."

"That's not what she interviewed for. You can't just switch the position on her like that."

She nudged Ashley's résumé closer to him. "She's qualified."

Jake lifted the résumé, but only because he needed the phone number on it. "Ronny was entry level, which pays less than what she gets now. She wouldn't make the move for that kind of salary."

"You don't know until you offer her the job. Besides, you could pay more because she brings more experience than Ronny did. You have to admit, he was a weird kid. Did I tell you what he said when I called about his no shows? He said working here was dangerous."

So he'd made a mistake hiring Ronny, but he didn't have to let Vanessa make one, too. "Why do you want to hire her?"

"Look at everything Harold's done."

"I don't want to make decisions based on him." He sighed. "Look. You'll be busy with roasting. That's your job title, right?"

She warily withheld a response.

"I'll have Gareth hire Ronny's replacement."

Her expression slackened. "I need to take some PTO." She tugged off her apron.

"It's nothing personal, Vanessa. We can't let Harold blind us."

She flung the apron onto the desk. "I've worked here for how long? I never got to make a hiring decision. Supposedly, this time, you were going to let me, but then you hijacked it. And you're handing the next chance right to the new guy? I'm not blind."

"I'm not even letting myself make the decision."

"You went to all the trouble of letting me post it and sit in on the interviews. Then you went and made this decision just fine." She marched out and slammed the door.

If she took it this badly, how would Ashley respond? *God, I'm trying to do the right thing here.*

Ashley's voice wavered when she picked up Jake's call.

He introduced himself, speaking quickly to keep from dwelling on how he hated this part of his role. "I'm calling to follow up on your interview. We've decided to move forward with a different candidate."

Silence.

"As other openings come up, we'll post them. You're welcome to apply."

Ashley drew a breath. "I asked Harold if I could try roasting a batch of coffee this morning. He said I couldn't, and I asked why he bought the roaster if he didn't intend to use it. He said, 'Oh, I'll use it' and started to rant about you."

He had to cut short the gossip about Harold. "Look, Ashley—"

"It was really weird, so I went away and came back later and asked again, and then he really lost it, but that time, I recorded the whole thing on my phone. Do you want to see it? He says he's going to shut you down. It was, like, insane stuff. The roaster's his grand plan, not that he's ever fired it up. In fact, I'm not sure it even works. He was trying to fix it, but heaven forbid I ask why he doesn't just use the warranty."

What a temptation that video was. He stumbled over an apology that he couldn't offer her a job. "But we'll keep you in mind in the future."

"OK. Thanks. Just watch out for Harold, all right?"

"Sure. Thanks."

If Harold thought he could compete with Hillside using a home roaster, he was insane.

~*~

I'm accepting.

Brooklyn sent the text and chewed her lip, waiting for Caleb to respond. It was Wednesday afternoon already.

You said you needed a higher salary to live in Greenly. Ask for what you had in mind and see what the counteroffer is.

She should've known he'd have a way to delay her decision further. At nearly 5:00 PM, if she countered their offer, they likely wouldn't respond until tomorrow. But if they wouldn't raise the salary, she'd still have to take the job. The clock—and her savings account balance—was ticking.

I'm not in a position to negotiate.

Sure, you are. Where's the recruiter in you? You know how to negotiate a salary.

Fine. She'd give it a shot.

~*~

Brooklyn had soup steaming on the stove when Caleb arrived. "I was trying to write the e-mail, but it just sounded…" She took two plates from the cupboard. "Lame. So I went to call them to accept without negotiating. When I picked up my phone, it started to ring. The place in Bethel called."

"And?"

"They offered the amount I was going to ask for from Greenly, and it's cheaper to live here."

He grinned. "Unbelievable."

He thought this was part of his miracle, but taking a job in Bethel, where she had no family or friends, would mean raising Gabriel with absolutely no help. Unless Jake did want to invest in a second location as Caleb hoped. Even if he did, what were the odds they could make a life together?

"What'd you do? You didn't turn them down, did you?"

"No. I told them I had another offer that I was considering, and I would get back to them by Friday. I e-mailed Greenly and told them I had a better offer and asked if they would be willing to increase the salary." She plated the sandwiches.

Caleb carried them to the table. "You're not excited."

"I don't want to stay here. I want to have family for Gabriel."

"Greenly doesn't have family, either."

"It'd be closer to church. I made some friends in the crochet club, and there are others there, too."

"Like Jake, if you're into that kind of thing." He poured their drinks.

"Do you really think he's changing?"

"Yes."

After they prayed, she blew on her steaming soup. "And you think he'll come here?"

"I'm banking on it."

That was safe enough for Caleb, who could sell the property he'd purchased to someone else. But Jake was most likely to stay in North Adams, and waiting for his arrival in Bethel could leave Brooklyn stranded.

~*~

On Thursday morning, Jake fixed Pastor Simeon's coffee and brought it to the table.

Pastor's recipe for a Sunday sermon—notes and Bibles—covered the tabletop. The man motioned to the spot across from him, and Jake spilled the story about Vanessa.

"She really thought I'd be OK with stealing one of Harold's employees."

"What would have given her that idea, do you think?"

"I've been angry at him. That's no secret."

"We talked about Psalm 4:4. The whole verse goes like this, 'Be angry, and do not sin. Ponder in your own hearts on your beds, and be silent.'"

"You think it should've been a secret."

He smiled. "What he did was public. Of course, David was wronged publically, too. We can follow the basic letter of the law and look OK at first glance, but God wants our hearts and our minds. If we don't trust him, that attitude shines through and influences the way people around us see us. Our attitudes can leave us open to missteps in all areas of our lives."

"That's why Mom took away Contact Point." And why Brooklyn left.

"You'd have to ask her about that."

From the window, the outreach's brick face and tinted windows stood out like an old friend in a crowd. When he'd talked to Mom on Sunday, she had assured him the right time would come for him to take it over, and he trusted the promise more than he trusted Vanessa to show up for work. Her shift would start in two minutes, but he had yet to spot her. "I don't know what it means to be silent in Harold's case."

"You know not to hire his employees. Sometimes all we get is one step at a time."

39

Vanessa burst through the side door, five minutes late for her shift, while Jake was still sitting with Pastor Simeon. Gareth would arrive soon, and he needed to talk to Vanessa first, so he excused himself from Pastor.

Vanessa was already cleaning a display case as if her job depended on it.

"I've been thinking."

She ignored him.

"We don't need to fill Ronny's job right now. Once business picks back up, we can fill it."

She pushed a handful of crumbs into her palm then dumped the bits into the trash. Instead of straightening up to talk, she leaned further into the case.

"You feel like I passed you over, and I'm sorry. You said hiring Ashley would hurt Harold, and I can't let my business be about a vendetta. She didn't interview well. We need staff who can deal with conflicts in ways that don't involve taking a video of someone losing their cool and then offering to share the footage."

"She did that?"

"When I called to decline her for the job, she asked if I wanted to see a video of Harold. Can you imagine if she got a clip of an angry customer and put it on social media?"

"Harold is an exception."

"Once in a while, we get exceptional customers. Remember your froth guy?"

Vanessa smiled, despite a fight to keep it from showing.

"Pursuing revenge would cost more than you think. More than is immediately apparent." Since his first talk with Pastor Simeon, his quiet times with God had gotten a lot less lonely. He wouldn't go back. "Promise to keep Harold out of it, and you can hire the next one."

"Fine. I'll ignore him. There's no way he can roast coffee like I can, anyway."

"Not even with Ashley on his side?"

Her cheeks flushed. "I may have given her a couple of roasting tips yesterday. But no. Not even with her."

"Don't worry about it. He won't let her touch the roaster. Besides, he hasn't bought a commercial one yet."

"Yeah, she's planning to do what I did. Make some and earn the job that way."

"Still not worried."

Harold wouldn't let her near the roaster if he intended it to be Hillside's downfall.

~*~

Jake split Gareth's first shift to accommodate the soccer game the new manager had to coach. During the break, Jake retreated to his apartment to read the Sermon on the Mount, because it had come to mind when he'd talked with Pastor Simeon. Jesus's command, spelled out in red letters, said to pray for his enemies. He gave it a shot, but if God interested

Himself in the heart and not in lip service, He saw right through Jake's prayer about blessing Harold.

Change my heart, Lord. Show me how to love Harold and how to represent You to him.

Better. He went downstairs.

"Jake," his mom called. She sat at a table tucked back along the wall.

Sylvia sat with her. Neither woman had a coffee, but Sylvia looked as though she could use one, if only as an outlet for her nervous hands.

He tried to read their faces, but Mom looked to Sylvia, who stared at him.

"You met Sylvia once?" Mom asked.

"Yeah. Hey, Sylvia. Welcome." He'd shake her hand, but she was checking over her shoulder toward Harold's Books.

"She says she was introduced as Sylvia Monroe last time, but she used to be Sylvia Keen. She came to me because she heard about the trouble you've been having, and she has some insight."

"I'll take anything that'll help me figure out how to handle him."

Sylvia straightened her shoulders. "Harold is a jealous man, but he doesn't harass everyone the way he does you. My insight isn't about how to handle him, but I can tell you why he persecutes you."

"I don't want to get into gossip, but if there's something you know that'll help me end this peacefully..."

Sylvia sank back against her chair.

"A peaceful resolution is why we came." Mom touched Sylvia's hand.

She nodded at the reminder. "Harold ran for mayor a few years before his brother and failed.

Sometime after that, he and I married, and he got into business, but he had ideas that Andy, our son, would succeed in politics. Redeem our little branch of the family.

"I accepted Jesus when Andy was in high school. Another choice of mine for Harold to ridicule, but I wasn't part of his big aspirations, so my faith didn't result in all-out war."

The coffee grinder grated into use. Jake leaned closer to hear.

"Andy's decision to follow Christ, however, did. He and Harold ended up cutting all ties while Andy was off at college. That's when Harold divorced me." Sylvia untangled her hands, gaining confidence. "You run a successful business right across the street from him, but I think what got him started on you is your faith. Add to that the fact that you mentor high school boys, and he thinks of you as the kind of person who drew Andy away from him. But when I tried to convince him to leave you and that poor young woman alone, I learned his real problem. You were becoming a father, and he'd lost his son. It's scary how angry his jealousy makes him."

"How scary?"

"He used to hit me. The only reason he stopped is that I wasn't around for him to do it anymore. But you're tied down by a building."

The counter crew started another loud drink, but no one tried to talk over it. When it quieted, Jake explained the roaster. "So if it puts you at ease, his plan seems to be to mimic my business and steal our sales. Next, he'll go for training in Seattle and maybe try to steal our new wholesale accounts."

"Seems like that plan lacks a certain pizzazz,

doesn't it?"

"You think he's planning something else?"

"I don't know, and neither of us wants to fall into gossiping." Her focus drifted toward Main Street, and she moved away from the table. "Maybe I already have. I just thought knowing why he hates you might help."

He rose, and she hurried out. He turned back to his mom. "Doesn't help much. It's not like I'll deny my faith to make him happy."

"Absolutely not."

"Do you think he's dangerous?"

"She seems to think he could be. He abused her for years. But I can't stay because I drove her." She squeezed his shoulder. "Trust God."

~*~

Gareth returned to learn closing shift duties with Jake. Once they'd locked the doors for the night, he sent Gareth to shut off the restroom lights while he stopped in the basement to check the roaster. As he reached the bottom of the steps, the sound of breaking glass sprinkled the air from somewhere above him. He raced to the top of the stairs.

Gareth's shadow moved toward the glowing windows along Main.

Jake flipped on lights as glass crunched under Gareth's feet. Three of the front windows had been smashed, and the jagged edges caught the light, framing a clear view of Main Street.

People loitered across the street, outside Harold's Books.

Gareth pointed at a tan, tumbled brick on one of

the tables. Two others lay on the floor. "Whoever it was has quite an arm."

"They're off the building next to Harold's." The abandoned carpet store had bricks like these loose in the alley.

A man peered through one of the gaping windows. "We called the police."

Witnesses. Perfect. "Did you see who it was?"

"Kids. They were just walking down the street, until all of a sudden, they started chucking stuff at the windows. Pretty dumb, considering how many people are around."

"Can you describe them?"

"Three kids. They were wearing hoodies with the hoods up. None of them were real big or anything."

"Middle schoolers?"

"No, they weren't short. They just weren't big, either. Like, not linebackers."

Jake glanced at Gareth.

The new hire lifted his hands. "I didn't see them."

Sirens grew in the quiet. By the time the onlooker gave his statement to the first officer, another policeman had arrived. They took a tour down the street, but other than the bricks, the kids had left no trace.

"Is there a reason someone would do this?" an officer asked.

Across the street, dim lights accented the structure of Harold's Books. *Ponder in your own hearts on your beds, and be silent.* A crime had been committed, and he could witness to that. But Gareth stood nearby, listening, and grudges against Harold could be passed on like wildfire. Anyway, this may not have been him. Vandalism lacked a certain pizzazz, and if Harold was involved, he hadn't done the dirty work himself. Unless they caught the culprits, there'd be no way to prove he had anything to do with this. Even then, Harold could make his problems with the justice system disappear.

The officer started to supply ideas. "Did you have to kick out any kids for loitering recently? Maybe fire someone?"

Ronny had said something weird when Vanessa called about his missed shifts. Something about the shop being a dangerous place to work. The kid's fear lined up with what Sylvia and Ashley said. Maybe Ronny had contact with the man, too. He could've helped delete the Easter basket e-mails, and he might have thrown the bricks. If so, a kid like Ronny would say something revealing to the police in a minute flat.

Jake could point that direction without making accusations. "We let someone go last week." He retrieved Ronny's information.

The officers left him with a report and a promise to keep an eye out for the kids. From the paper to the promise, the odds of resolution seemed flimsy.

Gareth took a broom to the glass. "It'll be covered by insurance, right?"

He'd have to look at the policy to see if it'd be worth reporting. The deductible and the possibility that Hillside's premiums would go up could prove too costly, but then gigantic windows like these would be expensive, too. And there was still no way to know what else Harold planned to do. "Can you stay long enough to help me hang some plywood?"

~*~

At two o'clock, Jake pounded in the last nail and sent Gareth home with assurances that his second day at work wouldn't be as eventful. Jake shut off the lights and crossed toward the stairs, but he stopped halfway through the dining room.

No two of Harold's attacks had been the same. Promising Gareth a more normal day had been foolish. Tomorrow and every day after could grow more eventful until Harold pressed the right button and put Hillside out of business.

He has no power You haven't given him, God.

Why had he fought for the books? Why escalate the feud with the book exchange? He'd confirmed Harold's war-like impression of Christians. If he'd just given up the books to begin with, the man would've backed off. If not, at least Jake's conscience would be clear. He sank into one of the chairs at a table facing the windows. He'd brought all of this on himself by not seeking peace. During his break that afternoon, he'd tried to memorize a chunk of the Sermon on the Mount, but only one phrase remained.

So if you are offering your gift at the altar and there remember that your brother has something against you, leave your gift there before the altar and go.

Leaving Hillside had been Caleb's recommendation. Jake hadn't deleted the text with the Bethel address. Brooklyn would be there. Right next door. His eyes closed at the thought of her.

God, I miss her. I miss enjoying work. I miss making a difference with the youth group. Most of all, I miss knowing I was doing the right thing. How did I get so far off track?

He folded his arms on the table and rested his head on them as he confessed a whole chain of missteps he'd taken with Brooklyn, Harold, Pastor, and

Mom. Pride and not trusting God. Taking matters into his own hands. Seeking vengeance.

Glass shattered like a taunt that his confession wasn't good enough.

He lifted his head.

Instead of another window, the sound had come from a bottle on the street. Anger pounded his chest, protesting he shouldn't have to give in to threats like Harold's. But no. Defensiveness had landed him here, where the last thing he had to lose was the shop, and that sat in danger, too.

He carried the police report to the apartment and set it on the computer desk. As he stepped away to go to bed, his vision caught on another folded set of papers. The report from Brooklyn's rape. He hooked it with his fingers, let his back slide down the wall, and sat on the floor to read the details he hadn't been able to stand in his dream. Three sentences in, his tears distorted his view of the paper, and he couldn't finish.

She'd said she was called to forgive her rapist and insisted he ought to forgive Harold. He'd claimed to want justice, not revenge. Justice would be better off lost forever than demanded at the price he was paying. And all over so much less than what Brooklyn had gone through.

"God, I need you to change me. Tell me what to do."

Without rising from the floor, he folded the report and slid it onto the desk. He waited, listening, but he only heard the echo of the verse Pastor Simeon had shared.

Be angry, and do not sin; ponder in your own hearts on your beds, and be silent.

Maybe the memory of the verse stemmed from his

own exhaustion, but it could also be God's way of telling him he'd come far enough for one night. He wiped his eyes, got up, and opened the chest in the living room. The blanket Brooklyn had made lay on top of the stack of spare pillows. He wrapped it around his shoulders and went to bed.

40

The light in the dream shone so brightly Jake couldn't see for the first few seconds. Voices echoed around him as they did in large, open museums. Mom spoke. And was that Dad?

He blinked at the white blindness, and forms took shape. Yes, Mom and Dad stood in front of him with more people before and behind them, a line that stretched clear out of the gigantic room. Beneath their feet, the golden floor shimmered. When he fixed his gaze forward, the light forced him to squint, narrowing his vision to minimize the pain. He and his parents stood near the front of the line, which ended at an ornate marble and gold table, an altar. Beside the altar, overseeing the process, stood an angel. The pure light came from somewhere above and beyond the table.

Though he wanted to watch the people ahead of him—what were they supposed to do when they reached the front of the line?—his eyes needed a rest from the light. He shifted his focus to the paper clamped between his fingers. Covered in embossed calligraphy, the sheets looked like diplomas. The thin, slanted letters in the center of the top one spelled out *Hillside*. The second said *Youth Leader*.

The line moved forward, and Jake followed, tilting his head to see over his dad's shoulder to the papers the older man held.

Father glinted on the top certificate. Dad shuffled

the papers. *Contact Point* adorned the second. The last certificate featured his full work title, complete with company logo.

The line progressed, and Jake's mom stepped up to the altar, where she laid her certificates and bowed her head for a moment.

"Well done." This Voice, unlike anything Jake had heard before, emanated from the light.

God.

Jake eyed the flimsy sheets of paper in his hand. This was his work on earth, a privilege extended to him so he could give it back to God. But would God want Hillside back with its broken windows and all the trouble he'd brought on it? And he'd walked away from being a youth leader.

Mom stepped to the side of the altar, and Dad moved ahead. After he offered up all three of his certificates, God repeated, "Well done."

His parents joined hands and walked away, leaving Jake to battle his shaking body and the urge to run the other direction. He forced himself forward and slid the papers onto the cool surface of the table.

"Leave your gift there before the altar and go."

He hadn't done well. The standard script of "well done" didn't apply to him. But God's voice didn't carry a reprimand. Only a command, an assignment. Jake's work wasn't done. But what other work was there for him to do, and who would protect the little that remained at Hillside if he left the shop unattended?

"Another place has been prepared for you." The angel's voice, though without the echo and power of God's, was deep with authority. "Have no fear. Nothing in the universe is unattended."

The force of the words woke Jake. His stomach continued to churn, as if he still faced the prospect of standing at the altar before God with little to show for his life besides a grudge match with Harold that had cost him Brooklyn and his youth ministry. He'd confessed his sin. He'd gotten right with God. *What do You want from me? What does this dream mean?*

The verse said to leave his gift on the altar. Did God want him to go to Bethel, leaving the shop open to whatever Harold had in the works? He could explain the dream no other way. But, like in his dream, his body resisted movement. There must be something he could do, some way he could right things with Harold, save the shop.

Nothing in the universe is unattended.

The truth sank deeper into him, loosening his muscles. Hillside would be better off in God's hands than in Jake's control. And leaving the shop would free him up to pursue Brooklyn the way she deserved to be pursued. The way he should've been pursuing her this whole time.

He packed a bag, got in his car, and drove from North Adams.

~*~

Caleb's apartment building wasn't locked, so Jake let himself in and knocked at the door that matched the number in the text Caleb had sent. Fatigue had been threatening to close his eyes for half of the drive, and now, at 4:00 AM, he could finally see how stupid the decision had been to come here. Scanning the hall for signs of disturbed tenants, his eyes hit on the doormat at the next door down. The word *hello* sloped across it in teal cursive. He'd seen that rug a million times at Brooklyn's old apartment. He could go over there, knock on her door and see her again.

"Jake?"

Continuing to watch Brooklyn's door, hoping he might've managed to wake her by knocking at his friend's apartment, he took a blind step toward Caleb's shocked voice.

"You're here." Laughter found its way into Caleb's voice.

Jake might never hear the end of showing up like this, in sweatpants cut off at the knees, a t-shirt and sandals, lugging an overstuffed backpack, half asleep.

But instead of mocking him or complaining, Caleb grinned.

Maybe Jake wasn't the crazy one here. "You know it's four in the morning."

"You say that like coming was my idea."

"I'm here, but I thought the 4:00 AM part would be a problem. I didn't even stop to look at the time until I was in the car." He dropped the backpack and sat on the couch. Caleb would probably appreciate an explanation for the early visit. "Have you heard the verse that says, *Leave your gift there before the altar and go?*"

Caleb approached, a laptop in hand.

Was he still dreaming? "Never mind. Just let me catch some sleep, and I'll get out of your hair."

Caleb was way too awake. "Don't leave without talking to me, OK?"

Jake sank deeper into the couch and pulled his feet onto the cushions, one sandal falling off. He kicked the other free. "Spare me if it's a lecture."

"Nothing of the sort."

~*~

The roar of a blender woke Jake. Caleb stood just in view of the couch, something tan sloshing around in the appliance. Jake sat up to glare. No clocks were in sight, but if his gritty eyes were any indication, it was still early.

Caleb poured the steaming, frothy liquid into a mug. "Did you know there's no place in town to get a latte?"

Jake had never seen Caleb use a blender in his life, and the man had chosen to break one out this particular morning? "Whatever that is, it is not a latte."

Caleb shrugged. "Looks like one." He typed on his phone, took the mug out of the apartment, and returned a moment later without it. "The way I see it, it's up to you to save the town from the lack of good coffee."

Jake groaned and leaned back, eyes closed again. "Tell me you didn't give that atrocity to Brooklyn." A pillow smacked his head.

"There's a space for sale that would make the perfect second location for you."

Jake rolled onto his side, holding the pillow over his ear. He needed sleep.

Caleb threw Jake's ankles onto the floor, and then dropped into the space he'd made. "Tell me this doesn't look like the ideal spot for another Hillside."

Jake blinked until his eyes focused on Caleb's laptop. A photo of a brick building in an historic downtown district covered the screen. "Another Hillside? The first one's giving me enough trouble."

"There's no competition, but there are a few gift

shops and drugstores within a block, and there's a theater around the corner that has some pretty well-attended plays and concerts. All the high school performances are there. Plus, no other lattes in town unless you count a certain fast food chain, and we both know you don't."

This was why Caleb had welcomed him in when he'd arrived, but why hadn't he just sent a link? He clicked through the pictures, but they didn't lend any clarity. "Why is this so important to you?"

"Because I bought it for you."

His hands lifted as if the keyboard had burned him. "You did what?"

"I closed on it yesterday. You won't believe what I got it for." He named a price.

If anyone else had said it, Jake would question them, but this was Caleb. And this kind of deal would explain why he'd been so eager at four in the morning. And again at 7:30 AM. Jake started through the pictures a second time.

"Come look at it, and see if that business plan doesn't write itself."

"A place was prepared…"

Caleb shook his head. "OK, I get it. You need more sleep."

"No. I'll go." Jake set aside the laptop and scooped up his backpack. "Only because the alternative is sitting idly by while you butcher lattes and feed them to Brooklyn."

~*~

Brooklyn picked up the mug from the hall and read Caleb's text again.

Rise and shine. Our miracle happened. I made you coffee, leaving it in the hall.

The mug didn't look much like coffee. It looked like milk, and if there was coffee under there, what were the odds he'd remembered she'd switched to decaf because of Gabriel? She could text him back and ask, but he'd feel bad if he got it wrong. She poured the milky coffee into the sink. If he asked how it was, she'd avoid answering by thanking him for thinking of her.

As she rinsed away the last of the liquid, she heard the low murmur of Caleb talking. Pretty early for a business call. But then another male voice responded. She couldn't make out words, only the most basic inflections and tones, but she'd recognize the second voice anywhere. Jake. His arrival was the miracle. Caleb had wanted her to take the job in Bethel because he was praying Jake would follow her here.

It seemed to be asking a lot, but if the miracle happened, Jake was here to stay. So, she needed to decline the Greenly job and take the one in Bethel.

Footsteps and the door sounding suggested Jake and Caleb left the apartment next door, laughing and joking as they went. Maybe he would be here to stay.

She waited until business hours then made the call to Greenly.

After, she dialed the company in Bethel. "Hi, this is Brooklyn Merrill. I'm calling about the job offer on the recruiter position."

"Let me grab the paperwork." After some rustling, the woman came back on the line. "You said you're Brooklyn?"

"Yes, I'm calling to accept the position."

There was a pause. "Let me put you on hold for a minute so I can check on some details."

Brooklyn paced, smiling. The rape and the pregnancy had been hard, yes, but she'd seen more miracles in the time since than she'd seen in her whole life. Someone had once told her that when life gets tough, God draws near. It was true. Not that she'd pick the trials she'd been through, but she wasn't as alone in this as she'd felt. She'd have a job, and Jake had come. God had never left her side through all of it.

"OK, thanks for waiting. We were expecting to hear from you yesterday at the latest. When we didn't, we offered the position to another candidate, and I'm afraid we can't rescind that offer."

Brooklyn stopped in front of the table she used as a desk. Her laptop sat on the surface, screensaver swirling. "I'm certain I said today. You—"

"I'm sorry, but the position has already been filled."

"I see. Thank you." The words choked her, and she hung up without saying more.

She stared at the phone for a good half hour, then curled up in bed. Hours later, she heard movement from Caleb's apartment. No voices. He might be alone, making this the time to tell him what had happened. He could adjust whatever he was trying to talk Jake into accordingly. She went to the hall and knocked.

"Door's open," Caleb shouted.

She leaned her head in.

He stuffed his wallet in his pocket and snatched keys from the counter. "I can't do dinner tonight. I'm off to Madison." His head swiveled in search of something as he stalked toward the bedroom. When he returned, he carried his cell phone in one hand, shoes in the other. "Jake's going to buy it."

She shook her head. "Buy what?"

"The building. From me. He's opening a new location. He'll be here for months, at least, while he gets it up and running."

"I turned down the Greenly job today."

He smiled and sat to put his shoes on.

"Because of your text, I called the place in Bethel to take that one."

More smiling and nodding.

"They thought they would hear from me yesterday. They offered the job to someone else this morning, before I called. It's gone."

He froze, his right shoe half on. "What?"

Brooklyn smiled, though her chest begged to sob. How had she been so foolish to decline one before accepting the other?

"They can't—seriously? They didn't even call to confirm before they made that assumption?"

Her panic hammered as her eyes flooded.

"Well." He tugged on his shoes and stood. "Well, it doesn't matter. God's up to something else. Jake's here, and I know you were concerned about his faith, but him showing up like that...you can trust this. It's meant to be. He's changed. The way he talks...everything's different."

"I have nothing to offer. I've never been a bigger mess."

Caleb assessed her as if to determine if he'd ever seen her worse off. He wouldn't come up with anything.

She was emotionally scarred. Unemployed. Pregnant. Living off charity. "I'm sorry about everything," she said. "How much you've had to do for me."

He waved it off. "Even Rosalie says she

understands."

The statement carried meaning he couldn't have intended to convey. He and Rosalie had talked about her. Rosalie had to be understanding to allow his relationship with Brooklyn. That must've been a strain, yet here Brooklyn stood.

She'd grown up taking care of herself. She'd paid her way through college and supported herself for years after that. Even the rape and the police, she'd handled alone. But now, taking a job seemed to be beyond her ability. She'd become the kind of woman she'd never meant to be. A burden.

"Brook." He shook his head. "It's OK."

"Nothing's OK."

His phone buzzed. He glanced at it, pressed a button, and put the cell away. "After Jake's dad died, there were times when he was so far gone I couldn't reach him. You did him more good than you'll ever know, and he's been waiting years to return the favor. It's taken an awful lot, but now that you're not on your A-game, you've finally got something you've never had before. Need. He's been waiting for years for you to need him."

"I don't want him to feel like he has to take care of me."

"Not like he has to. Like he finally gets to. You don't have any idea..." Caleb flexed his jaw. "Call it old-fashioned, sexist, quaint. Whatever it is, he'd be honored to help you, but he can only do it if you'll let him. And praise God, you're finally in a place where you don't have many other options. You've stood by your faith. You've made commendable decisions by it, and I could learn a lot from you—I do learn a lot—but God didn't put a lone human on earth and expect that to be good enough. It's not a sin to need help. You've held this off for—" He raised his hand toward her belly, indicating she'd held it off for about seven months. "Longer, even, but now, you're broken. And believe it or not, that's the perfect place to be."

His phone buzzed again. He checked it and offered her a faint smile. "Do me and Rosalie a favor." He scribbled on a slip of paper and handed it to Brooklyn. His slanted handwriting, all caps, spelled out an address. "He's still there. Go be your messy self. It'll be the best day of his life."

41

Jake recognized Vanessa's tone as the one she used to reserve for Ronny. "You've got a new hire wandering around, wondering what to do, and three plywood-covered windows. Where are you?"

He stood in the building Caleb bought, piles of to-do lists in front of him. Before calling, he'd snapped a picture of one with his phone and e-mailed the image to her. He'd forgotten he'd left Hillside mid-disaster. "You're showing Gareth the ropes?"

"Yes, because I'm a mind reader. I also have three companies coming to give us quotes on new windows."

"Great. I opened the claim with the insurance company last night. They'll be coming by, too. In the meantime, check your e-mail." He added a couple of items to the bottom of one of the lists while he half-listened to a couple more complaints about his irresponsibility.

"What is this?" She must've opened the attachment. "Is it for insurance? Because you forgot the roaster."

He checked the paper. The roaster didn't belong on these lists. "Do you have your poker face on?"

She hesitated. "Sure."

"It's a list of everything we need to open a second location, but I need you to not talk about that with anyone. Shut yourself in the office and double check my work."

She muffled a squeal. "You have a lot of explaining to do."

The door clicked behind him. Jake turned.

Brooklyn.

"Hello?" Vanessa's voice pinged through the phone. "When do I get the whole story?"

Brooklyn started a tour of the room, one hand jabbed against the small of her back as if she couldn't stand straight without it. Hard to imagine she had two more months of growing before Gabriel was here.

"Sure. I've got to go. Look at the list and e-mail me back." He hung up.

"Caleb told me to expect a miracle, but he didn't say he was trying to manufacture one." She smiled, rueful.

He nodded once. At least she'd chosen a point he could work with. "He went out on a limb, but he didn't manufacture this. I didn't even know this existed until this morning."

She walked the perimeter of the dining area. The storefront was smaller than Hillside, but then Bethel was a smaller city. The staffing budget he'd estimated covered less hours and had one fewer person per shift than Hillside, even with sales down the way they were. If things in Bethel went well, they could always expand.

She passed through a doorway into one of the back rooms. "Will you be using these?"

Stacks of old, metal tables and chairs stood in the storage area where she'd wandered. He waited for her to return. "I thought I might set up sidewalk seating."

"You are buying it?"

"If Caleb ever tells you he found a price that can't

be beat, believe him."

Dirt coated the windows, and stained carpet covered the floor, but the opportunity shone, even through the grime. Across the street sat a skateboard shop, a view exponentially better than Harold's Books. Caleb had lined up a contractor and promised to complete the remodel in two or three weeks. Jake had talked with his mom this morning, and she'd offered to either co-sign with him for the loan or fund the project herself using the savings Dad built up before he died. The whole thing could be up and running in under two months.

But none of that would matter to Brooklyn. In fact, compared with her, none of it mattered to him. He rounded up a table and chairs, which he set near her, in the center of the room.

"You were right to ask for more from me in how I handled Harold. After that day in the park, I tried going through the motions, but things only got worse. I needed to follow your example, forgive Harold. But forgiven or not, he's still causing problems."

Brooklyn rested a hand on her belly. A baby. A son he might get to know. Might get to help raise. Between that and her eyes, which caught light from the windows, he couldn't blink without missing her.

"Last night, someone threw bricks through the shop's windows."

Her eyebrows popped up. "Harold?"

"Kids. Whoever they are, I owe them because it helped bring me here."

A smile played at her mouth. "Maybe Caleb put them up to it."

How he'd missed the way she warmed his life. This was it. She needed the details he hadn't mentioned to Caleb. His reason for being here. "After the windows were broken, I had another dream." He related the details, ending with the angel telling him nothing in the universe was unattended. "His voice woke me up."

The facts he'd learned from his first dream about the assault had been proof the dream came from God. This time, no proof existed besides his own convictions. He plowed on. "After I squandered days questioning my first dream, I wasn't going to waste time again. I had a standing invitation from Caleb, so I came to Bethel, where a place really had been prepared for me." He lifted a hand to indicate the retail space.

Maybe she'd smile and say what he most wanted to hear—there was space for him in her life, too. But those pink cheeks weren't promising, as spellbinding as they were.

"Caleb's been buying my groceries."

"What?"

She brushed her forehead. "I don't have a job, and I botched the offers that came in. My mom thinks I want her to support me. As the responsibility of being a mom myself gets closer, I'm in awe of how much depends on a parent. I want to be like the best mom I know—yours—but she made a full-time job of it. I can't afford to do that." Her voice grew more unsteady, and tears tumbled out with her words. "I'm completely overwhelmed. I can't imagine taking it all on. I've never been at such a loss in my life."

He reached across the table and touched her arm. "You're OK, Brook."

She sniffed and blinked. "That's what Caleb says."

"Caleb's right."

"It doesn't feel like it." Her voice caught.

He pulled his chair next to her. When he rested his arm around her, she lowered her cheek to his shoulder. *Oh, God, how did I survive without her?* He wouldn't do it again. Not if he had any way to keep her. He'd seen a jewelry store down the street. Did rings have to be ordered in advance? Probably, if he wanted it to fit right, but he didn't know her ring size, anyway.

She leaned away to gather her things, forcing him to move his arm from around her. "Here I am, acting like my breakdowns are the reason you came to Bethel. I'm sure you have work to do." She peered around the room as if she could sense that his to-do lists lurked somewhere.

"No. Nothing right now." He ached to hold her in place, but he wouldn't repeat his mistakes, one of which was not honoring her convictions that they not spend time alone. "Do you want to get dinner later? Is there someplace in town?"

"I probably shouldn't. No job, remember?" She tossed him an apologetic smile and wiped her face, erasing the last of her tears.

She'd come to him. She let him touch her. Both she and Caleb kept calling his arrival a miracle. The time had come for his own leap of faith. "Do you remember the time I asked if you wanted to get dinner, and you said you'd go as long as it was your friend asking, and not a date?"

She couldn't hold eye contact. "Yes."

"It's not your friend asking this time."

A smile crept to her lips. "I could be ready by six."

~*~

Nervous energy sprang through Jake as he walked

down the block to the jewelry store. Bells jingled as he entered the small mom and pop shop. A bird-like lady with short hair and glasses stood behind one of the cases. Who in his right mind would propose on a first date with a woman he hadn't seen in weeks? And with a woman like Brooklyn, who'd told him plenty of times how she felt about dating and marriage.

But from the things she'd said and the way she leaned into him as she'd cried today, she may have changed her mind. The dream said a place had been prepared for him. No way that just meant a Bethel location for a business. "I'm shopping for an engagement ring."

The clerk smiled, her head tilted down so she could angle her vision over the glasses. "Wonderful. Congratulations. What style do you have in mind?"

He should've thought through this. On the chance she accepted, she'd wear this ring the rest of her life. He ought to know more about her taste in jewelry. *The rest of her life.* "Why don't you show me what you've got, and we'll go from there?"

42

Jake reserved a table at an Italian restaurant a few blocks from the space that would soon be his. The meal started quietly, but Brooklyn began to talk. He spoke only to ask questions intended to spark the next story.

He heard about her interviews and how she became Caleb's cook. She told him she'd found a new doctor so she wouldn't have to drive an hour to the hospital when Gabriel came. She talked about her childbirth class and asked if he'd be OK with his mom acting as her birth coach. "I haven't asked her yet. I didn't know what you'd think of it, and, honestly, if you and I weren't talking maybe that would've been awkward. But now, with things like this…"

"I can't think of anyone better."

The waiter interrupted to drop off the bill. Jake handed over his card right away, but it was too late to avoid a lull in the conversation.

Brooklyn ran her fingers over her hair, which was tied back, as it had been for months. Before she slipped her hand below the table, light caught the ring on her right hand.

"Let me see that," he said.

For a moment she seemed confused, but then she blushed. He left his hand on the table, waiting. When she laid her fingers across his, his instincts commanded him to hold on to her, tell her he loved her, and never let go again. He lifted her hand without tightening his grip.

The ring he'd bought today was very different. Where the fake was modern, the engagement ring was true vintage, a piece the jeweler had picked up at an estate sale after a couple who had been married sixty years passed away within months of each other. A ring with that kind of a marriage legacy seemed like a solid bet. But now he wasn't sure she'd like it.

"Tell me about this."

"It's fake."

"You don't say."

"Caleb thought it would make me look more stable to employers."

"You're not at an interview now."

"Oh." Her blush deepened, and she twisted the ring around her finger. "Anyway, I'm not wearing it like a wedding ring. It's just a reminder that people care about me."

"So all I'd have to do to get you to wear a ring is spend twenty dollars."

"I wouldn't argue against letting you spend more." She laughed nervously, as if she realized too late what she was inviting. She hid her hand away under the table, but the glimmer of a smile invaded her blushing cheeks.

The waiter returned with the receipt book, and a minute later, Jake held the door to let Brooklyn out of the restaurant. He hung back while she took a couple of steps down the sidewalk, the breeze playing in the wisps of hair that had come loose.

She turned back to look for him.

Clearing his throat, he stepped forward to take her hand.

They walked down the street. It was after seven, and most of the businesses were closed for the day.

They passed a Hispanic grocery, an appliance store, and a bakery. At the corner, their pace slowed. An old Catholic church dominated the next block.

"Have you found a good church here?" He struggled to hold her hand with the same loose, casual grip she used on him.

"I did find one." She gulped. "I was invited to a baseball game. They said to bring my husband, and I swear, I wasn't wearing the ring on my left hand."

He laughed. "What'd you say?"

"It was a passing comment, something this couple tossed out as they exited. To correct it, I would've had to shout after them. I didn't intend to keep everything a secret, but I don't know how to work in the truth with strangers. And if people know, do you think they'll treat Gabriel differently?"

"I doubt it, but there's a way to sidestep the questions."

She shook her head, confused.

He dipped his hand into his pocket and brought out the ring. The jeweler had called it art deco. The diamond wasn't the biggest Jake had seen, but nothing else at the store compared with the filigree on this one. The weight of the metal warmed his palm. He let go of her to lift the ring, his heart pumping with such worry that he could feel a pulse in his thumb as it held the band. "Wear this."

"Jake."

His name on her lips thrilled him. She packed surprise in the syllable, but not unhappiness. The fear began to drain away. A place had been prepared. Brooklyn was ready for this. He grinned and angled the ring between them so the diamond sparkled in the sunset. "This one's real." He reached for her left hand

and held it as he knelt in the middle of the sidewalk.

For a few seconds, her gaze fixed on the ring, but then she focused on his face. "You don't want a mess like me."

"If you'll have a mess like me, I absolutely want a mess like you."

She covered her mouth. Still, she hadn't told him to get up and forget the idea.

He slid the ring on her finger. "Brooklyn, will you marry me?"

She started to nod but then raised her eyes and blinked a few times. With a sniff, she tightened her fingers around his, and a tear dropped to her cheek. Instead of wiping it away, she held his hand with both of hers. "Yes."

It was a whisper, but it was a yes.

He got back to his feet. Holding both her hands, he lost his breath over the desire to kiss her. But he'd promised to save it until their wedding day. "Can we do it soon? A small ceremony?"

"We'll have to if the point is to not have to explain Gabriel."

"The point is I'm dying to kiss you."

She held his gaze as if she might feel the same way. If she kept it up another five seconds, he'd do it.

Four. Three. Two.

She turned and resumed their path toward the car. "Maybe we should put it off. There'll be a lot of waiting, no matter what we do."

He kept step with her.

A couple passed, walking the opposite direction, and she continued once they'd gone. "I want to bring Gabriel into a family, and I love you. But I'm really uncomfortable these days, and that'll only get worse.

On top of that..." She looked at the engagement ring, and then touched her hair. "This isn't how I want to introduce myself to my husband for the first time." She blew out a breath. "We'll have enough issues because of my history without adding to the mix." Her hand made smooth circles over her unborn son. Wait. She'd said yes. That made Gabriel *their* son. Close enough, anyway.

"If we married soon," she continued, "we could kiss on our wedding day and move in together, but I would want to wait until after he was born to take it much further than that. And healing after having a baby takes time. Afterward, we could take a honeymoon. Maybe we should put the whole thing off until then."

He'd thought he hated the promise to not kiss her. Which would be worse? Letting her bring Gabriel home to a place where he couldn't stay to help, or being there and having to keep his hands to himself? He'd rather be there, no question. "Married and living together, I'll be honest, abstinence will be...hard. But I want to marry you because I want to share our lives together. Intimacy is a part of that, but more importantly, I want to be here for you. Especially when Gabriel comes. I'd like to get married before he's born. That is, as long as you don't mind me spending time at the gym to blow off steam and sleeping on the couch when I know I can't be trusted."

Brooklyn tightened her grip on his hand and wrapped her other hand around his arm. "You have a new business to work on and when my mom had me, I actually came late. If we cut it close to the due date, you won't have to spend quite so many nights on the couch as you would if we got married next week. If he

Emily Conrad

comes early, we can get married at the hospital before we bring him home. Pastor Simeon would do that for us. As long as you really are OK with saving the honeymoon."

"I'll wait as long as it takes."

"Then I'll start planning."

43

Through the windows of the new coffee shop, Brooklyn watched cars hunt for parking spaces. The location was a copy of Hillside—wood floors, brown walls. She'd spent hours writing out the menu on the gigantic chalkboard. But her work, and more significantly, Jake and Vanessa's work, was paying off. The grand opening party had drawn many from their old church in North Adams, in addition to the people of Bethel.

The crowd meant most people had to stand as they socialized, but at thirty-seven weeks and counting, Brooklyn had scored a table near the door, where she planned to stay until her mother showed up. If her mother showed up.

The door swung open, and Lauren and Devin stepped in.

The teenage girl's face lit up on seeing her. "You look like you're ready to pop!"

"Two and a half weeks, if baby obeys his due date." Brooklyn smiled.

Devin's expression darkened. His and Lauren's baby had miscarried. Whether Lauren was faking being unaffected or had already somehow healed, Devin wasn't on board. He wandered off.

Lauren helped herself to one of the chairs at Brooklyn's table.

Brooklyn leaned to see if Jake had spotted Devin,

but a long line led to the register, where he and Vanessa were helping new employees learn the ropes in this trial by fire. He'd asked her to let him know if Devin arrived. Instead of wading through the crowd to reach him, she sent a text then turned to Lauren, who started gushing about her first experiences with college.

~*~

Jake passed the crowded couches and chairs, checking faces as he went.

"You've done wonderful work here," someone called out.

"Thank you. Thanks for coming all the way here for this." He repeated similar exchanges five times before he spotted a shape in one of the chairs at a table along the wall. People stood around the spot, their backs turned to whoever sat there alone. He excused himself as he bumped between them.

Devin sat at the table, hard at work on his phone.

Jake took the seat across from him.

People moved back into place, blocking off the table again.

"I heard you made it. Long day at work?"

Devin's mouth lifted in a crooked smile at seeing him. The kid had taken a job stocking shelves to convince Lauren to marry him, but she still wouldn't consider it. He turned the phone face down on the table. "It's always a long day, but, hey, carrying all those boxes, I'm ripped now."

Jake laughed. "Yeah, similar story here. Living with Caleb means I end up at the gym a lot more, but that's coming to an end."

"Are you moving back?" Devin talked sometimes

about Lauren leaving him behind by experiencing college without him. The hope in his voice at the idea of Jake returning confirmed that he might feel as if Jake had left him behind, too. This was why Jake had left his staff to fend for themselves at Brooklyn's text.

"Caleb. He put in an offer on a house in North Adams. He'll take Kelley's place, work with the youth group like I used to."

"Oh." Devin slouched. "Yeah. Cool."

"You ought to help him."

Devin stared at his phone. "I can't."

"Only youth group leaders have to be out of high school five years. There's no rule about who assists with the Bible study, and I didn't spend all that time mentoring you for nothing."

"I didn't realize I was a project."

"Not a project. The next generation. Someone to pick up where I left off. Caleb would lead the study, but you could be there to help the conversation along. Coming from you, a talk on purity would mean more."

Devin's gaze darted as if he wanted to make sure no one had heard that. A small frown formed as his eyes settled on something across the room.

Lauren was talking with Brooklyn.

Caleb and Rosalie stood there, too.

Jake lifted his chin toward the group. "She's still saying no?"

"Yeah."

"That's a lonely road." Jake's eyes rested on Brooklyn. What if she'd turned him down?

"Your wedding's next week."

"Trust me. I haven't forgotten what all those years felt like, before she said yes."

While Devin continued to watch Lauren, Jake

pushed an envelope across the table. The teen didn't look until Jake tapped it against his arm. The plain envelope was marked only with Devin's name in Jake's short, quick strokes.

Devin picked it up. It flopped, weighted down on one side. "What's this?"

"One of those keys opens the side door of the North Adams shop. The other two open the apartment there."

"To your place."

"Your place now." Jake smiled. "I'm not using it, and I figure it's not easy to be stuck living with your parents."

"I…can't afford rent. I'm saving money."

"No rent, but these keys come with a lot of strings attached."

Devin took the keys out of the envelope as if he had to feel their weight to confirm they were real.

"For one, spend some of the money you're not paying in rent to take at least two college classes a semester, even over summer."

Devin pulled his own keys from his pocket.

"Second condition is no spending alone time there with a girl until you've got one who's your wife. And I'm serious about that. Even Brooklyn and I don't spend time in each other's apartments alone anymore, and we're engaged."

Devin nodded. The importance of the rule was probably fresh enough on his mind that he'd obey.

"The third one's not exactly a condition. It's more of a personal favor." Jake smiled, but this wasn't a done deal yet.

Devin could still say no, even though he was currently jamming one of the keys under the end of his keyring. "A place to stay away from my parents? And a way to save some money for college so I can keep up with everybody? Whatever you need."

"Quit your job."

The key popped through, now attached to the ring. Still holding it apart from his other keys, Devin froze. "Even without rent, there're bills."

"Vanessa's moving to manage this location. She'll handle the wholesale accounts for the coffee roasting from here. That leaves Gareth to manage the actual roasting, shipping, and the employees. That's enough work for two people. He'll need another manager to help. I would consider it a personal favor if you'd take the job."

"I don't know anything about coffee."

"Remember how I said I didn't mentor you for nothing? Tell me how many times you've been late to work."

"Once. My mom took my car and didn't get back when she said she would. But it's been months, and I haven't missed a day."

"What makes a person a good boss?"

Devin wiped his hands on his shirt. "Being fair? Calling you on stuff but not making you feel like an idiot about it."

"Do you think you could do that?"

Devin looked as if he wanted to nod, but he chewed his lip instead.

Jake sat forward. "The mechanics of a job— making drinks, cleaning, customer service, even leadership—can be taught, and Gareth has experience at that. Other things like integrity and commitment and common sense can't be trained, and they're rare. Much rarer than you'd think."

Devin laughed. "I didn't think you'd have time to talk to me tonight."

"Nonsense." Jake slid his chair back as Lauren pushed through the crowd to join them.

"What are the keys for?"

Jake stood with a smile as Devin finished twisting the keys on his ring.

Lauren nudged his shoulder. "Seriously. What are they for? Did he give you a car?"

Holding in laughter, Jake turned away, but he could still hear Devin's answer.

"Better. A plan."

~*~

Brooklyn sat with Caleb, Rosalie, and Haley as the night wore on. More than half of Jake's customers had left by the time Caleb tilted his head toward the door and said, "Mayday."

Brooklyn's mom stood a couple of feet inside the shop, wearing dress pants, a frilly shirt, and a sour mouth.

Brooklyn stepped away to greet her. She'd said two words when she felt a hand encircle hers. Jake.

He reached out and shook hands with her mother. "Glad you made it." His tone rang with more sincerity than Brooklyn's had.

"Yes. Here I am." Her eyes clicked to a stop on their joined hands. Her smile pulled more condescending than congratulatory.

Jake signaled Vanessa, who manned the register, and then opened his hand toward the counter, motioning her mom that direction. "You have a free pass tonight. They'll set you up with whatever you order, on the house."

She headed for the counter without a cutting remark.

Brooklyn leaned against his arm. "She thinks he's yours."

Her mom gave Vanessa an order. Most customers paid half price tonight, but as promised, Vanessa accepted no money before turning to prepare the drink herself. Thank God she had made the move from Hillside.

Jake turned to Brooklyn. "Close enough, right? What's mine is yours and yours is mine. If that doesn't include Gabriel, I might have to call this whole thing off."

Her smile answered his. "How about my mother?"

"She's part of the package, too. I got her to come, didn't I?"

They'd decided together to mail the invite to her, but she came because of him. If Mom were still worried Brooklyn expected financial help, she wouldn't have put in an appearance.

That burden rested on Jake because he'd fought for it. He'd said he wanted Brooklyn to be a stay-at-home mom for as long as she thought it was best for Gabriel. He ran his thumb over the back of her hand. "We should invite her to the wedding."

The wedding, to which they'd only invited Haley, Devin, Elizabeth, Caleb and Jake's mom, was scheduled for next week in Pastor Simeon's office. If her mom could hold the insults tonight, there was hope for the wedding day, too. "I'll talk to her."

Vanessa finished making the drink then called Jake over.

With a squeeze on Brooklyn's hand, he left again.

44

Jake wrote and revised his wedding vows in a notebook. Once he had them figured out, he copied them on a fresh page, but as he set about memorizing them, he made a few more changes.

Now, Caleb held the scratched-up page and prompted Jake when he forgot a line as he practiced.

Jake's phone interrupted. He rose from the couch and crossed to the window that overlooked the field behind the Bethel apartments. The tree in the center of it had lost half its leaves already, though most were preparing for winter more slowly. He swiped his finger across the face of his phone. "Yeah, Devin."

"Harold's Books is on fire."

He pivoted back toward the living room. "Is this a wedding prank?"

Caleb dropped the notebook to the couch.

"No." Devin hesitated. "No. It's burning up. Some of the windows are, like, split and flames are coming out of the bottom two floors."

"You're serious. Harold's is burning down. Right now. As we speak." It was late, almost eleven o'clock, the night before the wedding.

Caleb stood, staring.

"This is really bad." Devin shouted like a play-by-play announcer. "I don't think places come back from something like this."

"Did you call the fire department?"

"Yeah. Not that I wanted to."

Jake nodded to Caleb to relate the answer.

"You really ought to see this," Devin said.

He'd be in North Adams tomorrow. He and Caleb would dress for the ceremony at Hillside before meeting Brooklyn at the church. A special trip to watch the place burn down would be spiteful.

"Oh, here they are. Fire trucks. I'm going downstairs."

"There's no one inside, right?"

"The place was completely dark a couple of hours ago. They've been closed since seven, so yeah, should be empty. Better be."

"OK." Jake pressed his fingers against the back of his neck. The movement was meant to be a massage, but brought back the feel of his father's hand on his shoulders, steering him away from trouble as a boy. "I'll see you in the morning. You remembered to pick up the tuxes today, right?"

"Yup. Right here. As long as Harold's doesn't send a spark across the street and burn us down, too."

"Don't even joke, Devin."

The call ended. The broken windows at Hillside were bad enough. A fire would be a million times worse. Was it really only a couple of months ago he'd spent hours dreaming this kind of disaster would strike Harold?

Caleb continued to stare. "The kid wouldn't have lit it, would he? As a wedding present?"

"No way."

"Harold wanted insurance money, then. It's his way of cashing out."

"He was pretty intent on staying in business, last I saw."

Caleb retook his seat, smirking. "Is it wrong to hope they discover it's insurance fraud? That way, they wouldn't cover a rebuild."

Jake refused to focus on it. He didn't want to reap the rewards of someone else's misfortune—even if that someone was Harold. Not anymore. He took one deep breath and rattled off his vows without pausing for air.

Caleb snorted. "Yeah, say them just like that tomorrow. You're the king of romance."

"You really want me to say them to you like I'm going to say them to her?"

"Good point." Caleb took the notebook. "Besides, you missed the one line you two both agreed to use. Seems like that'd be important."

Jake and Brooklyn had agreed to end with the same sentence. He hadn't forgotten. He had run out of air. "All right. From the top."

~*~

The dress, an inexpensive jersey knit, draped over Brooklyn in rich folds that lent even her, in week thirty-eight of her pregnancy, the beauty of an ancient Greek princess. She gazed into the full-length mirror as Haley brushed her hair.

"The practice run was good, right?" Haley asked. "Nothing you want to change?"

Brooklyn nodded slightly, enough that Haley would notice but not unintentionally tug a snarl. Margaret had set up the mirror for her in one of the church classrooms so that the space could act as a dressing room for the tiny ceremony. The dress shone in the sunlight that poured from the window.

A white dress.

For her, of all people. The woman who never planned to get married, whose mother had so little respect for the institution that she hadn't canceled her other plans to attend. Brooklyn, who'd been raped. Who was bearing the child of another man as she married the Davidson boy, as Elizabeth had called him.

Yes, a white dress. She let the thought thunder through her mind. Jake wanted her and never second-guessed her worth, and the only thing he didn't deserve from her was self-doubt, the very thing that had kept them apart for so many years. If she let that into her marriage, she'd be setting up their future for failure.

More than that, when she doubted herself this way, she doubted God's healing. Since God called her daughter and loved and redeemed her, she had no right to question her worth.

Haley ran her pointer finger along Brooklyn's scalp, separating a lock of hair to work with.

Brooklyn had bought Jake a wedding gift, a nice watch to replace the one he'd nicked and dented over the years, but now she wanted to give him something more. Something to show her commitment to not condemn herself anymore, a sign of God's healing. At such short notice before the ceremony, only one option presented itself.

"What if we leave my hair down?"

Haley's fingers froze and a smile took over her face. "Really? You've worn it up since...haven't you?"

Not naming the event seemed fitting. She was done letting that night define her. "I think it's time to change that. To start over."

Haley's excited nod jiggled the curls she'd styled in her own hair before beginning Brooklyn's. She began removing the bobby pins she'd placed. "He'll love this."

Half an hour later, Haley put down the curling iron and stepped back. Brooklyn's hair was a cascade of waves, restrained only by rhinestone pins that kept the locks from her eyes. Haley arranged the waves to fall down her back instead of over her shoulders. "Otherwise you'd never see the necklace."

Brooklyn touched the pearl on its delicate chain, a gift from Elizabeth.

"All set. Do you feel like a bride? Because you sure look like one."

"Yes." Very much so. Pure and happy. Loved and redeemed. Since the dream that brought Jake to Bethel, he'd often said that nothing in the universe was left unattended. He never spoke the connection, but God hadn't left her unattended that night in New Wilshire. He'd been caring for her, even then. He'd allowed her to escape with her life. No, with two lives—hers and Gabriel's. And now there'd be three lives, joined together by an awesome God. She ducked her head away from Haley and stood. "I'm going to stop in the bathroom quick before everything starts."

Haley giggled. "Want me to hold the dress for you?"

Brooklyn shook her head—the dress wasn't that fancy, and Haley knew it. In the restroom, she took a deep breath and bowed her head. "God, every day for the rest of my life, however many times a day I forget, remind me that I'm Yours and that I'm redeemed. I want to live my life with the joy You've promised, and I want to trust Your power to work evil for good. I don't deserve anything, but You gave Your Son to give me everything. I'm sorry for my doubts. Thank You for

Your love and Your grace." She glanced at herself. Haley was right; Jake would love to see her with her hair down. She loved to see herself this way, too. "And thank You for Jake. Bless our marriage, and allow us to bring glory to You as we live our lives together." After a slow breath, she nodded. Time to get married.

She returned to the classroom to find Haley standing at the window. Her friend turned, mouth pursed.

"What's going on?"

Haley shook her head. "Nothing. Jake's here, so don't look out there. Tradition for you to not see him, right?" But Haley was worried about something.

Brooklyn approached the window.

Jake stood in the lot, but he wasn't alone. Two police cars were parked near his sedan, and the officers spoke with him, their uniforms almost as dark as Jake's tux.

"He wouldn't be the first guy to get pulled over for speeding to his wedding." Haley's chuckle sounded forced. "I'll kill him for you. After the wedding, of course."

When Brooklyn stole another glance, Caleb's car was parked next to Jake's and both men were in conversation with the police. This was no speeding ticket.

Haley stood at her elbow until the group in the lot broke up.

Jake headed for the main doors, Caleb for the entrance closest to Brooklyn.

"Focus," Haley said. "This is it. Last check."

Brooklyn turned to the mirror and wiped at her eyeshadow as Haley smoothed her hair.

Gabriel gave a swift kick when a soft knock

sounded at the door.

"Come in."

Caleb opened the door, but only the crisp, black shoulder of his tux appeared. "Everyone decent?"

"See for yourself." Haley wiggled her fingers at Brooklyn and slipped out of the room.

Tugging the sleeve of his jacket, Caleb stepped in. His hair was freshly cut and styled, but he swiped his hand over it. Brooklyn had never seen him more ill at ease in his own skin, but she'd also never seen him more handsome. As his gaze settled on her, he stopped fidgeting. "You're beautiful, Brook."

"Thanks." She straightened his boutonniere. If Jake's was in the same condition, hopefully one of the women would notice and fix it before the service got underway. "You're pretty dashing yourself." She took the trio of calla lilies from the table and rested her free hand in the crook of his arm, but when he stepped toward the door, she held him back. "What was going on in the lot?"

The creases around his eyes faded as his smile died back. But then he winked. "A little wedding day fun. We'll all laugh about it later."

"So Harold's not trying to break up the wedding?"

"No." His voice was smooth and strong, reassuring. "I'll let Jake tell you about it another time. At the moment, there's nothing you need to worry about besides making that guy the happiest man in the world. Let me walk you down there."

She cast one last look at the mirror. Her stomach—what little of it Gabriel hadn't taken over—tightened. Unlike so many feelings that had jolted and turned her insides over the last eight and a half months, this wasn't guilt or anxiety. This was anticipation. Pure anticipation. And that reflection in the mirror? That woman really was beautiful. Glowing. Happy. Taking this step, getting married, was reclaiming her life. "I'm ready."

Caleb tightened his hold on her hand and led her down the hall. "Now, watch, because if you think you've ever seen him look happy before, this'll blow your mind. He's like a sparkler today."

"Didn't they make those illegal here?"

"Why do you think the police wanted to talk?" He grinned and pulled open the door to Pastor's office.

Jake and Pastor Simeon spoke near the desk while Margaret, Elizabeth, Haley, and Devin waited on the couch. As soon as Caleb led her into the room, everyone stood. And Caleb was right. When he handed her over, Jake's smile was subdued, but something about his eyes suggested joy a smile could never convey.

Pastor spoke, but the warmth of Jake's hand was louder than the traditional words of the ceremony.

It was Jake's movement that woke her to the fact that they had been told to face each other and join hands.

How had she become so blessed? The people in the room meant the world to her. This man who held her hand and seemed reluctant to look anywhere but into her eyes, this man wanted to commit his life to her.

At Pastor's prompting he comfirmed it, saying, "I do." His gaze didn't shift, his grip on her hands didn't falter.

As Pastor Simeon repeated the same words he'd asked Jake, Brooklyn's heart pounded air from her lungs. How did people do this in front of hundreds of witnesses? She was so breathless she wasn't sure she could speak clearly enough for the seven people in the room to hear. She squeezed Jake's hands to borrow strength. "I do."

No fitted ring would make it over her puffy fingers at this point. Even her engagement ring, which had initially been large, didn't fit anymore. But they'd left her wedding ring large, to be sized after Gabriel's birth.

Jake held her hand as if it was the hand of a princess and slid the diamond band onto her finger.

When her turn came, she had to twist the band to get it over his knuckle. When she glanced to make sure she hadn't hurt him, he tightened his hand around hers, his warmth already soaking through the white gold to her fingers.

"Jake and Brooklyn wrote personalized vows. Jake?"

Instead of reaching into his coat pocket for notes, Jake kept his hands firmly around hers. "Brooklyn, I love you and all the ways you've spurred me on to deeper faith, starting not all that long after we met in fifth grade. Trusting in God's faithfulness to enable me, I will strive to follow Christ's example in loving you with sacrificial love. I vow to put God first, you second, and myself last, as I lead, care for, and protect you. Whether it's my life on the line..." His serious expression gave way to a smile. "...Or which roast we brew in the morning..." Chuckles went up around the room, but his own face sobered. "...I will sacrifice for your best interest. I pledge you my love and my faithfulness from this day forward."

Her eyes were dangerously liquid. She worked a tissue out of the small pocket Elizabeth had sown into the waistband of the dress and dabbed at her face. She'd spent hours writing and memorizing her vows. In case she went blank, she'd written them on a card and tucked the card into the ribbon that held her flowers together. The vase with the lilies sat on a small table next to her, but her mind was clear enough. She tucked the tissue away.

"Jake, behind God, you are the love of my life. Through the years and through my darkest days, you have been a steady voice reminding me of my worth and value. My promise to you is to stick with you through dark days and sunny days, to listen to your voice, to submit to you as your wife the way the Bible instructs, and to care for you." She took a slow breath, savoring the last line. "I pledge you my love and my faithfulness from this day forward."

Pastor talked some more, but she missed his words as she watched tears gather in Jake's eyes. One fell, the others disappeared.

When Pastor Simeon finished the ceremony by saying Jake could kiss her, Jake stepped closer, his torso pressing lightly against the swell that was Gabriel. Before Jake could obey the pastor, Gabriel let loose another kick.

Jake stepped back, eyes fixed on her belly with an amazed smile.

Someone in the room shifted.

Caleb cleared his throat. "You did hear the man, right?"

Jake met Brooklyn's gaze, and then glanced at their audience. "Our son's not sure how he feels about all this romance stuff." He laughed and refocused on Brooklyn.

Even if Gabriel kicked again, she suspected Jake

wouldn't back off. He'd waited for this, their first kiss, too long. He ran one hand up her arm to her shoulder and rested the other on her waist. His breath brushed her lips. Why did her joints stiffen? Should she lean in more? But as soon as his mouth met hers, the worries melted. The kiss was over in the space of one missed breath, but if Jake was a sparkler today, she'd become a firework.

~*~

Jake led Brooklyn from the church to his car. Their reception would be a gift-opening party at his mom's house, and these few minutes would be his only chance to talk to her before the party broke up and they got to drive home. Where he'd get to spend the night with her. Granted, it'd be without the perks other newlyweds enjoyed, but at least he'd get to hold her close. And Gabriel. Maybe he'd feel the baby kick again. What a perfect end that had been to the ceremony, his first time feeling his son move.

"What did the police want?"

He turned the key and shifted into drive. "I wanted to talk to you about that. I just...are you sure you want to know today?"

Her expression hardened from curious to determined. "Yes."

He put the car back into park. He couldn't drive and talk about this at the same time. "Harold's Books burned down last night. Police found Ronny poking around this morning, trying to get to that roaster Harold bought."

"What does that have to do with you?"

Jake shook his head. "They must suspect I'm

involved, but today is the first time I've been back to North Adams since I left in August. I told them to check traffic cameras and cell phone records or whatever else it would take, and Caleb's an alibi for all of yesterday, when the fire happened."

Her hands had turned into a knot on her lap. "They won't arrest you, will they? The Keen family has a lot of sway."

"Nah. They're giving a guy a break on his wedding day."

"What about when it's not your wedding day?"

"They have no evidence. I'm innocent, I left it to God, and I'm leaving it with Him. Just watch. The whole thing'll be figured out before we have anything to worry about." The seatbelt zipped out more length as he leaned toward her and kissed her cheek. "I've been waiting for the chance to tell you. I've never seen a more beautiful woman in my life." He ran his fingers through the gold that was her hair, waited for her to smile, and then shifted the car in gear.

45

The week after the wedding, Vanessa drove back and forth to North Adams each day to train Devin and Gareth on using the coffee roaster, so Jake managed the morning shifts in Bethel. The smaller shop opened at seven, and unlocking the doors after the sky was lit left Jake surveying the sidewalk to see if anyone might be around to appreciate an earlier open time. No pedestrians. That didn't mean customers wouldn't come if they changed their hours.

He made his way to the back, where customers could enter directly from the parking lot. As he flipped the open sign on the rear door into place, a car pulled into the lot. Vanessa. It was Friday, and she ought to be traveling to North Adams for one last day of training. He pushed open the door for her. "Did they cancel on you?"

"I'm going there now. I just wanted to make sure you heard. I mean, I figured you did, but sometimes Bethel feels like a world away from back home, so I thought maybe you hadn't."

"Heard what?"

Vanessa lifted her chin, smug. "Ah, so you didn't. The coffee roaster Harold had was rigged to cause a fire. Two sets of prints were found on it, Harold's and Ashley's. Harold said Ashley and Ronny were both working for you, Ashley to start the fire, and Ronny to clean up the evidence." She pulled a tablet from her oversized purse.

Would Harold's lies convince authorities? Ronny had been on Hillside's payroll and there would be a long trail of communication between Ashley and one of his employees, Vanessa.

"Remember that I gave Ashley tips for roasting coffee? She tried to make a batch the night of the fire and admitted she did it without Harold's permission. She left it plugged in, and that's how the fire started. After she admitted all that, Harold tried to throw her under the bus for causing the fire. Then, she posted this." She tapped the screen of the tablet and passed it to him.

The video that played featured Harold ranting about Jake and how Harold would squash him. The roaster, semi-dismantled, was in the background. After a minute, Jake paused it and passed it back. Listening to much more would shake his resolve to leave Harold to God. "Why sabotage his own roaster?"

"That's where our friend Ronny comes in. He got this brilliant idea to post a video of his own. It's a long one, and I really should be getting on the road, but watch it sometime. He talks about all the things Harold hired him to do. It incriminates him as much as Harold." Shaking her head, Vanessa put the tablet back in her purse. "He was paid to delete the e-mails about the Easter basket order. Harold offered to pay him to switch my roaster for the faulty one, but Ronny figured there was no way to know when it would light up the shop, so he refused to plant it and stopped coming to work.

"That messed up Harold's plan because he didn't have a Hillside employee working for him anymore. No good way to get inside. So he had Ronny break the windows. That was supposed to make the roaster easier to get in. No picking locks. Just pull out the nails in the plywood. But Harold told Ronny to wait because you'd left town, and the new windows were in place before he acted."

Jake crossed his arms. "So the bad roaster stayed in the bookstore long enough for Ashley to test it, accidentally starting the fire. And Ronny tried to retrieve the roaster the morning of the wedding because Harold wanted to get back the proof."

Vanessa nodded. "The videos both have thousands of hits. Harold was arrested. I think his family's distancing themselves from the scandal. You were right. We didn't have to try to get revenge by stealing his employees or doing anything else, did we?"

This wasn't quite the insurance fraud Caleb had wished for, but whether Harold ended up staying in jail or not, the bookstore wouldn't be rebuilt.

Vanessa hefted her purse to her shoulder. "You don't look as happy as you ought to."

Harold was so lost, so far from God. "It's a lot to take in."

"Take your time." She patted his shoulder as she passed, exiting. But then her step clunked to a stop. "Hey, I've been meaning to tell you. After working with them for a week like this, I see why Gareth and Devin were great choices and why Ashley might not've worked out so well. They're both really, really dedicated and smart. Fast on their feet."

A customer entered and approached the counter.

"What do you think that says about you?"

"That I might make the wrong choice...?"

"No, that I hired you, too. And asked you to train

them and help out here when I know I won't be available for a few weeks after the baby. There's no one else I'd trust a brand new shop to." Jake took the spot behind the register to help the customer.

Vanessa's face flushed with a smile as she waved and left for North Adams.

~*~

On Saturday, Jake parked in his old spot behind Hillside. As he shut off the car, Vanessa called. He waited for her to leave a voicemail before he climbed out. The message asked if Brooklyn had gone into labor. She'd taken to asking that every time he left the shop. Brooklyn was due early next week, but she kept saying that the baby hadn't dropped yet and used that as proof that Gabriel would be late. He should've checked on her before driving off, but if he managed to stay out of Hillside, he could be home in an hour.

He locked the car. The sidewalk led him past the side door he'd used thousands of times. Despite living in Bethel for months, being here felt natural. In case Devin and Gareth were on duty, he kept his head down as he walked by the windows leading up to Main Street. He stopped on the corner and stared across the street.

Plywood had replaced most of the glass of Harold's Books, and tape and notices plastered the door. Black soot stained the formerly gleaming metal. The building had been gutted.

He'd watched Ronny's video, and the only mystery the clip didn't answer was how Harold had gotten the surveillance footage from Hillside's cameras. Probably a hired hacker, not that it mattered.

Jake glanced at Hillside's Main Street windows. The sun shone, transforming the glass into a translucent mirror that portrayed the charred remains of the bookstore while allowing a shallow view of a few faces inside the coffee shop. Each day since the fire, sales had been well above the comparable date from last year. A symbiotic relationship.

He fixed his gaze across the street one more time. He'd come because he needed to see it again before cleanup started. He wanted this image etched in his mind for the next time he was tempted to seek revenge. He'd been told many times to leave North Adams before he finally obeyed. If he'd stayed, Harold would've planted that roaster, and the fire department would've been called to Hillside instead of the bookstore. The coffee shop would be gutted and boarded up. If the fire had happened at night, while Jake slept, he might not have made it out alive.

God had been in control from the start and had provided the motivation he'd needed to get out of harm's way. Instead, Harold was paying the price. Had the man ignored warnings to drop his grudge? With Sylvia, Ashley, and Ronny all against what Harold was doing, someone must've confronted him. Neither business needed to burn.

God, thank you for keeping us out of harm's way. Even Harold. Forgive him. He needs You.

Jake's phone sounded, this time with a text from Brooklyn.

Five minutes apart. I'll let you know if it's a false alarm, but otherwise, we should go in in about an hour.

He started for his car as he replied. *I'll be there.*

46

Jake let himself in to the apartment. He'd intended to move his family back to North Adams, but things hadn't worked out that way. Yet. Caleb was house hunting for them. He would find the right place eventually, somewhere with a window seat and master suite to spoil Brooklyn—she deserved that and more—and a finished basement where he could set up a pool table and host the guys. In the meantime, at least they'd been able to move into a nicer apartment on January first.

Winter had come and gone, and he no longer had to plow through snow drifts to check in at the North Adams location. He'd driven today to meet with a grocery chain about carrying Hillside's roasts in their stores across the state. He smiled as he dropped his keys in the bowl Brooklyn put by the door.

The meeting marked the first time Devin had worn a tie in Jake's presence. Between Vanessa's experience marketing Hillside and Devin making a full-time job of taking the roasts to the next level, the meeting had gone smoothly. The chain placed a large order, and the team would come together to fill it—Jake, Devin, Vanessa, and Gareth each working their strengths to see the deal through while keeping both storefronts up and running.

He took a deep breath of the vanilla-scented air. Brooklyn must be burning another candle somewhere.

If he could smell it and not food, she wasn't making dinner. Maybe Gabriel had been a handful today. She'd let Jake's cooking skills get rusty in the months since they'd married, but he still knew how to boil water for noodles. There must be a jar of marinara around somewhere.

He stepped toward the kitchen, but Brooklyn came around the corner to meet him in the entryway, her long hair down. She didn't come close enough for him to touch the gentle curls on the ends before she raised a half sheet of paper. "Look. Finally."

He closed the gap between them. They'd lived out of each other's reach for far too much of their lives. With her in the circle of his arms, her shoulder against his chest, he accepted the paper from her.

A swirling blue pattern was at the top, printed in a narrow rectangle like something that might appear on a check or a car title.

"Gabriel's birth certificate," he said.

Because he wasn't the biological father, he'd had to go through the legal process of adopting Gabriel. It'd taken months to get the judge's ruling and to apply for the new birth certificate, the one that would list Jake as Gabriel's father. Legally. Binding, no matter what twists and turns life took.

Brooklyn kissed his cheek as his gaze raced to find it. There. Father. Jacob Ryan Davidson. He tightened his arms around Brooklyn.

"You've been Gabriel's father this whole time."

He nodded, but no slip of paper had ever meant more to him. Correction. The marriage license meant quite a bit, too. "Where is he? Sleeping?"

"I have him with a sitter for a couple of hours. Now that everything's done with that, it sort of feels like we can move on, doesn't it?"

He rubbed his hand higher on her back so that her hair brushed over his fingers. Before seeing the certificate, he'd convinced himself they didn't need all the loose ends tied up to feel like a family. They had everything. But now that he held the certificate, he nodded agreement. The official stamp of approval meant something, and he'd like to hold his son. Maybe they could go collect him from the sitter. The one they used most lived a few doors down.

"You wanted our kids to be close together, right?" Brooklyn tipped her face toward him, her chin resting on his chest.

This would explain the choice to get a sitter. He brushed his lips over hers, but she grinned and laughed instead of kissing him back.

Still gripping the birth certificate between the fingers of his right hand, he held her a small step away. She looked the same as she had since a few months after having Gabriel, but she kept beaming. "Are you saying you're pregnant?"

"I am." Her smile added a happy slant to her eyes. So beautiful. His Brooklyn. Another baby. This time next year, they'd be a family of four.

"Is it a girl?"

"You know it's too early for that." With a laugh, she guided his hand to her abdomen. "Baby's only about six weeks along. Besides, why a girl?"

"So she'll look like you."

"Gabriel has my eyes. I'd like it if our next took after you."

Jake pulled her into another hug. "Either way, the decision's in good hands."

"God's?" Her jaw moved against him as she

spoke.

He nodded, threading a hand through her hair to hold her close. "Nothing in the universe is unattended."

Thank you

We appreciate you reading this White Rose Publishing title. For other inspirational stories, please visit our on-line bookstore at www.pelicanbookgroup.com.

For questions or more information, contact us at customer@pelicanbookgroup.com.

White Rose Publishing
Where Faith is the Cornerstone of Love™
an imprint of Pelican Book Group
www.PelicanBookGroup.com

Connect with Us
www.facebook.com/Pelicanbookgroup
www.twitter.com/pelicanbookgrp

To receive news and specials, subscribe to our bulletin
http://pelink.us/bulletin

May God's glory shine through
this inspirational work of fiction.

AMDG

You Can Help!

At Pelican Book Group it is our mission to entertain readers with fiction that uplifts the Gospel. It is our privilege to spend time with you awhile as you read our stories.

We believe you can help us to bring Christ into the lives of people across the globe. And you don't have to open your wallet or even leave your house!

Here are 3 simple things you can do to help us bring illuminating fiction™ to people everywhere.

1) If you enjoyed this book, write a positive review. Post it at online retailers and websites where readers gather. And share your review with us at reviews@pelicanbookgroup.com (this does give us permission to reprint your review in whole or in part.)

2) If you enjoyed this book, recommend it to a friend in person, at a book club or on social media.

3) If you have suggestions on how we can improve or expand our selection, let us know. We value your opinion. Use the contact form on our web site or e-mail us at customer@pelicanbookgroup.com

God Can Help!

Are you in need? The Almighty can do great things for you. Holy is His Name! He has mercy in every generation. He can lift up the lowly and accomplish all things. Reach out today.

Do not fear: I am with you; do not be anxious: I am your God. I will strengthen you, I will help you, I will uphold you with my victorious right hand.
~Isaiah 41:10 (NAB)

We pray daily, and we especially pray for everyone connected to Pelican Book Group—that includes you! If you have a specific need, we welcome the opportunity to pray for you. Share your needs or praise reports at http://pelink.us/pray4us

Free Book Offer

We're looking for booklovers like you to partner with us! Join our team of influencers today and periodically receive free eBooks and exclusive offers.

For more information
Visit http://pelicanbookgroup.com/booklovers